Once there was a girl who ran away and joined a traveling carnival. She married a man she grew to hate—and gave birth to a child she could never love. A child so monstrous that she killed it with her own hands . . . Twenty-five years later, Ellen Harper has a new life, a new husband, and two normal children—Joey loves monster movies, and Amy is about to graduate from high school. But their mother drowns her secret guilt in alcohol and prayer. The time has come for Amy and Joey to pay for her sins . . .

Because Amy is pregnant.

And the carnival is coming to town.

THE FUNHOUSE

continued. . .

THE VOICE OF THE NIGHT

"A fearsome tour of an adolescent's psyche. Terrifying, knee-knocking suspense." —*Chicago Sun-Times*

THE BAD PLACE

"A new experience in breathless terror." —UPI

THE SERVANTS OF TWILIGHT

"A great storyteller." —*New York Daily News*

MIDNIGHT

"A triumph." —*The New York Times*

LIGHTNING

"Brilliant . . . a spine-tingling tale . . . both challenging and entertaining." —The Associated Press

THE MASK

"Koontz hones his fearful yarns to a gleaming edge." —*People*

WATCHERS

"A breakthrough for Koontz . . . his best ever." —*Kirkus Reviews*

TWILIGHT EYES

"A spine-chilling adventure . . . will keep you turning pages to the very end." —*Rave Reviews*

STRANGERS

"A unique spellbinder that captures the reader on the first page. Exciting, enjoyable, and an intensely satisfying read." —Mary Higgins Clark

continued . . .

DEMON SEED

"One of our finest and most versatile suspense writers."
—*The Macon Telegraph & News*

PHANTOMS

"First-rate suspense, scary and stylish."   —*Los Angeles Times*

WHISPERS

"Pulls out all the stops . . . an incredible, terrifying tale."
—*Publishers Weekly*

NIGHT CHILLS

"Will send chills down your back."   —*The New York Times*

DARKFALL

"A fast-paced tale . . . one of the scariest chase scenes ever."
—*The Houston Post*

SHATTERED

"A chilling tale . . . sleek as a bullet."   —*Publishers Weekly*

THE VISION

"Spine-tingling—it gives you an almost lethal shock."
—*San Francisco Chronicle*

THE FACE OF FEAR

"Real suspense . . . tension upon tension."
—*The New York Times*

DEAN KOONTZ

The Funhouse

BERKLEY BOOKS, NEW YORK

THE BERKLEY PUBLISHING GROUP
Published by the Penguin Group
Penguin Group (USA) Inc.
375 Hudson Street, New York, New York 10014, USA

USA / Canada / UK / Ireland / Australia / New Zealand / India / South Africa / China

Penguin Books Ltd., Registered Offices: 80 Strand, London WC2R 0RL, England
For more information about the Penguin Group, visit penguin.com.

THE FUNHOUSE
A Novel by Dean Koontz
Based on a screenplay by Larry Block

A Berkley Book / published by arrangement with Universal Studios Publishing Rights,
a division of Universal Studios Licensing, Inc.

For information, address: The Berkley Publishing Group,
a division of Penguin Group (USA) Inc.,
375 Hudson Street, New York, New York 10014.

ISBN: 978-0-425-25064-8

PUBLISHING HISTORY
Jove mass-market edition / November 1980
Berkley mass-market edition / June 1994
Berkley premium edition / March 2013

PRINTED IN THE UNITED STATES OF AMERICA

40 39 38 37 36 35 34 33 32 31 30

Cover photograph © by Philip Scalia/Alamy.
Cover design by Marc Cohen.

*This book is dedicated to
Marion Bush and Frank Scafati—
two people who are warmer
than the California sunshine.*

Contents

You gain strength, courage and confidence by every experience in which you really stop to look fear in the face. You are able to say to yourself, "I lived through this horror. I can take the next thing that comes along." You must do the thing you think you cannot do.

—Anna Roosevelt

Happy families are all alike; every unhappy family is unhappy in its own way.

—Leo Tolstoy

Don't look back. Something may be gaining on you.

—Satchel Paige

PROLOGUE

Ellen Straker sat at the small kitchen table in the Airstream travel trailer, listening to the night wind, trying not to hear the strange scratching that came from the baby's bassinet.

Tall oaks, maples, and birches swayed in the dark grove where the trailer was parked. Leaves rustled like the starched, black skirts of witches. The wind swept down from the cloud-plated Pennsylvania sky, pushing the August darkness through the trees, gently rocking the trailer, groaning, murmuring, sighing, heavy with the scent of oncoming rain. It picked up the hurlyburly sounds of the nearby carnival, tore them apart as if they were fragments of a flimsy fabric, and drove the tattered threads of noise through the screen that covered the open window above the kitchen table.

In spite of the wind's incessant voice, Ellen could still hear the faint, unnerving noises that issued from the bassinet at the far end of the twenty-foot trailer. Scraping and scratching. Dry rasping. Brittle crackling. A papery whisper. The harder she strained to block out those sounds, the more clearly she could hear them.

She felt slightly dizzy. That was probably the booze doing its job. She was not much of a drinker, but in the past hour she had tossed down four shots of bourbon. Maybe six shots. She couldn't quite remember whether she had made three or only two trips to the bottle.

She looked at her trembling hands and wondered if she was drunk enough to do something about the baby.

Distant lightning flashed beyond the window. Thunder rumbled from the edge of the dark horizon.

Ellen turned her eyes slowly to the bassinet, which stood in shadows at the foot of the bed, and gradually her fear was supplanted by anger. She was angry with Conrad, her husband, and she was angry with herself for having gotten into this. But most of all, she was angry with the baby because the baby was the hideous, undeniable evidence of her sin. She wanted to kill it—kill it and bury it and forget that it had ever existed—but she knew she would have to be drunk in order to choke the life out of the child.

She thought she was just about ready.

Gingerly, she got up and went to the kitchen sink. She poured the half-melted ice cubes out of her glass, turned on the water, and rinsed the tumbler.

Although the cascading water roared when it struck the metal sink, Ellen could still hear the baby. Hissing. Dragging its small fingers down the inner surfaces of the bassi-net. Trying to get out.

No. Surely that was her imagination. She couldn't possibly hear those thin sounds over the drumming water.

She turned off the tap.

For a moment the world seemed to be filled with absolutely perfect, tomblike silence. Then she heard the soughing wind once more; it carried with it the distorted music of a calliope that was piping energetically out on the midway.

And from within the bassinet: scratching, scrabbling.

Suddenly the child cried out. It was a harsh, grating screech, a single, fierce bleat of frustration and anger. Then quiet. For a few seconds the baby was still, utterly motionless, but then it began its relentless movement again.

With shaking hands, Ellen put fresh ice in her glass and poured more bourbon. She hadn't intended to drink any more, but the child's scream had been like an intense blast of heat that had burned away the alcohol haze through which she had been moving. She was sober again, and fear followed swiftly in the wake of sobriety.

Although the night was hot and humid, she shivered.

She was no longer capable of murdering the child. She was no longer even brave enough to approach the bassinet.

But I've got to do it! she thought.

She returned to the booth that encircled the kitchen table, sat down, and sipped her whiskey, trying to regain the courage that came with intoxication, the only sort of courage she seemed able to summon.

I'm too young to carry this burden, she thought. I don't have the strength to handle it. I admit that. God help me, I just don't have the strength.

At twenty Ellen Straker was not only much too young

to be trapped in the bleak future that now seemed to lie ahead of her; she was also too pretty and vibrant to be condemned to a life of unremitting heartache and crushing responsibility. She was a slender, shapely girl-woman, a butterfly that had never really had a chance to try out its wings. Her hair was dark brown, almost black; so were her large eyes; and there was a natural, rosy tint to her cheeks that perfectly complemented her olive-tone skin. Before marrying Conrad Straker, she had been Ellen Teresa Marie Giavenetto, the daughter of a handsome, Italian-American father and a Madonna-faced, Italian-American mother. Ellen's Mediterranean beauty was not the only quality about her that revealed her heritage; she had a talent for finding joy in small things, an expansive personality, a quick smile, and a warmth that were all quite Italian in nature. She was a woman meant for good times, for parties and dances and gaiety. But in her first twenty years of life, there had not been very much laughter.

Her childhood was grim.

Her adolescence was an ordeal.

Although Joseph Giavenetto, her father, had been a warm, good-hearted man, he had also been meek. He had not been the master of his own home, and he hadn't had a great deal to say about how his daughter ought to be raised. Ellen had not been soothed by her father's gentle humor and quiet love nearly so often as she had been subjected to her mother's fiery, religious zealotry.

Gina was the power in the Giavenetto house, and it was to her that Ellen had to answer for the slightest impropriety, real or imagined. There were rules, an endless list of them, which were meant to govern Ellen's behavior, and Gina was determined that every rule would be rigidly enforced and strictly obeyed. She intended to see that her daughter grew up to be a very moral, prim, God-fearing woman.

Gina always had been religious, but after the death of her only son, she became fanatically devout. Anthony, Ellen's brother, died of cancer when he was only seven years old. Ellen was just four at the time, too young to understand what was happening to her brother, but old enough to be aware of his frighteningly swift deterioration. To Gina, that tragedy had been a divine judgment leveled against her. She felt that she had somehow failed to please God, and that He had taken her little boy to punish her. She began going to Mass every morning instead of just on Sundays, and she dragged her little girl with her. She lit a candle for Anthony's soul every day of the week, without fail. At home she read the Bible from cover to cover, over and over again. Often, she forced Ellen to sit and listen to Scripture for hours at a time, even before the girl was old enough to understand what she was hearing. Gina was full of horrible stories about Hell: what it was like; what grisly tortures awaited a sinner down there; how easy it was for a wicked child to end up in that sulphurous place. At night young Ellen's sleep was disturbed by hideous, bloody nightmares based on her mother's gruesome tales of fire and damnation. And as Gina became increasingly religious, she added more rules to the list by which Ellen was expected to live; the tiniest infraction was, according to Gina, one more step taken on the road to Hell.

Joseph, having yielded all authority to his wife early in their marriage, was not able to exert much control over her even in ordinary times; and when she retreated into her strange world of religious fanaticism, she was so far beyond his reach that he no longer even attempted to influence her decisions. Bewildered by the changes in Gina, unable to cope with the new woman she had become, Joseph spent less and less time at home. He owned a tailor shop—not an extremely prosperous business but a reliably steady one—and he began to work unusually long hours. When he wasn't working he passed more time with his friends than he did with his family, and as a result Ellen was not exposed either to his love or to his fine sense of humor often enough to compensate for the countless, dreary hours during which she existed stoically under her mother's stern, somber, suffocating domination.

For years Ellen dreamed of the day she would leave home; she looked forward to that escape with every bit as much eagerness as a convict anticipating release from a real prison cell. But now that she was on her own, now that she had been out from under her mother's iron hand for more than a year, her future looked, incredibly, worse than it ever had looked before. Much worse.

Something tapped on the window screen behind the booth.

Ellen twisted around, looked up, startled. For a moment she couldn't see anything. Just darkness out there.

Tap-tap-tap.

"Who's there?" she asked, her voice as thin as tissue, her heart suddenly beating fast.

Then lightning spread across the sky, a tracery of fiery veins and arteries. In the flickering pulse of light, there were large white moths fluttering against the screen.

"Jesus," she said softly. "Only moths."

She shuddered, turned away from the frantic insects, and sipped her bourbon.

She couldn't live with this kind of tension. Not for long. She couldn't live in constant fear. She had to do something soon.

Kill the baby.

In the bassinet the baby cried out again: a short, sharp noise almost like a dog's bark.

A distant crack of thunder seemed to answer the child; the celestial rumbling briefly blotted out the unceasing voice of the wind, and it reverberated in the trailer's metal walls.

The moths went *tap-tap-tap.*

Ellen quickly drank her remaining bourbon and poured two more ounces into her glass.

She found it difficult to believe that she had wound up in this shabby place, in such anguish and misery; it seemed like a fever dream. Only fourteen months ago she had begun a new life with great expectations, with what had proved to be hopelessly naive optimism. Her world had collapsed into ruin so suddenly and so completely that she was still stunned.

Six weeks before her nineteenth birthday, she left home. She slipped away in the middle of the night, not bothering to announce her departure, unable to face down her mother. She left a short, bitter note for Gina, and then she was off with the man she loved.

Virtually any inexperienced, small-town girl, longing to escape boredom or oppressive parents, would have fallen for a man like Conrad Straker. He was undeniably handsome. His straight, coal-black hair was thick and glossy.

His features were rather aristocratic: high cheekbones, a patrician nose, a strong chin. He had startlingly blue eyes, a gas-flame blue. He was tall, lean, and he moved with the grace of a dancer.

But it wasn't even Conrad's looks that had most appealed to Ellen. She had been won by his style, his charm. He was a good talker, clever, with a gift for making the most extravagant flattery sound understated and sincere.

Running away with a handsome carnival barker had seemed wildly romantic. They would travel all over the country, and she would see more of the world in one year than she had expected to see in her entire life. There would be no boredom. Each day would be filled with excitement, color, music, and lights. And the world of the carny, so different from that of her small town in Illinois farm country, was not governed by a long, complex, frustrating set of rules.

She and Conrad were married in the best carnival tradition. The ceremony consisted of an after-hours ride on the merry-go-round, with other carnies standing as witnesses. In the eyes of all true carnival people, their marriage was as binding and sacred as if it had been performed in a church, by a minister, with a proper license in hand.

After she became Mrs. Conrad Straker, Ellen was certain that only good times lay ahead. She was wrong.

She had known Conrad for only two weeks before she had run off with him. Too late, she discovered that she had seen just the best side of him. Since the wedding, she had learned that he was moody, difficult to live with, and capable of violence. At times he was sweet, every bit as charming as when he had been courting her. But he could turn vicious with the unexpected, inexplicable suddenness of a wild animal. During the past year his dark moods had seized him with increasing frequency. He was sarcastic, petty, nasty, grim, and quick to strike Ellen when she displeased him. He enjoyed slapping, shoving, and pinching her. Early in the marriage, before she was pregnant, he had hit her in the stomach with his fist on two occasions. While she'd been carrying their child, Conrad had restricted his attacks, contenting himself with less brutal but nonetheless frightening abuse.

By the time she was two months pregnant, Ellen was almost desperate enough to go home to her parents. Almost. But when she thought of the humiliation she would have to endure, when she pictured herself begging Gina for another chance, when she thought of the smug self-righteousness with which her mother would greet her, she wasn't able to leave Straker.

She had nowhere else to go.

As she grew heavy with the child, she convinced herself that a baby would settle Conrad. He genuinely liked children; that was obvious because of the way he treated the offspring of other carnies. He appeared to be enchanted by the prospect of fatherhood. Ellen told herself that the presence of the baby would soften Conrad, mellow him, sweeten his temper.

Then, six weeks ago, that fragile hope was shattered when the baby arrived. Ellen hadn't gone to the hospital. That wasn't the true carny way. She had the baby at home, in the trailer, with a carnival midwife in attendance. The delivery had been relatively easy. She was never in any physical danger. There were no complications. Except . . .

The baby.

She shivered with revulsion when she thought of the baby, and she picked up her bourbon once more.

As if it sensed that she was thinking about it, the child squalled again.

"Shut up!" she screamed, putting her hands over her ears. "Shut up, shut up!"

It would not be quiet.

The bassinet shook, rocked, creaked, as the infant kicked and writhed in anger.

Ellen tossed down the last of the bourbon in her glass and licked her lips nervously and finally felt the whiskey-power surging into her again. She slid out of the booth. She stood in the tiny kitchen, swaying.

The dissonant music of the oncoming storm crashed louder than ever, directly over the fairgrounds now, building rapidly to a furious crescendo.

She weaved through the trailer and stopped at the foot of the bassinet. She switched on a lamp that produced a soft amber glow, and the shadows crawled away to huddle in the corners.

The child stopped struggling with its covers. It looked up at her, its eyes shining with hatred.

She felt sick.

Kill it, she told herself.

But the baby's malevolent glare was hypnotic. Ellen could not tear her eyes from its medusan gaze; she could not move; she felt as if she had been turned to stone.

Lightning pressed its bright face to the window again, and the first fat drops of rain came with the subsequent growl of thunder.

She stared at her child in horror, and beads of cold

sweat popped out along her hairline. The baby wasn't normal; it wasn't even close to normal, but there was no medical term for its deformity. In fact you couldn't rightly call it a child. It was not a baby. It was a *thing*. It didn't seem deformed so much as it seemed to belong to a species entirely different from mankind.

It was hideous.

"Oh, God," Ellen said, her voice quavering. "God, why me? What have I done to deserve this?"

The large, green, inhuman eyes of her offspring regarded her venomously.

Ellen wanted to turn away from it. She wanted to run out of the trailer, into the crackling storm, into the vast darkness, out of this nightmare and into a new dawn.

The creature's twisted, flared nostrils quivered like those of a wolf or a dog, and she could hear it sniffing eagerly as it sorted out her scent from the other odors in the trailer.

Kill it!

The Bible said, *Thou shalt not kill.* Murder was a sin. If she strangled the baby, she would rot in Hell. A series of cruel images flickered through her mind, visions of a Hell that her mother had painted for her during thousands of lectures about the terrible consequences of sin: grinning demons tearing ragged gobbets of flesh from living, screaming women, their leathery black lips slick with human blood; white-hot fire searing the bodies of sinners; pale worms feeding off still-conscious dead men; agonized people writhing painfully in mounds of indescribably horrible filth. Ellen was not a practicing Catholic, but that did not mean that she was no longer a Catholic in her heart. Years of daily Mass and nightly prayer, nineteen interminable years of Gina's mad sermons and stern admonitions could not be sloughed off and forgotten easily. Ellen still believed wholeheartedly in God, Heaven, and Hell. The Bible's warnings continued to hold value and meaning for her. *Thou shalt not kill.*

But surely, she argued with herself, that commandment did not apply to animals. You were permitted to kill animals; that was not a mortal sin. And this thing in the bassinet was just an animal, a beast, a monster. It was not a human being. Therefore, if she destroyed it, that act of destruction would not seal the fate of her immortal soul.

On the other hand, how could she be certain that it wasn't human? It had been born of man and woman. There couldn't be any more fundamental criterion for humanity than that one. The child was a mutant, but it was a *human* mutant.

Her dilemma seemed insoluble.

In the bassinet, the small, swarthy creature raised one hand, reaching toward Ellen. It wasn't a hand, really. It was a claw. The long, bony fingers were much too large to be those of a six-week-old infant, even though this baby was big for its age; like an animal's paws, the hands of this little beast were out of proportion to the rest of it. A sparse, black fur covered the backs of its hands and bristled more densely around its knuckles. Amber light glinted off the sharp edges of the pointed fingernails. The child raked the air, but it was unable to reach Ellen.

She couldn't understand how such a thing could have come from her. How could it possibly exist? She knew there were such things as freaks. Some of them worked in a sideshow in this very carnival. Bizarre-looking people. But not like this. None of them was half as weird as this thing that she had nurtured in her womb. Why had this happened? *Why?*

Killing the child would be an act of mercy. After all, it would never be able to enjoy a normal life. It would always be a freak, an object of shame, ridicule, and derision. Its days would be unrelievedly stark, bitter, lonely. Even the tamest and most ordinary pleasures would be denied it, and it would have no chance of attaining happiness.

Furthermore, if she were forced to spend her life tending to this creature, she wouldn't find any happiness of her own. The prospect of raising this grotesque child filled her with despair. Murdering it would be an act of mercy benefitting both herself and the pitiful yet frightening mutant now glaring at her from the bassinet.

But the Roman Catholic Church did not condone mercy killing. Even the highest motives would not save her from Hell. And she knew that her motives were not pure; ridding herself of this burden was, in part, a selfish act.

The creature continued to stare at her, and she had the unsettling feeling that its strange eyes were not merely looking *at* her but *through* her, into her mind and soul, past all pretension. It *knew* what she was contemplating, and it hated her for that.

Its pale, speckled tongue slowly licked its dark, dark lips.

It hissed defiantly at her.

Whether or not this thing was human, whether or not killing it would be a sin, she knew that it was evil. It was not simply a deformed baby. It was something else. Something worse. It was dangerous, both less and more than human. Evil. She felt the truth of that in her heart and bones.

Or am I crazy? she wondered. No. She couldn't allow doubt to creep in. She was not out of her mind. Grief-stricken, deeply depressed, frightened, horrified, confused—she was all of those things. But she was not crazy. She perceived that the child was evil, and in that regard her perception was not askew.

Kill it.

The infant screamed. Its gravelly, strident voice grated on Ellen's nerves. She winced.

Wind-driven sheets of rain drummed noisily against the trailer. Thunder picked up the night and vigorously rattled it again.

The child squirmed, thrashed, and managed to push aside the thin blanket that had been draped across it. Hooking its bony hands on the edges of the bassinet, gripping with its wicked claws, it strained forward and sat up.

Ellen gasped. It was too young to sit up on its own with such assurance.

It hissed at her.

The thing was growing at a frightening rate; it was always hungry, and she fed it more than twice as much as she would have fed an ordinary child; week by week she could see the amazing changes in it. With surprising, disquieting swiftness it was learning how to use its body. Before long it would be able to crawl, then walk.

And then what? How big and how mobile would it have to get before she would no longer have any control over it?

Her mouth was dry and sour. She tried to work up some saliva, but there was none.

A trickle of cold sweat broke from her hairline and wriggled down her forehead, into the corner of one eye. She blinked away the salty fluid.

If she could place the child in an institution, where it belonged, she would not have to murder it. But Conrad would never agree to giving up his baby. He was not the least bit revolted by it. He was not frightened of it, either. He actually seemed to cherish it more than he might have done a healthy child. He took considerable pride in having fathered the creature, and to Ellen his pride was a sign of madness.

Even if she could commit the thing to an institution, that solution would not be final. The evil would still exist. She knew the child was evil, knew it beyond the slightest doubt, and she felt responsible for bringing such a creature into the world. She could not simply turn her back and walk away and let someone else deal with it.

What if, grown larger, it killed someone? Wouldn't the responsibility for that death rest on her shoulders?

The air coming through the open windows was much cooler than it had been before the rain had begun to fall. A chilly draft brushed the back of Ellen's neck.

The child began trying to get out of the bassinet.

Finally summoning all of her bourbon-inspired courage, her teeth chattering, her hands trembling as if she were afflicted by palsy, she took hold of the baby. No. The *thing*. She must not think of it as a baby. She could not allow herself the luxury of sentiment. She must act. She must be cold, unmoved, implacable, iron-willed.

She intended to lift the loathsome creature, retrieve the satin-encased pillow that was under its head, and then smother it with the same pillow. She didn't want to leave any obvious marks of violence on the body. The death must appear to be natural. Even healthy babies sometimes died in their cribs without apparent cause; no one would be surprised or suspicious if this pitiful deformity passed away quietly in its sleep.

But as she lifted the thing off the pillow, it responded with such shocking fury that her plan instantly became unworkable. The creature squealed. It clawed her.

She cried out in pain as its sharp nails gouged and sliced her forearms.

Blood. Slender ribbons of blood.

The infant squirmed and kicked, and Ellen had great difficulty holding on to it.

The thing pursed its twisted mouth and spat at her. A viscous, foul-smelling glob of yellowish spittle struck her nose.

She shuddered and gagged.

The child-thing peeled its dark lips back from its mottled gums and hissed at her.

Thunder smashed the porcelain night, and the lights in the trailer blinked once, blinked twice, and lightning coruscated through the brief spell of blackness before the lamps came on again.

Please, God, she thought desperately, don't leave me in the dark with this thing.

Its bulging, green eyes seemed to radiate a peculiar light, a phosphorescent glow that appeared, impossibly, to come from within them.

The thing screeched and writhed.

It urinated.

Ellen's heart jackhammered.

The thing tore at her hands, scratching, drawing blood. It gouged the soft flesh of her palms, and it ripped off one of her thumbnails.

She heard an eerie, high-pitched ululation quite unlike anything she had heard before, and she didn't realize for several seconds that she was listening to her own shrill, panicked screaming.

If she could have thrown the creature down, if she could have turned away from it and run, she would have done just that, but suddenly she found that she was unable to release it. The thing had a fierce grip on her arms, and it wouldn't let go.

She struggled with the inhumanly ferocious child, and the bassinet almost tipped over. Her shadow swayed wildly across the nearby bed and up the wall, bobbing against the rounded ceiling. Cursing, straining, trying to keep the creature at arm's length, she managed to shift her left hand to its throat, and then her right hand, and she squeezed hard, bearing down, gritting her teeth, repelled by the savagery she felt rising within herself, frightened by her own newly discovered capacity for violence, but determined to choke the life out of the thing.

It wasn't going to die easily. Ellen was surprised by the rigid, resistant muscles in its neck. It crabbed its claws higher on her arms and dug its nails into her again, making ten fresh puncture wounds in her skin; and the pain prevented Ellen from putting all of her strength into the frantic attempt to strangle the thing.

It rolled its eyes, then refocused on her with even more evident hatred than before.

A silvery stream of thick drool oozed out of one corner of its mouth and down its pebbled chin.

The twisted mouth opened wide; the dark, leathery lips writhed. A snaky, pale, pointed tongue curled and uncurled obscenely.

The child pulled Ellen toward it with improbable strength. She could not keep it safely at arm's length as she wanted. It drew her relentlessly down toward the bassinet, and at the same time it pulled itself up.

Die, damn you! Die!

She was bent over the bassinet now. Leaning into it. Her grip on the child's throat was weakened by her new position. Her face was only eight or ten inches from the creature's repugnant countenance. Its rank breath washed over her. It spat in her face again.

Something brushed her belly.

She gasped, jerked.

Fabric ripped. Her blouse.

The child was kicking out with its long-toed, clawed feet. It was trying to gouge her breasts and stomach. She attempted to draw back, but the thing held her close, held her with demonic power and perseverance.

Ellen felt dizzy, fuzzy, whiskey-sick, terror-sick, and her vision blurred, and her ears were filled with the roaring suction of her own breath, but she couldn't seem to breathe fast enough; she was light-headed. Sweat flew off her brow and spattered the child as she wrestled with it.

The thing grinned as if it sensed triumph.

I'm losing, she thought desperately. How can that be? My God, it's going to kill me.

Thunder pounded the sky, and lightning burst from the broken night. A mallet of wind struck the trailer broadside.

The lights went out.

And stayed out.

The child fought with renewed fury.

It was not weak like a human infant. It had weighed almost eleven pounds at birth, and it had gained, phenomenally, more than twelve pounds in the past six weeks. Almost twenty-three pounds now. And no fat. Just muscle. A hard, sinewy, gristly infant, like a young gorilla. It was as strong and energetic as the six-month-old chimpanzee that performed in one of the carnival's more popular sideshows.

The bassinet toppled with a crash, and Ellen stumbled over it. She fell. With the child. It was close against her now. No longer safely at arm's reach. It was on top of her. Gurgling. Snarling. Its taloned feet found purchase on her hips, and it tried to tear through the heavy denim jeans she was wearing.

"No!" she shouted.

A thought snapped through her mind: *I've got to wake up!*

But she knew she was already awake.

The thing continued to hold her right arm, its nails hooked in her flesh, but it let go of her left arm. In the blackness she sensed the hooked claw reaching for her throat, her vulnerable jugular vein. She turned her head aside. The small yet incredibly long-fingered, deadly hand brushed past her throat, barely missing her.

She rolled, and then the child-thing was on the bottom. Whimpering, teetering on the wire of hysteria, she tore her right arm loose of the creature's steely grip, at the expense of new pain, and she felt for its arms in the darkness, found its wrists, held its hands away from her face.

The thing kicked at her stomach again, but she avoided its short, powerful legs. She managed to put one of her knees on its chest, pinning it. She bore down on it with all of her weight; the creature's ribs and breastbone gave way beneath her. She heard something crack inside the thing. It wailed like a banshee. Ellen knew, at last, that she had a chance to survive. There was a sickening crunch, a wet sound, a horrible mashing, squashing, and all the fight went out of her adversary. Its arms went slack and stopped trying to resist her. The creature abruptly fell silent, limp.

Ellen was afraid to take her knee off its chest. She was certain that it was faking death. If she shifted her weight, if she gave it the slightest opening, the thing would move as fast as a snake, strike at her throat, and then disembowel her with its spiky feet.

Seconds passed.

Then minutes.

In the darkness she began an urgent, whispered prayer: "Jesus, help me. Saint Elena, my patron saint, plead for me. Mary, Mother of God, hear me, help me. Please, please, please. Mary, help me, Mary, please . . ."

The electric power was restored, and Ellen cried out at the unexpected light.

Under her, on its back, blood still running from its nostrils and its mouth, the child-thing stared up at her with glistening, bulging, bloodshot eyes. But it couldn't see her. It was looking into another world, into Hell, to which she had dispatched its soul—if it had a soul.

There was a lot of blood. Most of it wasn't Ellen's.

She released the child-thing.

It didn't return magically to life, as she had half expected it would. It didn't attack.

It looked like a huge, squashed bug.

She crawled away from the corpse, keeping one eye on it as she went, not entirely convinced that it was dead. She did not have sufficient strength to stand up just yet. She crept to the nearest wall and sat with her back against it.

The night air was heavy with the coppery odor of blood, the stench of her own sweat, and the clean ozone of the thunderstorm.

Gradually, Ellen's stentorian breathing subsided to a soft, rhythmic lullaby of inhalation, exhalation, inhalation . . .

As her fear dwindled along with the steady deceleration of her heartbeat, she became increasingly aware of her pains; there was a multitude of them. She ached in every joint and every muscle from the strain of wrestling with the child. Her left thumb was bleeding where the nail had been ripped off; the exposed flesh stung as if it were being eaten away by acid. Her scratched, scraped fingers burned, and the gouged palm of her right hand throbbed. Both of her forearms had been scored repeatedly by the thing's sharp fingernails. Each upper arm was marked by five, ugly, oozing punctures.

She wept. Not just because of the physical pain. Because of the anguish, the stress, the fear. With tears she was able to wash away much of her tension and at least a small measure of her heavy burden of guilt.

—*I'm a murderer.*

—*No. It was just an animal.*

—*It was my child.*

—*Not a child. A thing. A curse.*

She was still arguing with herself, still trying to find a comfortable set of rationalizations that would allow her to live with what she had done, when the trailer door flew open and Conrad came inside, backlighted by a strobe-flutter of lightning. He was wearing a plastic raincoat, streaming water; his thick black hair was soaked, and strands of it were plastered across his broad forehead. Wind rushed in at his heels and, like a big dog, circled the room, sniffing inquisitively at everything.

Raw, throat-tightening fear gripped Ellen again.

Conrad pulled the door shut. Turning, he saw her sitting on the floor with her back against the wall, her blouse torn, her arms and hands bleeding.

She tried to explain why she had killed the child. But she couldn't speak. Her mouth moved, but nothing came out of it except a dry, frightening rasping.

Conrad's intensely blue eyes looked puzzled for a moment. Then his gaze traveled from Ellen to the bloody, crumpled child that was on the floor a few feet from her.

His powerful hands curled into large, hard fists. "No," he said softly, disbelievingly. "No . . . no . . . no . . ."

He moved slowly toward the small corpse.

Ellen looked up at him with growing trepidation.

Stunned, Conrad knelt beside the dead creature and stared at it for what seemed like an eternity. Then tears began to track down his cheeks. Ellen had never seen him cry before. Finally he lifted the limp body and held it close. The child-thing's bright blood dripped onto the plastic raincoat.

"My baby, my little baby, my sweet little boy," Conrad crooned. "My boy . . . my son . . . what's happened to you? What did she do to you? What did she do?"

Ellen's burgeoning fear gave her new strength, though not much. Bracing herself against the wall with one hand, she got to her feet. Her legs were shaky; her knees felt as if they would buckle if she dared take even one step.

Conrad heard her move. He looked back at her.

"I . . . I had to do it," she said shakily.

His blue eyes were cold.

"It attacked me," she said.

Conrad put down the body. Gently. Tenderly.

He isn't going to be that tender with me, Ellen thought.

"Please, Conrad. Please understand."

He stood and approached her.

She wanted to run. She couldn't.

"You killed Victor," Conrad said thickly.

He had given the child-thing a name—Victor Martin Straker—which seemed ludicrous to Ellen. More than ludicrous. Dangerous. If you started calling it by name, you started thinking of it as a human baby. And it wasn't human. It *wasn't*, damn it. It was evil. You couldn't let your guard down for a moment when you were around it; sentiment made you vulnerable. She refused to call it Victor. And she even refused to admit that it had a sexual identity. It wasn't a little boy. It was a little *beast*.

"Why? Why did you kill my Victor?"

"It attacked me," she said again.

"Liar."

"It did!"

"Lying bitch."

"Look at me!" She held up her bleeding hands and arms. "Look what it did to me."

The grief on Conrad's face had given way to an expression of blackest hatred. "You tried to kill him, and he fought back in self-defense."

"No. It was awful. Horrible. It clawed me. It tried to tear out my throat. It tried to—"

"Shut up," he said between clenched teeth.

"Conrad, you *know* it was violent. It scratched you sometimes. If you'll just face the truth, if you'll just look into your heart, you'll have to admit I'm right. We didn't create a child. We created a *thing*. And it was bad. It was evil, Conrad. It—"

"I told you to shut your filthy mouth, you rotten bitch."

He was shaking with rage. Flecks of foamy spittle dotted his lips.

Ellen cringed. "Are you going to call the police?"

"You know a carny never runs to the cops. Carnies handle their own problems. I know exactly how to deal with disgusting filth like you."

He was going to kill her. She was sure of it.

"Wait, listen, give me a chance to explain. What kind of life could it have had anyway?" she argued desperately.

Conrad glared at her. His eyes were filled with cold fury but also with madness. His wintry gaze pierced her, and she felt almost as if slivers of ice were being driven through her by some slow, silent, barely perceptible but nonetheless devastating explosion. Those were not the eyes of a sane man.

She shivered. "It would have been miserable all its life. It would have been a freak, ridiculed, rejected, despised. It wouldn't have been able to enjoy even the most ordinary pleasures. I didn't do anything wrong. I only put the poor thing out of its misery. That's all I did. I saved it from years and years of loneliness, from—"

Conrad slapped her face. Hard.

She looked frantically left and right, unable to see even the slightest opportunity for escape.

His sharp, clean features no longer looked aristocratic; his face was frightening, stark, carved by shadows into a ferocious, wolflike visage.

He moved in even closer, slapped her again. Then he used his fists—once, twice, three times, striking her in the stomach and the ribs.

She was too weak, too exhausted, to resist him. She slid inexorably toward the floor and, she supposed, toward death.

Mary, Mother of God!

Conrad grabbed her, held her up with one hand, and continued to slap her, cursing her with each blow. Ellen lost count of the number of times he struck her, and she lost the ability to distinguish each new pain from the myriad old pains with which she was afflicted, and the last thing she lost was consciousness.

After an indeterminable period of time, she drifted back from a dark place where guttural voices were threatening her in strange languages. She opened her eyes, and for a moment she didn't know where she was.

Then she saw the small, ghastly corpse on the floor, only a few feet away. The gnarled face, frozen for all time in a vicious snarl, was turned toward her.

Rain drummed hollowly on the rounded roof of the trailer.

Ellen was sprawled on the floor. She sat up. She felt terrible, all busted up inside.

Conrad was standing by the bed. Her two suitcases were open, and he was throwing clothes into them.

He hadn't killed her. Why not? He had intended to beat her to death, she was certain of that. Why had he changed his mind?

Groaning, she got to her knees. She tasted blood; a couple of her teeth were loose. With tremendous effort, she stood.

Conrad shut the suitcases, carried them past her, pushed open the trailer door, and threw the luggage outside. Her purse was on the kitchen counter, and he threw that out after the bags. He wheeled on her. "Now you. Get the hell out and don't ever come back."

She couldn't believe that he was going to let her live. It had to be a trick.

He raised his voice. "Get out of here, slut! Move. *Now!*"

Wobbly as a colt taking its first steps, Ellen walked past Conrad. She was tense, expecting another attack, but he did not raise a hand against her.

When she reached the door, where windblown rain lashed across the threshold, Conrad said, "One more thing."

She turned to him, raising one arm to ward off the blow she knew had to come sooner or later.

But he wasn't going to hit her. He was still furious, but now he was in control of himself. "Some day you'll marry someone in the straight world. You'll have another child. Maybe two, three."

His ominous voice contained a threat, but she was too

dazed to perceive what he was implying. She waited for him to say more.

His thin, bloodless lips slowly peeled back in an arctic smile. "When you have children again, when you have kids *you* love and cherish, I'll come and take them away from you. No matter where you go, no matter how far away, no matter what your new name may be. I'll find you. I swear I will. I'll find you, and I'll take your children just like you took my little boy. I'll kill them."

"You're crazy," she said.

His smile became a wide, humorless, death's-head grin. "You won't find a place to hide. There won't be one safe corner anywhere in the world. Not one. You'll have to keep looking over your shoulder as long as you live. Now get out of here, bitch. Get out before I decide to kick your damned head in after all."

He moved toward her.

Ellen quickly left the trailer, descended the two metal steps into the darkness. The trailer was parked in a small clearing, with trees bracketing it, but there was nothing directly overhead to break the falling rain; in seconds Ellen was soaked to the skin.

For a moment Conrad was outlined in the amber light that filled the open doorway. He glowered at her. Then he slammed the door.

On all sides of her, trees shook in the wind. The leaves made a sound like hope being crumpled and discarded.

At last Ellen picked up her purse and her muddy suit-cases. She walked through the motorized carny town, passing other trailers, trucks, cars; and under the insistent

fingers of the rain, every vehicle contributed its tinny notes
to the music of the storm.

She had friends in some of those trailers. She liked
many of the carnival people she'd met, and she knew a lot
of them liked her. As she plodded through the mud, she
looked longingly at some of the lighted windows, but she
did not stop. She wasn't sure how her carny friends would
react to the news that she had killed Victor Martin Straker.
Most carnies were outcasts, people who didn't fit in anywhere else; therefore, they were fiercely protective of their
own, and they regarded everyone else as a mark to be
tapped or fleeced in one way or another. Their strong
sense of community might even extend to the horrid
child-thing. Furthermore, they were more likely to side
with Conrad than with her, for Conrad had been born of
carny parents and had been a carny since birth, while she
had been converted to the roadshow life only fourteen
months ago.

She walked.

She left the grove and entered the midway. Unob-
structed, the storm pummeled her more forcefully than it
had done in the grove; it pounded the earth, the gravel
footpaths, and the patches of sawdust that spread out from
some of the sideshows.

The carnival was shut down tight. Only a few lights
burned; they swung on wind-whipped wires, creating amor-
phous, dancing shadows. The marks had all gone home,
banished by the foul weather. The fairgrounds were
deserted. Ellen saw no one other than two dwarves in yellow rain slickers; they scurried between the silent carousel
and the Tilt-a-Whirl, past the gaudily illustrated kootch

show, glancing at Ellen, their eyes moon-bright and inquisitive in the darkness under their rain hoods.

She headed toward the front gate. She looked back several times, afraid that Conrad would change his mind and come after her.

Tent walls rippled and thrummed and snapped in the wind, pulling at anchor pegs.

In the sheeting rain that was now laced with tendrils of fog, the dark Ferris wheel thrust up like a prehistoric skeleton, weird, mysterious, its familiar lines obscured and distorted and made fantastic by the night and the mist.

She passed the funhouse, too. That was Conrad's concession. He owned it, and he worked there every day. A giant, leering clown's face peered down at her from atop the funhouse; as a joke, the artist had modeled it after Conrad's face. Ellen could see the resemblance even in the gloom. She had the disconcerting feeling that the clown's huge, painted eyes were watching her. She looked away from it and hurried on.

When she reached the main gate of the county fairgrounds, she stopped, abruptly aware that she had no destination in mind. There was no place for her to go. She had no one to whom she could turn.

The hooting wind seemed to be mocking her.

Later that night, after the storm front passed, when only a thin, gray drizzle was falling, Conrad climbed onto the dark carousel in the center of the deserted midway. He sat on one of the gaily painted, elaborately carved benches, not on a horse.

Cory Baker, the man who operated the merry-go-round, stood at the controls behind the ticket booth. He switched on the carousel's lights. He started the big motor, pushed a lever, and the platform began to turn backwards. Calliope music piped loudly, but it wasn't able to dispel the dreary atmosphere that surrounded this ceremony.

The brass poles pumped up and down, up and down, gleaming.

The wooden stallions and mares galloped backwards, tail-first, around, around.

Conrad, the sole passenger, stared straight ahead, tight-lipped, grim.

Such a ride on a carousel was the traditional carnival way to dissolve a marriage. The bride and groom rode in the usual direction, forward, when they wanted to wed; either of them could obtain a divorce by riding backwards, alone. Those ceremonies seemed absurd to outsiders, but to carnies, their traditions were less ridiculous than the straight world's religious and legal rituals.

Five carnies, witnesses to the divorce, watched the merry-go-round. Cory Baker and his wife. Zena Penetsky, one of the girls from the kootch show. Two freaks: the fat lady, who was also the bearded lady; and the alligator man, whose skin was very thick and scaly. They huddled in the rain, watching silently as Conrad swept around through the cool air, through the hollow music and the fog.

After the carousel had made half a dozen revolutions at normal speed, Cory shut down the machine. The platform gradually slowed.

As he waited for the carousel to drift to a stop, Conrad thought about the children Ellen would have one day. He raised his hands and stared at them, trying to envision his fingers all red with the blood of Ellen's offspring. In a couple of years she would remarry; she was too lovely to remain unattached for long. Ten years from now she could have at least one child. In ten years Conrad would start looking for her. He would hire private investigators; he would spare no expense. He knew that, by morning, Ellen would not take his threat seriously, but *he* did. And when he found her years from now, when she felt safe and secure, he would steal from her that which she valued most.

Now, more than at any other time in his mostly unhappy life, Conrad Straker had something to live for. Vengeance.

Ellen spent the night in a motel near the county fairgrounds.

She didn't sleep well. Although she had bandaged her wounds, they still burned, and she couldn't find a comfortable position. Worse than that, every time she dozed off for a few minutes, she was plagued by bloody nightmares.

Awake, staring at the ceiling, she worried about the future. Where would she go? What would she do? She didn't have much money.

Once, at the deepest point of her depression, she considered suicide. But she quickly dismissed that thought. She might not be condemned to Hell for having killed the child-thing, but she surely would be damned for taking her own life. To a Catholic, suicide was a mortal sin.

Having forsaken the Church in reaction to her mother's zealous support of it, having been without faith for a few years, Ellen discovered that she now *believed*. She was a Catholic again, and she longed for the cleansing of confession, for the spiritual uplift of the Mass. The birth of that grotesque, malevolent child, and especially her recent struggle with it, had convinced her that there were such things as abstract evil and abstract good, forces of God and forces of Satan at work in the world.

In the motel bed, with the covers drawn up to her chin, she prayed often that night.

Toward dawn she finally managed to get a couple of hours of uninterrupted, dreamless sleep, and when she woke up she did not feel depressed. A shaft of golden sunlight pierced the high window and came to rest upon her, and as she luxuriated in the warmth and brightness, she began to feel that there was hope for the future. Conrad was behind her. Forever. The monstrous child was gone. Forever. The world was filled with interesting possibilities. After all the sadness and pain and fear that she had endured, she was long overdue for her share of happiness.

Already, she had put Conrad's threat out of her mind.

It was Tuesday, August 16, 1955.

ONE

AMY HARPER

1

On the night of the senior prom, Jerry Galloway wanted to make love to Amy. His desire didn't surprise her. He always wanted to make love. He was always pawing at her. He couldn't get enough of her.

But Amy was beginning to think she'd had enough of Jerry. Too much of him, in fact. She was pregnant.

Whenever she thought about being pregnant, she got a hollow, cold sensation in her chest. Afraid of what she would have to face in the days ahead—the humiliation, her father's disappointment, her mother's fury—she shivered.

Several times during the evening, Jerry saw her shivering, and he thought she was just bothered by a draft from the gymnasium's air conditioning. She was wearing a lacy, green, off-the-shoulder gown, and he kept suggesting that she put her shawl over her shoulders.

They danced only a few of the fast songs, but they

didn't miss a single slow number. Jerry liked slow dancing. He liked to hold Amy close, pressing her tight against him as they glided somewhat clumsily around the floor. He whispered in her ear while they danced; he told her that she looked terrific, that she was the sexiest thing he had ever seen, that all of the guys were surreptitiously staring at her cleavage, that she made him hot, real hot. He pressed so tightly against her that she could feel his erection. He *wanted* her to feel it because he wanted her to know that she turned him on. To Jerry's way of thinking, his erection was the greatest compliment he could pay her.

Jerry was an ass.

As Amy allowed him to maneuver her around the crowded room, as she permitted him to rub his body against her under the pretense of dancing, she wondered why she had let him touch her in the first place. He was such a creep, really.

He was handsome, of course. He was one of the handsomest boys in the senior class. A lot of girls thought Amy had made a wonderful catch when she'd latched on to Jerry Galloway.

But you don't give your body to a guy just because he's good-looking, she told herself. My God, you've got to have higher standards than that!

Jerry was handsome, but he wasn't nearly as intelligent as he was good-looking. He wasn't witty, clever, kind, or more than minimally considerate. He thought he was cool, and he was good at playing Joe College; but there was no substance to him.

Amy looked around at the other girls in their silks and satins and laces and chiffons, in their low-cut bodices, in their Empire-waist dresses, in their backless gowns and long skirts and pumps, in their elaborate hairdos and carefully applied makeup and borrowed jewelry. All those girls were laughing and pretending to be ultra-sophisticated, glamorous, even world-weary. Amy envied them. They were having so much fun.

And she was pregnant.

She was afraid she was going to cry. She bit her tongue and held back the tears.

The prom was scheduled to last until one o'clock in the morning. Afterwards, from one-thirty until three o'clock, there was an extravagant breakfast buffet in one of the town's nicest restaurants.

Amy had been allowed to come to the prom, but she hadn't been given permission to attend the breakfast. It was all right with her father, but, as usual, her mother objected. Her father said she could stay out until three because this was a special night, but her mother wanted her home by ten, three whole hours before the prom ended. Amy always had to be home by ten on weekends, nine o'clock on school nights. Tonight, however, her father interceded on her behalf, and her mother grudgingly compromised; Amy didn't have to be home until one o'clock. Her mother didn't like making that concession, and later, in a hundred small telling ways, she would make Amy pay for it.

If Mother could have her way, Amy thought, if Daddy didn't stick up for me now and then, I wouldn't be permitted to date at all. I wouldn't be permitted to do anything except go to church.

"You're dynamite," Jerry Galloway whispered as he took

her in his arms for another dance. "You make me so hot, baby."

Dear, dear Mother, Amy thought bitterly, just look at how well all your rules and regulations have worked. All your prayers, all those years you dragged me to Mass three or four or five times a week, all those nightly recitations of the rosary that I had to take part in before I could go to sleep. You see, Mother? See how well all of that has worked? I'm pregnant. Knocked up. What would Jesus think about that? And what will you think about that when you find out? What will you think about having a bastard grandchild, Mother?

"You're shivering again," Jerry said.

"Just a chill."

A few minutes after ten o'clock, while the orchestra was playing "Scarborough Fair," and while Jerry was pushing Amy around the dance floor, he suggested they cut out and spend the rest of the night together, in their own way, just the two of them, just (as he so transparently put it) proving their love to each other. This was supposed to be a special night for a girl, a time to store up good memories, not just another cheap opportunity to screw around in the backseat of her boyfriend's car. Besides, they had arrived at the dance only two and a half hours ago. Jerry's eagerness was unseemly and more than a little selfish. But after all, she reminded herself, he was just a horny teenager, not a real man, and certainly not a romantic. Besides, she couldn't really enjoy herself anyway, not with everything she had to worry about. She agreed to leave with him, although what she had in mind for the remainder of the evening was much different from the steamy makeout session he was contemplating.

As they left the gymnasium, which the decorating committee had tried desperately to transform into a ballroom, Amy glanced back wistfully, taking one last look at the crepe paper and the tinsel and the carnations made out of Kleenex tissues. The lights were low. A revolving, mirrored globe hung above the dance floor, turning slowly, casting down splinters of color from its thousand facets. The room should have looked exotic, magical. But it only made Amy sad.

Jerry owned a meticulously restored, fussily maintained, twenty-year-old Chevrolet. He drove out of town, along narrow, winding Black Hollow Road. Eventually he pulled off on a single-lane dirt track near the river and squeezed the car in among the high brush and the scattered trees. He switched off the headlights, then the engine, and he rolled down his window a couple of inches to let in a warm current of fresh night air.

This was their usual parking spot. It was here that Amy had gotten pregnant.

Jerry slid out from behind the wheel. He smiled at her, and his teeth looked phosphorescent in the calcimined moonlight that streamed through the trees and the windshield. He took Amy's right hand and put it firmly on his crotch. "Feel that, baby? See how you get to me?"

"Jerry—"

"No girl has ever gotten to me like you do."

He slipped one hand in her bodice, feeling her breasts.

"Jerry, wait a minute."

He leaned toward her, kissed her neck. He smelled of Old Spice.

She took her hand off his crotch and resisted him.

He didn't take the hint. He removed his hand from her bodice only long enough to reach behind her for the zipper to her dress.

"Jerry, damn it!" She shoved him away.

He blinked stupidly. "Huh? What's wrong?"

"You're panting like a dog."

"You turn me on."

"A knothole would turn you on."

"What's that supposed to mean?"

"I want to talk," she said.

"Talk?"

"People do, you know. They talk before they screw."

He stared at her for a moment, then sighed and said, "All right. What do you want to talk about?"

"It's not what I *want* to talk about," she said. "It's what we *have* to talk about."

"You aren't making sense, baby. What is this—a riddle or something?"

She took a deep breath and blurted out the bad news: "I'm pregnant."

For a few seconds the night was so perfectly still that she could hear the soft gurgling of the river washing along the shore twenty feet away. A frog croaked.

"Is this a joke?" Jerry asked at last.

"No."

"You're really pregnant?"

"Yes."

"Oh, shit."

"Ah," she said sarcastically, "what an eloquent summary of the situation."

"Did you miss your period or what?"

"I missed it last month. And I'm overdue this month again."

"You been to a doctor?"

"No."

"Maybe you aren't."

"I am."

"You aren't getting big."

"It's too early to show."

He was silent for a while, staring out at the trees and the black, oily river beyond. Then: "How could you do this to me?"

His question stunned her. She gaped at him, and when she saw he was serious, she laughed bitterly. "Maybe I wasn't paying much attention in biology class, but the way I understand it, *you* did it to *me*, not the other way around. And don't try to blame it on parthenogenesis, either."

"Partho-what?"

"Parthenogenesis. That's when the female gets pregnant without having to find a male to fertilize her egg."

With a note of hope in his voice, he said, "Hey, is that possible?"

God, he was a dolt. Why had she ever given herself to him? They had nothing in common. She was artistically inclined; she played the flute, and she liked to draw. Jerry had no interest whatsoever in the arts. He liked cars and sports, and Amy had little tolerance for conversation about either of those things. She liked to read; he thought books were for girls and sissies. Except for sex, cars, and football, no subject could engage him for more than ten minutes; he had a child's attention span. So why had she given herself to him? *Why?*

"Oh, sure," she said in answer to his question. "Sure, parthenogenesis might be possible—if I was an insect. Or a certain kind of plant."

"You're sure it can't happen to people?" he asked.

"God, Jerry, you can't really be that dumb. You're putting me on, aren't you?"

"Hell, I never listened to old Amoeba Face Peterson in biology," Jerry said defensively. "That stuff always bored my ass off." He was silent for a minute, and she waited, and finally he said, "So what are you going to do?"

"I'll get an abortion," she said.

He brightened up immediately. "Yeah. Yeah, that's the best thing. It really is. That's smart. That's the best thing for both of us. I mean, you know, we're too young to be tied down with a kid."

"We'll cut school on Monday," she said. "We'll find a doctor and set up an appointment to have it done."

"You mean you want me to go with you?"

"Of course."

"Why?"

"For Christ's sake, Jerry, I don't want to go by myself. I don't want to face it alone."

"There's nothing to be scared of," he said. "You can handle it. I know you can."

She glared at him. "You're coming with me. You've got to. For one thing, you'll have to approve the doctor's fee. Maybe we'll have to shop around for the best price." She shuddered. "That's up to you."

"You mean . . . you want me to pay for the abortion?"

"I think that's fair."

"How much?"

"I don't know. Probably a few hundred."

"I can't," he said.

"What?"

"I can't pay for it, Amy."

"You've had a real good job the past two summers. And you work weekends most of the year."

"Stocking shelves in a grocery store doesn't pay a whole hell of a lot, you know."

"Union wages."

"Yeah, but—"

"You bought this car and fixed it up. You have a pretty good savings account. You've bragged about that often enough."

He squirmed. "I can't touch my savings."

"Why not?"

"I need every dollar for California."

"I don't understand."

"Two weeks from now, after graduation, I'm going to blow this stupid town. There ain't any future here for me. Royal City. What a laugh. There's nothing royal about this dump. And it sure ain't a city. It's just fifteen thousand people living in a dump in the middle of Ohio, which is just another, bigger dump."

"I like it."

"I don't."

"But what do you expect to find in California?"

"Are you kidding? There's a million opportunities out there for a guy with a lot on the ball."

"But what do you expect to find there for *you*?" she asked.

He didn't understand what she meant; he didn't feel her slip the needle in. "I just told you, baby. In California, there's more opportunities than anywhere else in the world. Los Angeles. That's the place for me. Hell, yes. A guy like me can go real far in a city like L.A."

"Doing what?"

"Anything."

"Such as?"

"Absolutely anything."

"How long have you been planning to go to L.A.?"

Sheepishly, he said, "For about a year now."

"You never told me."

"I didn't want to upset you."

"You were just going to quietly disappear."

"Hey, no. No, I was going to keep in touch, baby. I even figured maybe you'd come along with me."

"Like hell you did. Jerry, you *have* to pay for the abortion."

"Why can't *you* pay for it?" He was whining. "You had a job last summer. You've been working weekends just like me."

"My mother controls my savings account. There's no way I can withdraw that much cash without telling her why I need it. No way."

"So tell her."

"God, I can't. She'd kill me."

"She'd scream a lot, and you'd probably be grounded for a while. But she'll get over it."

"She won't. She'll kill me."

"Don't be stupid. She won't kill you."

"You don't know my mother. She's very strict. And she's . . . mean sometimes. Besides, we're a Catholic family. My mother is very devout. Very, very devout. And to a devout Catholic, abortion is a terrible sin. It's murder. My father even does some free legal work for the Right-to-Life League. He's not so fanatical about religion as my mother is. He's a pretty straight guy, but I don't think he'd ever approve an abortion. And I *know* my mother wouldn't. Not in a million years. She'd make me have the baby. I know she would. And I can't. I just can't. Oh, God, I can't."

She started to cry.

"Hey, baby, it's not the end of the world." He put an arm around her. "You'll come through this okay. It's not as bad as you think. Life goes on, you know."

She didn't want to lean on him for either emotional or physical support. Not on *him*, of all people. But she couldn't help it. She put her head on his shoulder, despising herself for this weakness.

"Easy," he said. "Take it easy. Everything's going to be just fine."

When the tears finally stopped flowing, she said, "Jerry, you've got to help me. You've *got* to, that's all."

"Well . . ."

"Jerry, please."

"You know I would if I could."

She sat up straight, dabbing at her eyes with her handkerchief. "Jerry, part of the responsibility is yours. Part of—"

"I can't," he said firmly, taking his arm away from her.

"Just lend me the money. I'll pay you back."

"You can't pay me back in just two weeks. And I'll need every dollar I've got when I go to California the first of June."

"Just a loan," she said, not wanting to beg but having no choice.

"I can't, can't, can't!" He shouted like a child throwing a tantrum. His voice was high, screechy. "Forget it! Just forget it, Amy! I need every penny I've got for when I get out of this stinking town."

Oh God, I hate him!

And she hated herself, too, for what she'd let him do.

"If you don't at least lend me the money, I'll call your parents. I'll tell them I'm carrying your child. I'll put the heat on you, Jerry." She didn't think she really had the nerve to do something like that, but she hoped the threat of it would make him be reasonable. "God help me, I'll even make you marry me if that's the last resort, but I won't go down alone."

"What do you want from me, for Christ's sake?"

"Just a little help. Decency. That's all."

"You can't make me marry you."

"Maybe not," she admitted. "But I can cause you a lot of trouble, and maybe I can force you to contribute to the support of the baby."

"You can't force me to do anything if I'm in another state. You can't make me pay up from California."

"We'll see about that," she said, although she thought he was probably right.

"Anyway, you can't prove I'm the father."

"Who else?"

"How should I know?"

"You're the only one I've been doing it with."

"I sure wasn't the first," he said.

"You bastard."

"Eddie Talbot was the first."

"I haven't done anything with anyone else since I started going with you six months ago."

"How do I know that's true?"

"You *know*," Amy said, loathing him. She wanted to kick him and hit him and scratch his face until it was a bloody mess, but she restrained herself, hoping she might yet gain some concession from him. "It *is* your baby, Jerry. There's no doubt about that."

"I never came inside you," he argued.

"A couple of times you did. Once is all it takes."

"If you tried to nail me in court or something like that, I'd get five or six friends to swear they'd been in your pants during the past couple of months."

"In my whole life there's never been anyone but Eddie and then you!"

"In court it'd be your word against theirs."

"They'd be committing perjury."

"I've got good buddies who'd do anything to protect me."

"Even destroy my reputation?"

"What reputation?" he asked, sneering.

Amy felt sick.

It was hopeless. There was no way she could force him to do the right thing. She was alone.

"Take me home," she said.

"Gladly," he said.

The drive back to town took half an hour. During that time neither of them said a word.

The Harper house was on Maple Lane, a solidly middle-class neighborhood of well-manicured lawns and shrubs, fresh paint, and two-car garages. The Harpers lived in a two-story, neo-colonial house, white with green shutters flanking the windows. Lights were on downstairs, in the living room.

As Jerry pulled the Chevy to the curb and braked in front of the house, Amy said, "We'll probably be passing each other in the halls during final exam week. And we'll see each other at graduation two weeks from now. But I guess this is the last time we'll be talking."

"Bet on it," he said coldly.

"So I wouldn't want to miss this opportunity to tell you what a rotten son of a bitch you are," she said as evenly as she could.

He stared at her but said nothing.

"You're an immature little boy, Jerry. You're not a man, and you'll probably never be a man."

He didn't respond. They were parked beneath a street light, and she could see his face clearly; he was impassive.

She was angered by his refusal to react to her. She wanted to leave with the knowledge that she had hurt him as badly as he had hurt her with his comment about her reputation. But she was not very good at vituperation. She didn't have a talent for quarreling. Ordinarily she preferred to live and let live, but in this case the injustice she had suffered at Jerry's hands was so great that she felt an uncharacteristic urge to retaliate. She steeled herself to make one last attempt to sting him.

"One other thing I want to tell you as sort of a favor to your next girlfriend," Amy said. "There's another way you're like a little boy, Jerry. You make love like a little boy. You're immature in that department, too. I kept hoping you'd get better at it, but you never did. You know how many times you managed to make me come? Three times. Out of all those nights we made love, I climaxed only three times. You're clumsy, rough, and quick on the trigger. A regular minuteman. Do your next girlfriend a favor and at least read a couple of books about sex. Eddie Talbot wasn't all that great, but compared to him you're really a lousy fuck."

She saw his face darken and tighten as she spoke, and she knew she had finally gotten to him. Feeling a sick sort of triumph, she opened her door and started to get out.

He grabbed her wrist and held her in the car. "You know what you are? You're a pig, that's what."

"Let go of me," she said sharply, trying to pry herself loose of him. "If you don't let go, I just might tell you how that pathetic little thing between your legs measures up to Eddie Talbot, and I'm sure you don't want to hear that."

She heard herself, and she didn't like how hard and sluttish she sounded; however, at the same time, she took a fierce, primitive delight in the shock that was visible in his face.

Several times over the past six months, she had sensed his sexual insecurity, and now it was quite evident indeed. He was furious. He did not merely let go of her wrist; he flung it away from him, as if he suddenly realized he was holding on to a snake.

As she got out of the car, he said, "You bitch! I hope your old lady *does* make you keep the kid. And you know what? I hope the damned thing's not right. Yeah. I hope it's not right. I hope it's not normal. You're such a smart-mouthed bitch, I hope you're stuck with some drooling little creep who's not normal. Your smart mouth wouldn't get you out of that one."

She looked in at him and said, "You're disgusting." Before he could respond, she slammed the door.

He threw the Chevy in gear, stomped on the accelerator, and drove away with a protracted squeal of tires.

In the ensuing silence, a night bird shrieked.

Amy moved through a cloud of acrid blue smoke that smelled of burning rubber, and she started up the walk toward the house. After a couple of steps, she began to tremble violently.

When her father had approved of her staying out later than usual, he had said, *The senior prom is a special night in a girl's life. It's an event. Like a sixteenth birthday or a twenty-first. There's really not another night quite like the night of a girl's senior prom.*

As it turned out, there was a perverse sort of truth in what he had said. Amy had never lived through a night quite like this one. And she hoped she'd never know another one like it, either.

Prom night. Saturday, May 17, 1980.

That date would be burned in her memory forever.

When she reached the front door, she paused, her hand resting on the knob. She dreaded going into the house. She didn't want to face her mother tonight.

Amy didn't intend to reveal the fact that she was pregnant. Not just yet. In a few days, perhaps. In a week or two. And only if she were left with no other choice. In the meantime she would search diligently for other exits from her predicament, even though she didn't have much hope of finding another way out.

She didn't want to talk to her parents now because she was so nervous, so upset over Jerry's treatment of her that she didn't trust herself to keep the secret. She might let something slip by accident or out of a subconscious need for punishment and pity.

Her hand, damp with sweat, was still on the doorknob.

She considered just walking away, leaving town, starting a new life. But she had nowhere to go. She had no money.

The load of responsibility she had shouldered was almost too much for her. And when Jerry had lashed out in a childish attempt to hurt her, when he had wished a deformed baby on her, he had added another weight to the burden she bore. She didn't believe that Jerry's curse had any real power, of course. But it *was* possible that her mother would force her to have the baby, and it *was* possible that the baby would be deformed and forever dependent upon her. The chance of that happening was small, but not so small that she could put it out of her mind; misfortune of that nature befell people all the time. Crippled children were born every day. Legless and armless babies. Misshapen babies. Brain-damaged children. The list of possible birth defects was very long—and very frightening.

Again, a night bird cried. It was a mournful sound that matched her mood.

Finally she opened the door and went into the house.

2

Thin, talcum-white, with streaming hair the color and texture of spiderwebs, dressed all in white, Ghost hurried along the busy carnival midway. He moved like a pale column of smoke, slipping effortlessly through the narrowest gaps in the crowd; he appeared to flow with the currents of the night breeze.

From the funhouse barker's platform, four feet above the midway, Conrad Straker watched the albino. Straker had stopped in the middle of his come-on spiel the instant he had seen Ghost approaching. Behind Straker, the raucous funhouse music blared continuously. Every thirty seconds the giant clown's face—a much larger, more sophisticated, and more animated version of the face that had topped his first funhouse, twenty-seven years ago—winked down at the passersby and let out a recorded, four-bark laugh: "*Haa, haa, haa, haaaaa.*"

As he waited for the albino, Straker lit a cigarette. His hand shook; the match bobbled.

At last Ghost reached the funhouse and pulled himself up onto the barker's platform. "It's done," he said. "I gave her the free ticket." He had a cool, feathery voice that nevertheless carried clearly above the carnival din.

"She wasn't suspicious?"

"Of course not. She was thrilled to have her fortune told for free. She acted like she really believed that Madame Zena could see into the future."

"I wouldn't want her to think she'd been singled out," Straker said worriedly.

"Relax," Ghost said. "I gave her the usual dumb story, and she bought it. I said my job was to wander up and down the midway, giving out free tickets for this and that, just to stir up interest. Public relations."

Frowning, Straker said, "You're positive you approached the right girl?"

"The one you pointed out."

Above them, the enormous clown's face broadcast another tiny burst of laughter.

Taking small, quick, nervous drags on his cigarette, Straker said, "She was sixteen or seventeen. Very dark hair, almost black. Dark eyes. About five foot five."

"Sure," Ghost said. "Like the others, last season."

"This one was wearing a blue and gray sweater. She was with a blond boy about her age."

"That's the one," Ghost said, combing his lank hair with his long, slender, milky-white fingers.

"Are you sure she used the ticket?"

"Yes. I walked her straight to Zena's tent."

"Maybe this time . . ."

"What does Zena do with these kids you steer to her?"

"While she tells their fortunes, she finds out as much about them as she can—their names, their parents' names, a lot of things like that."

"Why?"

"Because I want to know."

"But why do you want to know?"

"That's none of your business."

Behind them, inside the enormous funhouse, several young girls screamed at something that popped out at them from the darkness. There was a phony quality to their squeals of terror; like thousands of teenage girls before them, they were pretending to be frightened witless, so that they would have an excuse to cuddle closer to the young men beside them.

Ignoring the screams behind him, Ghost stared intently at Straker; the albino's almost colorless, semitransparent eyes were disconcerting. "Something I have to know. Have you ever . . . well . . . have you ever touched one of these kids I've sent to Zena?"

Straker glared at him. "If you're asking me whether I've sexually molested any of the young girls and boys in whom I've shown an interest, the answer is no. That's ridiculous."

"I sure wouldn't want to be a part of something like that," Ghost said.

"You've got an ugly, dirty little mind," Straker said, disgusted. "I'm not looking for fresh meat, for God's sake. I'm searching for one child in particular, someone special."

"Who?"

"That's none of your business." Excited, as always, by

the prospect of finally, successfully concluding his long search, Conrad said, "I've got to get over to Zena's tent. She's probably just about finished with the girl. This could be the one. This could be the one I've been looking for."

In the funhouse, their voices muffled by the walls, the girls screamed again.

As Straker turned toward the platform steps, anxious to hear what Zena had discovered, the albino put a hand on his arm, detaining him. "Last season, in almost every town we hit, there was a kid who caught your eye. Sometimes two or three kids. How long have you been looking?"

"Fifteen years."

Ghost blinked. For a moment a pair of thin, translucent lids covered but did not fully conceal his strange eyes. "Fifteen years? That doesn't make sense."

"To me, it makes perfect sense," Straker said coldly.

"Look, last year was my first season working for you, and I didn't want to complain about anything until I understood your routines better. But that business with the kids really bugged me. There's something creepy about it. And now it's starting all over again this year. I just don't like being a part of it."

"Then quit," Straker said sharply. "Go to work for someone else."

"But, except for this one thing, I like the job. It's good work and good pay."

"Then do what you're told, take your paycheck, and shut up," Straker said. "Or get the hell out. It's your choice."

Straker tried to pull away from the albino, but Ghost would not relinquish his hold on the larger man's arm. His bony, clammy, death-white hand had a surprisingly strong grip. "Tell me one thing. Just to set my mind at ease."

"What is it?" Straker asked impatiently.

"If you ever find who you're looking for, do you intend to hurt him . . . or her?"

"Of course not," Straker lied. "Why would I hurt him?"

"Well, I don't understand why you're so obsessed with this search, unless—"

"Look," Straker said, "there's a woman to whom I'm deeply indebted. I've lost track of her over the years. I know she has children by now, and every time I see a kid who resembles her, I check it out. I figure I might be lucky enough to stumble across her daughter or son, find her, and repay the debt."

Ghost frowned. "You're going to an awful lot of trouble just to—"

"It's an awfully big debt," Straker said, interrupting him. "It's on my conscience. I won't rest easy until I repay it."

"But the chance that she'd have a kid that looks like her, the chance that her kid will come wandering past your funhouse some day . . . Do you realize what a long shot that is?"

"I know it's unlikely," Straker said. "But it doesn't cost me anything to keep an eye out for kids who resemble her. And crazier things happen."

The albino looked into Straker's eyes, searching for signs of deception or truth.

Straker was not able to read anything in Ghost's eyes, for they were too strange to be interpreted. Because they were without color, they were also without character. White and faded pink. Watery. Bottomless eyes. The albino's gaze was piercing but cold, emotionless.

At last Ghost said, "All right. I guess if you're just trying to find someone to repay an old debt . . . there's nothing wrong with me helping you."

"Good. It's settled. Now I've got to talk to Gunther for a minute, and then I'm going over to Zena's. You take over the pitchman's roost for me," Straker said, finally managing to pull free of the albino's moist hand.

Inside the funhouse a new chorus of girlish voices wailed in a shrill imitation of horror.

As the huge clown's face spat out another mechanical laugh, Straker hurried across the barker's platform, beneath a banner that proclaimed THE BIGGEST FUNHOUSE IN THE WORLD! He descended the wooden steps, went past the red-and-black ticket booth, and paused for a moment near the boarding gate where several ticket holders were stepping down into the brightly painted gondolas that would carry them through the funhouse.

Conrad looked up at Gunther, who was standing on a six-foot-square platform to the left of the boarding gate and four feet above it. Gunther was waving his long arms and growling at the marks below him, pretending to threaten them. He was an impressive figure, better than six and a half feet tall, more than two hundred and fifty pounds of bone and muscle. His shoulders were enormous. He was dressed all in black, and his entire head was covered by a Hollywood-quality Frankenstein monster mask that disappeared under his collar. He was also wearing monster gloves—big, green rubber hands streaked with fake blood—that extended beneath the cuffs of his jacket. Suddenly Gunther noticed Conrad looking up at him, and he turned, favoring him with an especially fierce growl.

Straker grinned. He made a circle with the thumb and forefinger of his right hand, giving Gunther a sign of approval.

Gunther capered around the platform in a clumsy monster dance of delight.

The people waiting to board the gondolas laughed and applauded the monster's performance.

With a fine sense of theater, Gunther abruptly turned vicious once more and roared at his audience. A couple of girls screamed.

Gunther bellowed and shook his head and snarled and stamped his foot and hissed and waved his arms. He enjoyed his work.

Smiling, Straker turned away from the funhouse and walked into the river of people that flowed along the midway. But as he drew nearer to Zena's tent, his smile faded. He thought of the dark-haired, dark-eyed girl he'd seen from the barker's platform a short while ago. Maybe this was the one. Maybe this was Ellen's child. After all these years, the thought of what she'd done to his little boy still filled him with a fiery rage, and the possibility of revenge still made his heart beat faster, still caused his blood to race with excitement. Long before he reached Zena's tent, his smile had metamorphosed into a scowl.

Dressed in red and black and gold, wearing a spangled scarf and a lot of rings and too much mascara, Zena sat alone in the dimly lighted tent, waiting for Conrad. Four candles burned steadily inside four separate glass chimneys, casting an orange glow that did not reach into the corners. The only other light was from the illuminated crystal ball that stood in the center of the table.

Music, excited voices, the spiels of pitchmen, and the clatter of the thrill rides filtered through the canvas walls from the midway.

To the left of the table, a raven stood in a large cage, head cocked, one shiny black eye focused on the crystal ball.

Zena, who called herself Madame Zena and pretended to be a Gypsy with psychic powers, had not a drop of Romany blood in her and actually couldn't see anything in the future other than the fact that tomorrow the sun would rise and subsequently set. She was of Polish extraction. Her full name was Zena Anna Penetsky.

She had been a carny for twenty-eight years, since she was just fifteen, and she had never longed for another life. She liked the travel, the freedom, and the carnival people.

Once in a while, however, she grew weary of telling fortunes, and she was disturbed by the endless gullibility of the marks. She knew a thousand ways to con a mark, a thousand ways to convince him (after he had already paid for a palm reading) to shell out a few more dollars for a purportedly more complete look into his future. The ease with which she manipulated people embarrassed her. She told herself that what she did was all right because they were only marks, not carnies, and therefore not *real* people. That was the traditional carny attitude, but Zena could not be that hard all the time. Now and then she was troubled by guilt.

Occasionally she considered giving up fortune-telling. She could take a partner, someone who had done the palm-reading scam before. It meant sharing the profits, but that didn't worry Zena. She also owned a bottle-pitch joint and a very profitable grab joint, and after overhead she netted more each year than any half dozen marks earned at their boring jobs in the straight world. But she continued to play Gypsy fortune-teller because she had to do *something*; she wasn't the kind of person who could just sit back and take it easy.

By the age of fifteen, she had been a well-developed woman, and she had begun her carnival career as a kootch dancer. These days, as she became increasingly dissatisfied with her role as Madame Zena, she frequently considered opening a girl show of her own. She even toyed with the idea of performing again. It might be a kick.

She was forty-three, but she knew she could still excite a tentful of horny marks. She looked ten years younger than she was. Her hair was chestnut-brown and thick, untouched by gray; it framed a strong, pleasing, unlined face. Her eyes were a rare shade of violet—warm, kind eyes. Years ago, when she'd first worked as a kootch dancer, she'd been voluptuous. She still was. Through diet and exercise, she had maintained her splendid figure, and nature had even cooperated by miraculously sparing her large breasts from the downward drag of gravity.

But even as she fantasized about returning to the stage, she knew the hootchie-kootchie was not in her future. The kootch was just another way of manipulating the marks, no different from fortune-telling; in essence it was the very thing that she needed to get away from for a while. She would have to think of something else she could do.

The raven stirred on its perch and flapped its wings, interrupting her thoughts.

An instant later Conrad Straker entered the tent. He sat in the chair where the marks always sat, across the table from Zena. He leaned forward, anxious, tense. "Well?"

"No luck," Zena said.

He leaned even closer. "Are you positive we're talking about the same girl?"

"Yes."

"She was wearing a blue and gray sweater."

"Yes, yes," Zena said impatiently. "She had the ticket that Ghost had given her."

"What was her name? Did you find out her name?"

"Of course. Laura Alwine."

"Her mother's name?"

"Sandra. Not Ellen. Sandra. And Sandra is a natural blonde, not a brunette like Ellen was. Laura gets her dark hair and eyes from her father, she says. I'm sorry, Conrad. I pumped the girl for a lot of information while I was telling her fortune, but none of it matches what you're looking for. Not a single detail of it."

"I was sure she was the one."

"You're always sure."

He stared at her, and gradually his face grew red. He looked down at the tabletop, and he became rapidly, visibly angrier, as if he saw something in the grain of the wood that outraged him. He slammed his fist into the table. Slammed it down once, twice. Hard. Half a dozen times. Then again and again and again. The tent was filled with the loud, measured drumbeat of his fury. He was shaking, panting, sweating. His eyes were glazed. He began to curse, and he sprayed spittle across the table. He made strange, harsh, animal noises in the back of his throat, and he continued to pound the table as if it were a living creature that had wronged him.

Zena wasn't startled by his outburst. She was accustomed to his maniacal rages. She had once been married to him for two years.

On a stormy night in August 1955, she had stood in the rain, watching him ride backwards on the carousel. He had looked so very handsome then, so romantic, so vulnerable and brokenhearted that he had appealed to both her carnal and maternal instincts, and she had been drawn to him in a way she had never been drawn to another man. In February of the following year, they rode the carousel forward, together.

Just two weeks after the wedding, Conrad flew into a rage over something Zena did, and he struck her—repeatedly. She was too stunned to defend herself. Afterward he was contrite, embarrassed, appalled by what he had done. He wept and begged forgiveness. She was certain that his fit of violence was an aberration, not ordinary behavior. Three weeks later, however, he attacked her again, leaving her badly bruised and battered. Two weeks after that, when he was seized by another fit, he tried to hit her, but she struck first. She rammed a knee into his crotch and clawed his face with such frenzy that he backed off. Thereafter, forewarned, always watching for the first sign of one of his oncoming rages, she was able, after a fashion, to protect herself.

Zena worked hard at the marriage, trying to make it last in spite of her husband's explosive temper. There were two Conrad Strakers; she hated and feared one of them, but she loved the other. The first Conrad was a brooding, pessimistic, violence-prone man, as unpredictable as an animal, with a shocking talent and taste for sadism. The second Conrad was kind, thoughtful, even charming, a good lover, intelligent, creative. For a while Zena believed that a lot of love and patience and understanding would change him. She was convinced that the frightening Mr. Hyde personality would fade completely away, and that in time Conrad would settle down and be just the good Dr. Jekyll. Instead, the more love and understanding she gave him, the more frequently he became violent and abusive, as if he were determined to prove that he was not worthy of her love.

She knew that he despised himself. His inability to like himself and be at peace in his own mind, the frustration generated by his incurable self-hatred—*that* was the root of his periodic, maniacal rages. Something monstrous had happened to him a long, long time ago, in his formative years, some unspeakable childhood tragedy that had scarred him so deeply that nothing, not even Zena's love, could heal him. Some horror in his distant past, some terrible disaster for which he felt responsible, gave him bad dreams every night of his life. He was consumed by an unquenchable guilt that burned in him year after year with undiminished brightness, turning his heart, piece by piece, into bitter ashes. Many times Zena had tried to learn the secret that gnawed at Conrad, but he had been afraid to tell her, afraid that the truth would repel her and turn her against him forever. She had assured him that nothing he told her would make her loathe him. It would have been good for him to unburden himself at last. But he could not do it. Zena could learn only one thing: the event that haunted him had transpired on Christmas Eve, when he was only twelve years old. From that night forward, he had been a changed person; day by day, he had become ever more sour, increasingly violent. For a brief spell, after Ellen gave him his much-wanted child, even though it was a hideously deformed baby, Conrad had begun to feel better about himself. But when Ellen killed the child, Conrad sank even deeper into despair and self-hatred, and it wasn't likely that anyone would ever be able to draw him out of the psychological pit into which he had cast himself.

After struggling for two years to make their marriage work, after living in fear of Conrad's rage all that time, Zena had finally faced the fact that divorce was inevitable. She left him, but they didn't cease to be friendly. They shared certain bonds that couldn't be broken, but it was clear to both of them that they couldn't live together happily. She rode the carousel backwards.

Now, as Zena watched Conrad venting his rage on the table, she realized that most, if not all, of her love for him had been transformed into pity. She felt no passion anymore—just an abiding sorrow for him.

Conrad cursed, sputtered through bloodless lips, snarled, pounded the table.

The raven flapped its shiny, black wings and cried shrilly in its cage.

Zena waited patiently.

In time Conrad grew tired and stopped thumping the table. He leaned back in his chair, blinking dully, as if he were not quite sure where he was.

After he was silent for a minute, the raven became silent, too, and Zena said, "Conrad, you aren't going to find Ellen's child. Why don't you just give up?"

"Never," he said, slightly hoarse.

"For ten years you had a bunch of private detectives on it. One after the other. Several at the same time. You spent a small fortune on them. And they didn't find anything. Not a clue."

"They were all incompetent," he said sullenly.

"For years you've been looking on your own without any luck."

"I'll find what I'm after."

"You were wrong again tonight. Did you really think you'd stumble across her kids *here*? At the Coal County, Pennsylvania, Spring Fair? Not a very likely place, if you ask me."

"As likely as any other."

"Maybe Ellen didn't even live long enough to start a family with another man. Have you thought of that? Maybe she's long dead."

"She's alive."

"You can't be sure."

"I'm positive."

"Even if she's alive, she might not have children."

"She does. They're out there—somewhere."

"Damn it, you have no reason to be so sure of that!"

"I've been sent signs. Portents."

Zena looked into his cold, crystalline blue eyes, and she shivered. Signs? Portents? Was Conrad still only half-mad—or had he gone all the way over the edge?

The raven tapped its beak against the metal bars of its cage.

Zena said, "If by some miracle you do find one of Ellen's kids, what then?"

"I've told you before."

"Tell me again," she said, watching him closely.

"I want to tell her kids what she did," Conrad said. "I want them to know she's a baby killer. I want to turn them against her. I want to use all of my power as a pitchman to convince them that their mother is a vicious, despicable human being, the worst kind of criminal. A baby killer. I'll make them hate her as much as I hate her. In effect, I'll be taking her kids away from her, though not as brutally as she took my little boy."

As always, when he talked about exposing Ellen's past to her family, Conrad spoke with conviction.

As always, it sounded like a hollow fantasy.

And as always, Zena felt that he was lying. She was sure that he had something else in mind, an act of revenge even more brutal than what Ellen had done to that strange, disturbing, mutated baby twenty-five years ago.

If Conrad intended to kill Ellen's children when (and if) he found them, Zena wanted no part of that. She didn't want to be an accomplice to murder.

Yet she continued to assist him in his search. She helped him only because she didn't believe he would ever find what he was looking for. Helping him seemed harmless;

she was merely humoring him. That was all. Nothing more than humoring him. His quest was hopeless. He would never find Ellen's kids, even if they did exist.

Conrad looked away from her, turned his gaze on the raven.

The bird fixed him with one of its oily black eyes, and as their gazes locked, the raven froze.

Outside, on the midway, there was calliope music. The hundred thousand sounds of the closing-night crowd blended into a rhythmic susurration like the breathing of an enormous beast.

In the distance the giant, mechanical funhouse clown laughed and laughed.

3

When Amy stepped into the house at a quarter till twelve, she heard muffled voices in the kitchen. She thought her father was still awake, though he usually went to bed early Saturday night in order to get up in time for the first Mass on Sunday, thus freeing the rest of the day for his hobby— building miniature sets for model train layouts. When Amy got to the kitchen, she found only her mother. The voices were on the radio; it was tuned to a telephone talk show on a Chicago station, and the volume was turned low.

The room smelled vaguely of garlic, onions, and tomato paste.

There wasn't much light. A bulb burned above the sink, and the hood light was on over the stove. The radio dial cast a soft green glow.

Ellen Harper was sitting at the kitchen table. Actually, she was slumped over it, arms folded on the tabletop, head resting on her arms, her face turned away from the doorway where Amy stopped. A tall glass, half-full of yellow liquid, was within Ellen's reach. Amy didn't have to sample the drink to know what it was; her mother always drank the same thing—vodka and orange juice—and too much of it.

She's asleep, Amy thought, relieved.

She turned away from her mother, intending to sneak out of the room and upstairs to bed, but Ellen said, "You."

Amy sighed and looked back at her.

Ellen's eyes were blurry, bloodshot; the lids drooped. She blinked in surprise. "What're you doing home?" she asked groggily. "You're more than an hour early."

"Jerry got sick," Amy lied. "He had to go home."

"But you're more than an hour early," her mother said again, looking up at her in puzzlement, still blinking stupidly, struggling to penetrate the alcohol haze that softened the outlines of her thoughts.

"Jerry got sick, Mama. Something he ate at the prom."

"It was a *dance*, wasn't it?"

"Sure. But they had food. Hors d'oeuvres, cookies, cakes, punch, all kinds of stuff. Something he ate didn't agree with him."

"Who?"

"Jerry," Amy said patiently.

Her mother frowned. "You're sure that's all that happened?"

"What do you mean?"

"Seems . . . funny to me," Ellen said thickly, reaching for her unfinished drink. "Suspicious."

"What could possibly be suspicious about Jerry getting sick?" Amy asked.

Ellen sipped the vodka and orange juice. She studied Amy over the rim of the glass, and her stare was sharper than it had been a minute ago.

Exasperated, Amy spoke before her mother had a chance to make any accusations. "Mama, I didn't come home late. I came home *early*. I don't think I deserve to be subjected to the usual third degree."

"Don't you get smart with me," her mother said.

Amy looked down at the floor, shifted nervously from one foot to the other.

"Don't you remember what Our Lord said?" Ellen asked. "'Honor thy father and thy mother.' That's what He said. After all these years of church services and Bible readings, hasn't *anything* sunk into your head?"

Amy didn't respond. From experience she knew that respectful silence was the best way to deal with her mother at times like this.

Ellen finished her drink and got up. Her chair barked against the tile floor as she scooted it backwards. She came around the table, weaving slightly, and stopped in front of Amy. Her breath was sour. "I've tried hard, so very hard, to make a good girl out of you. I've made you go to church. I've forced you to read the Bible and pray every day. I've preached at you until I'm blue in the face. I've taught you all the right ways. I've done my best to keep you from going wrong. I've always been aware that you could go either way. Either way. Good or bad." She swayed, put a hand on Amy's shoulder to steady herself. "I've seen the potential in you, girl. I've seen that you have the potential for evil. I pray my heart out to Our Lady every day to look over you and guard you. There's a darkness deep inside you, and it must never be allowed to come to the surface."

Ellen leaned very close, put a hand under Amy's chin, lifted the girl's head, and met her eyes.

Amy felt as if ice-cold snakes were uncoiling inside her.

Ellen stared at her with a peculiar, drunken intensity, with the burning gaze of a fever victim. She seemed to be looking into her daughter's soul, and there was a mixture of fear and anger and hard-edged determination in her expression.

"Yes," Ellen said, whispering now. "There's a darkness in you. You could slip so easily. It's in you. The weakness. The difference. Something bad is in you, and you have to fight it every minute. You have to be careful, always careful."

"Please, Mama . . ."

"Did you let that boy touch you tonight?"

"No, Mama."

"Unless you're married, it's a dirty, filthy thing. If you slip, the Devil will have you. The thing inside you will come to the surface for everyone to see. And no one must ever see it. No one must know what you've got inside you. You've got to wrestle with that evil, keep it caged."

"Yes, Mama."

"Letting the boy touch you—that's an awful sin."

Getting drunk out of your mind every night is a sin, too, Mama. Using booze to escape from your worries is sinful. You use booze and the Church the same way, Mama. You use them to forget your troubles, to hide from something. What are you hiding from, Mama? What are you so afraid of?

Amy wished she could say all of that. She didn't dare.

"Did he touch you?" her mother asked.

"I told you—no."

"He touched you."

"No."

"Don't lie to me."

"We went to the prom," Amy said shakily, "and he got sick, and he brought me home. That's all, Mama."

"Did he touch your breasts?"

"No," Amy said, unsettled, embarrassed.

"Did you let him put his hands on your legs?"

Amy shook her head.

Ellen's hand tightened on the girl's shoulder, the talonlike fingers digging painfully deep. "You touched him," she said, her words slurring just a bit.

"No," Amy said. "I didn't."

"You touched him between the legs."

"Mama, I came home *early*!"

Ellen stared at her for several seconds, searching for the truth, but at last the fire went out of her dark eyes; the debilitating effects of the booze became evident again, and her eyelids drooped, and the flesh of her face sagged on her bones. When she was sober she was a pretty woman, but when she was drunk she looked haggard, much older than she looked otherwise. She let go of Amy, turned away, tottered back to the table. She picked up her empty glass, carried it to the refrigerator, dropped a couple of ice cubes into it. She added a little orange juice and a lot of vodka.

"Mama, can I go to bed now?"

"Don't forget to say your prayers."

"I won't forget."

"Say the rosary, too. It wouldn't hurt you."

"Yes, Mama."

Her long dress rustling noisily, Amy hurried upstairs. In her bedroom she switched on a lamp and stood by the bed, shuddering.

If she failed to raise the abortion money, if she had to tell her mother, she couldn't expect her father to intercede. Not this time. He would be angry and would agree to any punishment her mother proposed.

Paul Harper was a moderately successful attorney, a man who was in control in the legal arena, but at home he relinquished nearly all authority to his wife. Ellen made the domestic decisions, large and small, and for the most part, Paul was happy to be relieved of the responsibility. If Ellen insisted Amy carry the baby to term, Paul Harper would support that decision.

And Mama *will* insist on it, Amy thought miserably.

She looked at the Catholic icons her mother had placed around the room. A crucifix hung at the head of the bed, and a smaller one hung above the door. A statuette of the Virgin Mary was on the nightstand. Two more painted religious statuettes stood on the dresser. There was also a painting of Jesus; He was pointing to his Sacred Heart, which was exposed and bleeding.

In her mind Amy heard her mother's voice: *Don't forget to say your prayers.*

"Fuck it," Amy said aloud, defiantly.

What could she ask God to do for her? Give her money for an abortion? There wasn't much chance of *that* prayer being answered.

She stripped off her clothes. For a couple of minutes she

stood in front of a full-length mirror, studying her nude body. She couldn't see any sure signs of pregnancy. Her belly was flat.

Gradually the medical nature of her self-inspection changed to a more intimate, stimulating appraisal. She drew her hands slowly up her body, cupped her full breasts, teased her nipples.

She glanced at the religious statuettes on the dresser.

Her nipples were erect.

She slid her hands down her sides, reached behind, squeezed her firm buttocks.

She looked at the painting of Jesus.

Somehow, by flaunting her body at the image of Christ, she felt she was hurting her mother, deeply wounding her. Amy didn't understand why she felt that way. It didn't make sense. The painting was only a painting; Jesus wasn't really here, in the room, watching her. Yet she continued to pose lasciviously in front of the mirror, caressing herself, touching herself obscenely.

After a minute or two she caught sight of her own eyes in the mirror, and that brief glimpse into her own soul startled and disconcerted her. She quickly put on her flannel nightgown.

What's wrong with me? she wondered. Am I really bad inside, like Mama says? Am I evil?

Confused, she finally knelt at the side of her bed and said her prayers after all.

A quarter of an hour later, when she pulled back the covers, there was a tarantula on her pillow. She gasped, jumped—and then realized that the hideous thing was only a painted-rubber novelty item. She sighed wearily, put the phony spider in the drawer of her nightstand, and got into bed.

Her ten-year-old brother, Joey, never missed a chance to play a practical joke on her. Ordinarily, when she encountered one of his tricks, she went looking for him, pretending to be furious, threatening him with grave bodily harm. Of course she wasn't capable of hurting the boy. She loved him very much. But her mock anger was the part of the game that Joey enjoyed most. Usually, in retaliation for his pranks, Amy did nothing more than hold him down and tickle him until he promised to be good.

Right now he was in bed, probably awake in spite of the late hour, waiting for her to storm into his room. But tonight she would have to disappoint him. She wasn't in the mood for their usual routine, and she didn't have the energy for it, either.

She got into bed and switched off the light.

She couldn't sleep.

She thought about Jerry Galloway. She had told him the truth when she had ridiculed his skills as a lover. She had seldom had an orgasm. He was a clumsy, ignorant, thoughtless bedmate. Yet she had let him touch her night after night. She got little or no pleasure out of the affair, but she allowed him to use her as he wished. Why? *Why?*

She wasn't a bad girl. She wasn't wild or loose, not deep down in her heart. Even while she let Jerry use her, she hated herself for being so easy. Whenever she made out with a boy in a parked car, she felt awkward, embarrassed, out of place, as if she were trying to be someone else and not herself.

She wasn't a lazy girl, either. She had ambition. She planned to go to Royal City Junior College, then to Ohio

State, majoring in art. She would get a job as a commercial artist, and she would labor at fine arts in her spare time, nights and weekends, and if she found that she had enough talent to make a good living as a painter, she would quit the nine-to-five job and create wonderfully beautiful pictures for sale in galleries. She was determined to build a successful, interesting life.

But now she was pregnant. Her dreams were ashes.

Maybe she didn't deserve happiness. Maybe she *was* bad, just deep-down rotten.

Did a good girl spread her legs in the backseat of a boy's car nearly every night of the week? Did a good girl get knocked up while she was still in high school?

The dark minutes of the night unwound like black thread from a spinning spool, and Amy's thoughts unwound, too—tangled and confusing thoughts. She couldn't make up her mind about herself; she couldn't decide whether she was basically a good person or a bad one.

In her mind Amy could hear her mother's voice again: *There's a darkness in you. Something bad is in you, and you have to fight it every minute.*

Suddenly, Amy wondered if her sluttish behavior was just an attempt to spite her mother. That was an unsettling thought.

Speaking softly to the blackness around her, she said, "Did I let Jerry knock me up just because I knew the news would shatter Mama? Am I destroying my own future just to hurt that bitch?"

She was the only one who knew the answer to her own question; she would have to look for it within herself.

She lay very still beneath the covers, thinking.

Outside, the wind stirred the nearby maple trees.

In the distance a train whistle sounded.

The door scraped open, and floorboards creaked beneath the carpet as someone walked into the room.

The noise woke Joey Harper. He opened his eyes and looked at the alarm clock, which was visible in the pale glow of the night-light. 12:36.

He had been asleep an hour and a half, but he wasn't groggy. He was instantly awake and alert, for he was anticipating Amy's reaction to the tarantula in her bed. He had set his alarm for one o'clock because that was when she was supposed to come home; apparently she had returned early.

Footsteps. Soft. Sneaky. Coming closer.

Joey tensed under the sheets, but he continued to feign sleep.

The footsteps stopped at the side of his bed.

Joey felt a giggle building in him. He bit his tongue and struggled to hold back his laughter.

He sensed her leaning toward him. She was inches away.

He was going to wait a few seconds longer, and then, when she was on the verge of tickling him, he was going to yell in her face and scare the dickens out of her.

He kept his eyes closed, breathed shallowly and evenly, and counted off the seconds: One . . . two . . . three . . .

He was just about to shout in her face when he realized that the person bending over him wasn't Amy. He smelled sour, alcohol-tainted breath, and his heart began to pound.

Unaware that Joey was awake, his mother said, "Sweet, sweet, little Joey. Little baby-boy angel. Sweet, precious little angel face." Her voice was eerie. She spoke in an odd, half-whispered, half-crooned, throaty, silky stream of slurred words.

He wished desperately that she would go away. She was very drunk, worse than usual. She had come into his room several other nights when she'd been in this condition. She had talked to him, thinking he was asleep. Maybe she came in a lot more nights than he knew; maybe some nights he *was* asleep. Anyway, he knew what was coming. He knew what she was going to say and do, and he dreaded it.

"Little angel. You look like a little snoozing angel, a baby angel, lying there so innocent, so tender, sweet." She leaned even closer, bathing his face with her pungent breath. "But what're you like inside, little angel? Are you sweet and good and pure all the way through?"

Stop it, stop it, stop it! Joey thought. Please, don't do this again, Mama. Go away. Get out of here. *Please.*

But he didn't speak to her, and he didn't move. He didn't let her know he was awake because when she was like this he was afraid of her.

"You look so pure," she said, her alcohol-thickened voice growing even softer, even more blurry. "But maybe that angel face is just the surface . . . the mask. Maybe you're just putting on an act for me. Huh? Are you? Maybe . . . underneath . . . maybe you're just like the other one. Are you, little angel? Under that sweet face, are you like the other one, the monster, the thing he called Victor?"

Joey never had been able to figure out what she was

talking about when she sneaked in here at night and mumbled drunkenly at him. Who was Victor?

"If I produced one like you, why not another?" she asked herself aloud, and Joey thought she sounded a little bit afraid now. "This time . . . maybe it's a monster *inside*. In the mind. A monster *inside* . . . hiding in a normal body . . . behind such a nice face . . . waiting. Waiting to come out when no one's looking. Just waiting patiently. Both you and Amy. Huh? Wolves in sheep's clothing. Could be. Sure. Could be that way. What if it is? Huh? When will it happen? When will the thing come out of you for everyone to see? Can I turn my back on you, little angel? Can I ever be safe? Oh, God. Oh, Jesus, Jesus, help me. Mary, help me. I should never have had children. Not after the first one. I can never be sure of what I've created. Never. What if . . ."

Increasingly numbed by the liquor she had drunk, her tongue and lips became less and less able to form the words she wanted to say, and she lowered her voice so far that Joey could barely hear her, even though she was less than a foot from him. "What if . . . someday . . . what if I have to kill you, little angel?" Softer, softer, word by terrible word, softer. "What if . . . I have . . . to kill . . . you . . . like I had to kill . . . the other one . . . ?"

She began to weep quietly.

Joey was suddenly chilled to the bone, and he was worried that his shivering would disturb the sheets and draw her attention. He was afraid she would discover that he had heard every word.

Eventually her stifled weeping subsided.

Joey was sure she could hear his pounding heart.

He felt strange. He was afraid of her, but he was also sorry for her. He wanted to hug her and tell her everything would be all right—but he didn't dare.

Finally, after what seemed like hours but was surely only a minute or two, she left the bedroom, gently pulling the door shut after her.

Under the covers Joey curled into a tight, fetal ball.

What did it all mean? What had she been talking about? Was she just drunk? Or was she crazy?

Although he was scared, he was also a little bit ashamed of himself for thinking such things about his own mother.

Nevertheless, he was glad he had the wan, milky glow of the weak night-light. He sure didn't want to be alone in the dark right now.

In the nightmare Amy had given birth to a bizarrely deformed baby—a disgusting, vicious thing that looked more like a crab than like a human being. She was in a small, poorly lighted room with it, and it was coming after her, snapping at her with its bony pincers and arachnoid mandibles. The walls held narrow windows, and each time she passed one of them she saw her mother and Jerry Galloway on the far side of the glass; they were looking in at her and laughing. Then the baby scuttled along the floor, closed in fast, and seized her ankle in one of its spiny pincers.

She woke up, sat up in bed, a scream caught in the back of her throat. She choked it down.

Just a dream, she told herself. Just a bad dream courtesy of Jerry Galloway. Damn him!

In the gloom to her right, something moved.

She snapped on the bedside lamp.

Curtains. Her window was open a couple of inches to provide ventilation, and a mild breeze stirred the curtains.

Outside, a block or two away, a dog howled mournfully.

Amy looked at the clock. Three in the morning.

She sat there for a while, until she had calmed down, but when she switched off the light she couldn't get back to sleep. The darkness was oppressive and threatening in a way it hadn't been since she was a small child.

She had the curious, disturbing feeling that, outside, in the night, something terrible was bearing down on the Harper house. Like a tornado. But not a tornado. Something else. Something weird, worse than a mere storm. She had a premonition—not quite the right word, but the only word that came close to describing what she was feeling—an icy premonition that some relentlessly destructive force was closing in on her and the entire family. She tried to imagine what it could be, but no explanation occurred to her. The impression of danger remained formless, nameless, but powerful.

The sensation was, in fact, so electrifying, so unshakable, that she finally had to get up and go to the window, even though she felt foolish for doing so.

Maple Lane was dozing peacefully, wrapped in unthreatening shadows. And beyond their street, the suburban south side of Royal City rose on a series of gentle, low hills; at this hour there was only a sprinkling of lights.

Farther south, at the edge of the town and above it, lay the county fairgrounds. The fairgrounds were dark now, deserted, but in July, when the carnival arrived, Amy would be able to stand at her window and see the blaze of colored lights, the far-off, magical blur of the steadily turning Ferris wheel.

The night was filled only with the familiar. There was nothing new in it, nothing dangerous.

The feeling that she was standing in the path of a fiercely destructive, oncoming storm faded, and exhaustion replaced it. She returned to bed.

Only one threat loomed over the Harper household, and that was her pregnancy, the inescapable consequences of her sin.

Amy put her hands on her belly, and she thought about what her mother would say, and she wondered if she would always be as alone and helpless as she was now, and she wondered what was coming.

4

At the refreshment stand near the carousel, there were five people in line ahead of Chrissy Lampton and Bob Drew.

"I hate to waste time waiting like this," Chrissy said, "but I really want that candy apple."

"It won't take long," Bob said.

"There's so much more I want to do."

"Relax. It's only eleven-thirty. The carnival won't shut down until at least one o'clock."

"But it's the last night," Chrissy said. She took a deep breath, savoring the blend of aromas that permeated the night: popcorn, cotton candy, garlic-flavored french fries, hot roasted peanuts, and more. "Ahhhh! My mouth is watering. I've been stuffing myself all night, and I'm still famished. I can't believe I've eaten so much!"

"It's partly the excitement," Bob said. "Excitement burns up calories. And all those thrill rides. You were scared half to death on most of those rides, and fear burns up calories even faster than strenuous exercise." He was seriously trying to analyze her unusual appetite. Bob was an accountant.

"Listen," Chrissy said, "why don't you wait in line and get the candy apples while I find the ladies' room. I'll meet you over there by the merry-go-round in a few minutes. That way we'll kill two birds at the same time."

"With one stone," Bob said.

"Huh?"

"The expression is, 'We'll kill two birds with one stone.'"

"Oh. Sure."

"But I don't think it applies here exactly," Bob said. "Not quite. Anyway, you go ahead to the ladies'. We'll meet at the carousel like you said."

Sheesh! Chrissy thought. Are all accountants like this?

She walked away from the refreshment stand, through the damp wood shavings that covered the ground, through the calliope-blast from the merry-go-round, past a high-striker where a muscular young man slammed a sledgehammer into a scale and rang a bell overhead to impress his date, past a dozen pitchmen who were spieling a mile a minute, trying to get people to play all sorts of games where you could win a teddy bear or a kewpie doll or some other piece of junk. A hundred attractions played a hundred different songs, but somehow the various strains of music didn't sound the least bit discordant when they came together; everything fused into a single, strange, but appealing melody. The carnival was a river of noise, and Chrissy waded through it, grinning happily.

Chrissy Lampton loved the Coal County Spring Fair. It was always one of the high spots of the year. The fair,

Christmas, New Year's Eve, Thanksgiving, the Halloween dance at the Elks' Club, the Las Vegas Nights at St. Thomas's Church (one in April, one in August)—those were the only days of excitement in the entire year, the only events worth looking forward to in all of Coal County.

She remembered part of a funny and rather dirty little song that had made the rounds when she'd been in high school:

Everyone who lives here has the zits;
Good old Coal County sure is the pits.
Anybody with a brain has got to split
Cause this is where God squats when he gets the shits.

In high school she used to laugh at that song. But now, at the still-tender age of twenty-one, grimly aware of how limited her future was in this place, she didn't find those lyrics very humorous.

Someday she would move to New York or Los Angeles, to a place with opportunities. She intended to split as soon as she had six months' worth of living expenses in her savings account. She already had enough for five months.

Soaking up the color and glamour of the carnival as she walked, Chrissy headed toward the amusements that stood at the fringe of the midway, behind which she expected to find a comfort station within a couple of hundred feet. The public restrooms were in cinder-block buildings scattered around the perimeter of the fairgrounds.

As she made her way through the crowd, a pitchman at a duck-shoot game gave her a loud wolf-whistle.

She grinned and waved in reply.

She felt terrific. Even though she was temporarily stuck in Coal County, she had a wonderful, sparkling future. She knew she was good-looking. She had a lot of smarts, too. With those qualities she could carve out a niche for herself in the big city in record time, easily within six months. Currently she was a typist, but that was strictly short-term.

Another pitchman, this one working a wheel of fortune, heard the first barker's whistle, and he whistled at her, too. Then a third carny joined the fun, whistled, called to her teasingly.

She felt as if she would live forever.

Ahead of her the big clown's face atop the funhouse laughed shrilly.

The funhouse, which stood next to Freak-o-rama, was at the eastern edge of the midway, and Chrissy figured there would be a comfort station somewhere behind it. She turned in beside the big, rambling structure, with the freak show on her right, and she walked through the narrow alley between the two attractions, away from the crowds and the lights and the music.

The air was no longer redolent with cooking food. It smelled of wet wood shavings, grease, and gasoline from the large, thrumming generators.

Inside the funhouse, chains clanked, banshees howled, ghosts laughed spookily, ghouls cackled, the wheels of the cars clattered incessantly along the winding track, and haunting music swelled and faded, swelled and faded. A girl screamed. Then another. Then three or four at once.

They're acting like little kids, Chrissy thought scornfully. They're so pathetically eager to be thrilled, so willing to accept the shabby illusions in there, anything to be briefly transported from the drab reality of life in Coal County, Pennsylvania.

An hour or two ago, when she had ridden through the funhouse with Bob Drew, she had screamed, too. Now, remembering her own hysteria, she was a little bit ashamed of herself.

As she stepped over cables and ropes, cautiously picking her way toward the rear of the funhouse, she realized that, a few years from now, after she had had a chance to experience classier thrills, after she had grown accustomed to more sophisticated excitements, she would find the carnival tawdry and juvenile instead of exotic and glamorous.

She was almost at the end of the long, narrow passageway. It was darker here than she had expected.

She stumbled over a fat electric cable.

"Damn!"

She regained her balance, squinted at the ground ahead.

There was just enough light to create impenetrable, purple-black shadows on all sides.

She thought of turning back, but she really had to pee, and she was sure there was a bathroom nearby.

At last she reached the end of the alley and turned the corner into the darkness behind the funhouse, looking for one of the brightly lighted comfort stations.

She almost walked into the man.

He was standing against the rear wall of the funhouse, in an exceedingly deep pool of velvety shadows.

Chrissy yelped in surprise.

She couldn't see his face, but she *could* see that he was big. Very big. Huge.

An instant after she registered his presence, even as she

gasped in shock, even as she saw how large he was, she
realized that he was waiting for her. She started to scream.

He struck her on the side of the head with such brutal
force that it was a miracle her neck didn't snap.

The scream died in her throat. She dropped to her knees,
then toppled onto her side in the dirt, stunned, numbed,
unable to move, struggling desperately to remain conscious.
Her mind was a dully glinting blade skating on a crescent of
silvery ice, with mile-deep, black water on both sides.

She was vaguely aware of being lifted and carried.

She couldn't resist him; she had no strength at all.

A door creaked noisily.

She forced her eyes open and saw that she was being
carried out of the dark night, into an even darker place.

Her heart was beating so hard that it seemed to ham-
mer the air out of her lungs each time she tried to draw a
breath.

He dropped her rudely onto a hard, wooden floor.

Get up! Run! she told herself.

She couldn't move. She seemed paralyzed.

Hinges squealed as he pushed the door shut again.

This can't be happening! she thought.

A sliding bolt rasped into place, and the man grunted
with what she took to be satisfaction. She was locked in
with him.

Dizzy, confused, weak as a baby, but no longer in danger of losing consciousness, she tried to figure out where
she was. The room was perfectly black, as utterly lightless
as the inside of the Devil's pocket. The wooden floor was
crude, and it was filled with vibrations, the muffled sound
of machinery.

Someone screamed. Then someone else. The air was split by a maniacal laugh. Music swelled. The vibrations in the floor resolved into the *clackety-clackety-clack* of steel wheels on a metal track.

She was in the funhouse. Probably in the service area. Behind the tracks on which the cars moved.

A trickle of strength seeped into Chrissy's body again, but she was barely able to lift one hand to her bruised temple. She expected to find her skin and hair wet and sticky with blood, but they were dry. The flesh was tender but apparently unbroken.

The stranger knelt on the floor beside her.

She could hear him, sense him, but not see him; however, even in this pitch-black hole, she was aware of his great size; he loomed.

He's going to rape me, she thought. God, no. Please. Oh, please don't let him do it.

This stranger was breathing curiously. Sniffing. Snuffling. Like an animal. Like a dog trying to get her scent.

"No," she said.

He grunted again.

Bob will come looking for me, she told herself hopefully, frantically. Bob will come; he's got to come; he's got to come and save me, good old Bob, please, God, please.

She was succumbing to a rapidly burgeoning panic as her head cleared and as the terrible danger became more and more evident to her.

The stranger touched her hip.

She tried to pull back.

He held her.

She was gasping, shaking. The temporary paralysis

faded; the numbness in her limbs vanished. Abruptly she was awash in pain from the blow to the head that she had suffered a few minutes ago.

The stranger moved his hand up her belly to her breasts and ripped open her blouse.

She cried out.

He slapped her, jarring her teeth.

She realized that it was useless to call for help in a fun-house. Even if people heard her above all the music, above the recorded howling and wailing of the ghosts and mon-sters, they would think she was just another thrill-seeker startled by a pop-up pirate or a jack-in-the-box vampire.

The man tore off her bra.

She was no match for him physically, but enough of her strength had returned for her to offer some resistance, and she couldn't just lie there, waiting for him to take her. She reached for his hands, grabbed them, intending to push them away, but with a shock she discovered that they were not ordinary hands. They weren't a man's hands. Not ex-actly. They were . . . different.

Oh, God.

She became aware of two green ovals in the blackness. Two softly shining, green spots. Floating above her.

Eyes.

She was looking into the stranger's eyes.

What sort of man has eyes that shine in the dark?

Bob Drew stood at the carousel with one candy apple in each hand, waiting for Chrissy. After five minutes he started to eat his own apple. After ten minutes he grew impatient and began to pace. After fifteen minutes he was angry with Chrissy; she was a gorgeous girl, fun to be with, but she was sometimes flighty and frequently inconsiderate.

After twenty minutes his anger began to give way to mild concern; then he began to worry. Maybe she was sick. She had eaten an incredible amount and variety of junk. It would be amazing if she *didn't* upchuck sooner or later. Besides, you never knew for sure how clean and whole-some carnival food was. Maybe she had gotten a bad hot dog or had unwittingly eaten some piece of filth along with her chiliburger.

Considering that possibility, he began to feel queasy himself. He stared at his half-eaten candy apple and finally dropped it into a trash barrel.

He wanted to find her and satisfy himself that she was all right, but he didn't think she would be too happy to see him while her breath still stank of vomit. If she had just been sick in the ladies' room, she would want time to freshen up, patch her makeup, and put herself back together.

After twenty-five minutes he threw Chrissy's candy apple in the trash with his own.

After half an hour, bored by the endlessly galloping horses and by the rhythmically flashing brass poles, increasingly concerned about Chrissy, he went searching for her. Earlier, he had watched her walk away from the refreshment stand, admiring her round bottom and her shapely calves, and then she had vanished in the crowd. A minute or two later, he thought he had seen her golden head as she left the midway near the funhouse, and now he decided to look in that area first.

Between the funhouse and the freak show, a five-foot-wide

path led back to an open space behind the amusements, the outer ring of the fairgrounds, where the restrooms were located. Toward the end of the passageway, the shadows were so dark and thick that they seemed tangible, like black drapes, and the night was surprisingly lonely here, considering that the busy midway was only fifty or sixty feet behind him.

Peering uneasily into the shadows, Bob wondered if Chrissy had encountered more serious trouble than just an upset stomach. She was a *very* pretty girl, and these days, when so many people seemed to have lost all respect for the law, there were more than a few men prowling around who thought nothing of taking what they wanted from a pretty girl, regardless of whether or not she wanted them to have it. Bob supposed that there were even more men of that stripe in the carnival than there were in the real world.

With growing trepidation he reached the end of the path and stepped into the open area behind the funhouse. He looked right, then left, and saw the comfort station. It was sixty yards away, rectangular, gray, made of cement blocks, perched in the center of a tightly circumscribed pool of bright yellowish light. He couldn't see the entire structure, only a third of it, because there was a row of ten or twelve big carnival trucks parked in the intervening hundred and eighty feet. Here the darkness was even deeper; the trucks were only hulking outlines, and they made him think of slumbering, primeval beasts.

He took only two steps toward the distant comfort station before putting his foot down on something that nearly sent him sprawling. When he regained his balance, he reached down and picked up the treacherous object.

It was Chrissy's red clutch purse.

Bob Drew's heart began to sink into a bottomless well.

At the far end of the funhouse, at the front of it, out on the midway, the giant clown's face sprayed the night with a brittle, shrapnel laugh.

Bob's mouth was dry. He swallowed hard, tried to squeeze out some saliva. "Chrissy?"

She didn't answer.

"Chrissy, for God's sake, are you there?"

A door squealed on unoiled hinges. Behind him.

The music and screaming inside the funhouse got louder as the door opened.

Bob turned toward the noise, feeling something he had not felt in many years, not since he had been a small boy alone in his dark bedroom with the terrifying conviction that some hideous creature was hiding in the closet.

He saw a forest of shadows, all but one of them perfectly still, but that one was moving fast. It came straight at him. He was seized by powerful, shadow hands.

"No."

Bob was thrown against the rear of the funhouse with such incredible force that the wind was knocked out of him, and his head snapped back, and his skull cracked hard into the wooden wall. Trying to placate his burning lungs, he sucked desperately on the night air; it was cold against his teeth.

The shadow swooped down on him again.

It didn't move like a man.

Bob saw green, glowing eyes.

He brought up one arm to protect his face, but his assailant struck lower than that; Bob took a sledgehammer punch in the stomach. At least, for one hopelessly optimistic moment, he *thought* he had been punched. But the shadow-thing hadn't struck him with its fist. Nothing as clean as that. It had slashed him. He was badly cut. A wet, sickening, sliding, dissolving sensation filled him. Stunned, he reached down, put one trembling hand on his belly, and gagged with revulsion and horror when he felt the size of the wound.

My God, I've been disemboweled!

The shadow stepped back, crouching, watching, snorting and sniffing like a dog, although it was much too big to be a dog.

Gibbering hysterically, Bob Drew tried to hold his bulging intestines inside his body. If they slipped out of him, there was no chance that he could be sewn up and restored to health.

The shadow-thing hissed at him.

Bob was too deep in shock to feel more than the thinnest edge of the pain, but a red veil descended over his vision. His legs turned to water and then began to evaporate from under him. He leaned against the wall of the funhouse, aware that he had little chance of survival even if he stayed on his feet, but also aware that he had no chance at all if he fell. His only hope was to hold himself together. Get to a doctor. Maybe they could sew him up. Maybe they could put everything back in place and prevent peritonitis. It was a long shot. Very long. But maybe . . . if he just didn't fall . . . He couldn't allow himself to fall. He must not fall. He *wouldn't* fall.

He fell.

* * *

The carnies called it "slough night" and looked forward to it with true Gypsy spirit. The last night of the engagement. The night they tore down. The night they packed up and got ready to move on to the next stand. The carnival shed itself of the town in much the same way that a snake sloughed off its dead, dirty, unwanted skin.

To Conrad Straker, slough night was always the best night of the week, for he continued to hope, against all reason, that the next stop would be the one at which he would find Ellen and her children.

By one-thirty in the morning, the last of the marks was gone from the Coal County, Pennsylvania, fairgrounds. Even before then, some pieces of the show began to come down, although most of the job still lay ahead.

Conrad, who owned two small concessions in addition to the enormous funhouse, had already overseen the breaking down of those enterprises. One was a pitch-and-dunk, which he had shuttered and folded around one o'clock. The other was a grab joint, so named because it was a fast-food place with no chairs for the marks to sit down; they had to grab their food and eat on the fly. He had closed the grab joint earlier, around midnight.

Now, in the cool, mid-May night, he worked on the funhouse with Gunther, Ghost, his other full-time employees, a couple of local laborers looking to make forty bucks each, and a pair of freelance roughies who traveled with the show. They broke the joint apart and loaded it into two large trucks that would carry it to the next stand.

Because Conrad's funhouse could legitimately boast of being the largest in the world, because it offered the marks solid thrills for their money, and because the ride was long and dark enough to allow teenage boys to cop a few feels from their dates, it was a popular and profitable concession. He had spent many years and a lot of money adding to the attraction, letting it grow organically into the finest amusement of its kind on earth. He was proud of his creation.

Nevertheless, each time the funhouse had to be erected or torn down, Conrad hated the thing with a passion that most men couldn't generate for any inanimate object except, perhaps, a larcenous vending machine or a bullheaded billing computer. Although the funhouse was cleverly designed—a genuine marvel of prefabricated construction and easy collapsibility—putting it up and then sloughing it seemed equal, at least in Conrad's mind, to the most spectacular and arduous feats of the ancient Egyptian pyramid builders.

For more than four hours, Conrad and his twelve-man crew swarmed over the structure, illuminated by the big, generator-powered midway lights. They lowered and dismantled the giant clown's face, took down strings of colored lights, rolled up a couple thousand feet of heavy-duty extension cords. They pulled off the canvas roof and folded it. Grunting, sweating, they disconnected and stacked the gondola tracks. They removed the mechanical ghouls, ghosts, and ax murderers that had terrorized thousands of marks, and they wrapped the animated figures in blankets and other padding. They unbolted wooden wall panels, disassembled beams and braces, took up slabs of plank flooring, skinned their knuckles, knocked down the ticket booth, guzzled soda, and packed generators and transformers and a mess of machinery into the waiting trucks, which were checked periodically by Max Freed or one of his assistants.

Max, superintendent of transportation for Big American Midway Shows—BAM to its employees and fellow travelers—supervised the tearing down and loading of the huge midway. Next to the famous E. James Strates organization, BAM was the largest carnival in the world. It was no ragbag, gilly, or lousy little forty-miler; it was a first-rate show. BAM traveled in forty-four railroad cars and more than sixty enormous trucks. Although some of the equipment belonged to the independent concessionaires, not to BAM, every truckload had to pass Max Freed's inspection, for the carnival company would bear the brunt of any bad publicity if one of the vehicles proved to be less than roadworthy and was the cause of an accident.

While Conrad and his men dismantled the funhouse, a couple of hundred other carnies were also at work on the midway—roughies, concessionaires, animal trainers, jointees, wheelmen, pitchmen, jam auctioneers, short-order cooks, strippers, midgets, dwarves, even the elephants. Except for the men, now sleeping soundly, who would drive the trucks off the lot a few hours from now, no one could call it a night until his part of the show was bundled and strapped down and ready to hit the road.

The Ferris wheel came down. Partially dismantled, it looked like a pair of gigantic, jagged jaws biting at the sky.

Other rides were quickly and efficiently torn apart. The

Sky Diver. The Tip Top. The Tilt-a-Whirl. The carousel. Magical machineries of fun, all locked away in ordinary-looking, dusty, greasy vans.

One minute the tents rippled like sheets of dark rain. The next minute they lay in still, black puddles.

The grotesque images on the freak-show banners—all painted by the renowned carnival artist David "Snap" Wyatt—fluttered and billowed between their moorings. Some of the large canvases portrayed the twisted, mutant faces of a few of the human oddities who made their living in Freak-o-rama, and these appeared to leer and wink and snarl and sneer at the carnies who labored below, a trick of the wind as it played with the canvas. Then the ropes were loosened, the pulley wheels squeaked, and the banners slid down their mooring poles to the pitchman's platform, where they were rolled up and put away—nightmares in large cardboard tubes.

At five-thirty in the morning, exhausted, Conrad surveyed the site where the funhouse had stood, and he decided he could finally go to bed. Everything had been broken down. A small pile of gear remained to be loaded, but that would take only half an hour and could be left to Ghost, Gunther, and one or two of the others. Conrad paid the local laborers and the freelance roughies. He instructed Ghost to supervise the completion of the job and to obtain final approval from Max Freed; he told Gunther to do exactly what Ghost wanted him to do. He paid an advance against salary to the two fresh-eyed roughies who, having just gotten up from a good sleep, were prepared to drive the trucks to Clearfield, Pennsylvania, which was the next stand; Conrad would follow later in the day in his thirty-four-foot Travelmaster. At last, aching in every muscle, he trudged back to his motor home—which was parked among more than two hundred similar vehicles, trailers, and mobile homes—in the back lot, at the west end of the fairgrounds.

The nearer he drew to the Travelmaster, the slower he moved. He dawdled. He took time to appreciate the night. It was quiet, serene. The breezes had blown away to another part of the county, and the air was preternaturally still. Dawn was near, although no light yet touched the eastern horizon. Earlier, there had been a moon; it had set behind the mountains not long ago. Now there were only scudding, slightly phosphorescent clouds, silver-black against the darker, blue-black sky. He stood at the door of his motor home and took several deep breaths of the crisp, refreshing air, not eager to go inside, afraid of what he might find in there.

At last he could delay no longer. He steeled himself for the worst, opened the door, climbed into the Travelmaster, and switched on the lights.

There wasn't anyone in the cockpit. The kitchen was deserted, and so was the forward sleeping area.

Conrad walked to the rear of the main compartment and paused, trembling, then hesitantly slid open the door to the master bedroom. He snapped on the light.

The bed was still neatly made, precisely as he'd left it yesterday morning. There wasn't a dead woman sprawled on the mattress, which was what he had expected to find.

He sighed with relief.

A week had passed since he had found the last woman. He would shortly find another. He was certain of that, grimly certain. The urge to rape and kill and mutilate came at weekly intervals now, far more frequently than had once been the case. But apparently it had not happened tonight.

Feeling marginally better, he went into the small bathroom to take a quick, hot shower before going to bed—and the sink in there was streaked with blood. The towels were darkly stained, sodden, lying in a pile on the floor.

It *had* happened.

In the soap dish, a cake of Ivory sat in a slimy puddle; it was red-brown with blood.

For nearly a minute Conrad stood just inside the doorway, staring apprehensively at the shower stall. The curtain was drawn. He knew he had to whisk it aside and see if anything waited behind it, but he dreaded making that move.

He closed his eyes and leaned against the doorjamb, weary, pausing until he could regain sufficient strength to do what must be done.

Twice before, he had found something waiting for him in the shower stall. Something that had been ripped and crushed, broken and chewed on. Something that had once been a living human being but wasn't anymore.

He heard the shower curtain rattling back on its metal rod: *snickety-snickety-snick.*

His eyes snapped open.

The curtain was still closed, hanging limply, unstirred. He had only imagined the sound.

He let out his breath in a *whoosh!*

Get on with it, he told himself angrily.

He licked his lips nervously, pushed away from the

jamb, and went to the shower stall. He gripped the curtain with one hand and quickly jerked it aside.

The stall was empty.

At least this time the body had been disposed of. That was something to be thankful for. Handling the disgusting remains was a chore that Conrad hated.

Of course he would have to learn what had been done with the latest corpse. If it hadn't been taken far enough away from the fairgrounds to deflect police suspicion from the carnival, he would have to go out soon and move it.

He turned away from the shower stall and began to clean up the bloody bathroom.

Fifteen minutes later, badly in need of a drink, he fetched a glass, a tray of ice cubes, and a bottle of Johnnie Walker from the kitchen. He carried those items into the master bedroom compartment, sat on the bed, and poured two or three ounces of Scotch for himself. He sat back, propped up by three pillows, and sipped the whiskey, trying to attain a state of calm that would at least permit him to hold his glass without constantly rattling the ice in it.

A mimeographed copy of Big American Midway's season schedule was on the nightstand. It was tattered from much handling. Conrad picked it up.

From early November until the middle of April, BAM, like other carnivals, shuttered for the off-season. Most of the carnies, people from every roadshow there was, wintered in Gibsonton, Florida—known as "Gibtown" to show-folk—where they had created a year-round community of their own kind, a carny Shangri-La, a retreat, a place where the bearded lady and the man with three eyes could get together for a drink at the neighborhood bar without anyone staring at them. But from April through October, Big American traveled incessantly, settling into a new town every week, pulling up its fragile roots six days later.

As he sipped his Scotch, Conrad Straker read through the Big American schedule, letting his eyes linger on each line of it, savoring the names of the towns, trying to get a psychic fix on one of them, trying to figure out in which burg he would (at long last) come across Ellen's children.

He hoped she had at least one daughter. He had plans for her son if she had a son, but he had special plans for her daughter.

Gradually, after he poured a few more ounces, he felt the Scotch having its desired effect. But as always, the names of the towns on the season schedule settled his nerves more effectively than whiskey ever could.

At last he put the list aside and looked up at the crucifix that was fastened to the wall above the foot of the bed. It was hanging upside down. And Christ's suffering face had been carefully painted black.

A votive candle in a clear glass container stood on the nightstand. Conrad kept it lighted around the clock. The candle was black; the burning wax produced a strange, dark flame.

Conrad Straker was a devout man. Without fail he said his prayers every night. But he didn't pray to Jesus.

He had converted to a satanic religion twenty-two years ago, not long after Zena had divorced him. He contemplated death with great pleasure, eagerly anticipating the descent into Hell. He knew that was his destiny. Hell. His rightful home. He was not afraid of it. He would be at peace there. Satan's favored acolyte. He belonged in Hell. It was his rightful home. After all, since that tragic, fiery Christmas Eve when he was twelve years old, he had lived in one sort of hell or another, day and night, night and day, without relief.

The outside door opened at the front end of the Travelmaster, and the trailer rocked as it took in its other lodger, and the door closed with a bang.

"I'm back here!" Conrad called, not bothering to get up from the bed.

There was no answer, but he knew who was there.

"You left the bathroom a mess when you cleaned up," Conrad shouted.

Heavy footsteps headed toward him.

The following Sunday, a man named David Clippert and a dog named Moose were hiking in the spring-fresh Coal County hills, two miles from the fairgrounds.

Shortly before four o'clock, as they were crossing a grassy hill, Moose, gamboling ahead of his master, came across something in a small patch of brush that he found unusually interesting. He raced around in a circle, staying in the grass, not entering the brush, but fascinated by whatever he had spotted in there. He barked several times, stopped to sniff something, then dashed in a circle again and loudly announced his discovery.

From twenty yards behind the dog, David couldn't see what all the fuss was about. He had a pretty good idea, though. Most likely it was a flurry of butterflies flitting back and forth through the weeds. Or perhaps a tiny lizard that had frozen on a leaf but had failed to evade Moose's sharp eyes. At most it was a field mouse. Moose wouldn't stay close to anything larger than that. He was a big, silken-coated Irish setter, strong and friendly and good of heart, but he was a coward. If he had come upon a snake, a fox, or even a rabbit, he would have vamoosed with his tail between his legs.

As David drew nearer the waist-high brush—mostly milkweed and brambles—Moose slunk off, whining softly.

"What is it, boy?"

The dog took up a position fifteen feet away from his find, looked beseechingly at his master, and whimpered.

Strange behavior, David thought, frowning.

It wasn't like Moose to be frightened off by a butterfly or a lizard. Once the big mutt zeroed in on prey like that, he was a formidable adversary, absolutely ferocious, indomitable.

A few seconds later, when David reached the brush and saw what had drawn the dog's attention, he stopped as if he had walked into a brick wall.

"Oh, Jesus."

A great river of arctic air must have changed course in the sky, for the warm May afternoon was suddenly cold, blood-freezing cold.

Two dead bodies, a man and a woman, were sprawled in the brush, supported in a partially upright position by the interweaving blackberry vines. Both corpses were facing up, arms spread wide, almost as if they had been crucified on those thorny branches. The man had been disemboweled.

David shuddered, but he didn't turn away from that gruesome sight. In the late 1960s he had served two tours of duty as a battlefield medic in Vietnam before he was wounded and sent home: he had seen gut wounds of all kinds, bellies ripped open by bullets, by bayonets, and by the shrapnel from antipersonnel mines. He was not squeamish.

But when he took a closer look at the woman, when he saw what had been done to her, he cried out involuntarily, quickly turned away from her, stumbled a few steps into the grass, dropped to his knees, and was violently, wrackingly sick.

5

The Dive was *the* teenage hangout in Royal City. It was on Main Street, four blocks from the high school. There wasn't anything special about it, so far as Amy could see. A soda fountain. A short-order grill. Ten tables with oil-cloth draped over them. Eight shiny, red leatherette booths. Half a dozen pinball machines in an alcove in the back. A jukebox. That was it. Nothing fancy. Amy figured there had to be a million places just like it spread all over the country. She knew of four others right here in little old Royal City. But for some mysterious reason, perhaps herd instinct, perhaps because the name of the establishment sounded like the kind of sleazy dump their parents would disapprove of, Royal City's teenagers congregated at The Dive in greater numbers than they did anywhere else in town.

Amy had been a waitress at The Dive for the past two

summers, and she was going to work there full-time again starting the first of June, until the junior college opened in September. She also pulled a few hours of hash-slinging during the school year, around the holidays and on most weekends. She took a small allowance out of her earnings, hardly enough for pocket money, and the rest went into her savings account for college.

On Sunday, the day following the senior prom, Amy worked from noon until six. The Dive was exceptionally busy. By four o'clock she was worn out. By five o'clock she was amazed that she could still stand. As the shift-change neared, she caught herself glancing at the clock every few minutes, willing the hands to move faster, faster.

She wondered if her uncharacteristic lack of energy could be explained by her pregnancy. Probably. Some of her strength was being diverted to the baby. Even this early on, it was bound to have its effect on her. Wasn't it?

Dwelling on her pregnancy depressed her. Depressed, she found the time crawling by even slower than before.

A few minutes before six, Liz Duncan came into The Dive. She looked smashing. She was wearing skin-tight French jeans and a mauve and blue sweater that appeared as if it had been knitted on her. She was a pretty blonde with an extremely cute figure. Amy saw boys looking up from all over the room as Liz walked through the door.

Liz was alone, currently between boyfriends. She was always between boyfriends but never for long; she went through guys the way Amy went through a box of Kleenex. Yesterday evening Liz had gone to the prom with a one-night stand. It seemed to Amy that every relationship Liz had with a boy was a one-night stand, even if it went on for as long as a month or two; Liz never desired anything lasting. Unlike other high school girls, she was repelled by the thought of exchanging rings and going steady with just one guy. She liked variety, and she seemed to thrive on impermanence. She was the Bad Girl of the senior class, and some of her exploits were legendary among her peers. She didn't give a damn what anyone thought of her.

Amy was drawing two frosted mugs of root beer from the soda fountain when Liz breezed up to the counter and said, "Hey, kid, how's it going?"

"I'm frazzled," Amy said.

"You get off soon?"

"Five minutes."

"Doing anything after?"

"No. I'm glad you came in. I have to talk to you."

"Sounds mysterious."

"It's important," Amy said.

"Think the house will treat us to cherry Cokes?"

"Sure. There's an empty booth over there. You stake a claim to it, and I'll join you as soon as I get off work."

A few minutes later Amy brought the Cokes to the booth and sat down opposite Liz.

"What's up?" Liz asked.

Amy stirred her Coke with a straw. "Well . . . I need to . . ."

"Yeah?"

"I need to . . . borrow some money."

"Sure. I can let you have ten anyway. Will that help?"

"Liz, I've got to raise at least three or four hundred bucks. Probably more."

"You serious?"

"Yes."

"Jesus, Amy, you know me. When it comes to money, my hands have grease on them. The stuff just slips away. My folks give it to me pretty much whenever I ask, and then, next thing I know—*zip!* It's a fuckin' miracle that I've got *ten* bucks I can let you have. But three or four hundred!"

Amy sighed and nodded. "I was afraid you'd say that."

"Listen, if I had it I'd give it to you."

"I know you would."

Whatever other faults Liz might have—and she had her share—miserliness was not one of them.

"What about your savings?" she asked Amy.

Amy shook her head. "I can't touch my bank account without Mama's approval. And I'm hoping she won't find out about this."

"About what? What do you need big bucks for?"

Amy started to speak, but her voice caught in her throat. She was reluctant to reveal her awful secret, even to Liz. She sipped her Coke, buying time to reconsider the wisdom of sharing her misery with her friend.

"Amy?"

The Dive bristled with noise: clicking, beeping, ringing pinball machines; hard-driving rock and roll on the juke-box; a babble of voices; bursts of laughter.

"Amy, what's wrong?"

Blushing, Amy said, "I guess I'm being ridiculous, but I . . . I'm just . . . too embarrassed to tell you."

"That *is* ridiculous. You can tell me anything. I'm your best friend, aren't I?"

"Yes."

That was true; Liz Duncan was her best friend. In fact, Liz was just about her only friend. She didn't spend much time with any of the other girls her age. She hung out almost exclusively with Liz, and that was odd when you thought about it. She and Liz were so different from each other in so many ways. Amy studied hard and did well in school; Liz couldn't care less about her grades. Amy wanted to go to college; Liz abhorred the idea. Amy was introverted, downright shy on occasion; Liz was outgoing, bold, even brassy at times. Amy liked books; Liz preferred movies and Hollywood fan magazines. In spite of the fact that Amy was in rebellion against her mother's excessive religious fervor, she still believed in God; but Liz said that the whole concept of God and life after death was a crock. Amy didn't care much for booze or pot and used them only when she wanted to please Liz; but Liz said that if there was a God—which she assured Amy there was not—he would be worth worshipping just because he had created liquor and marijuana. Even though the two girls differed in countless ways, their friendship flourished. The main reason it flourished was that Amy worked very hard to make a success of it. She did pretty much what Liz wanted to do, said what she figured Liz wanted to hear. She never criticized Liz, always humored her, always laughed at her jokes, and nearly always agreed with her opinions. Amy had put an enormous amount of time and energy into making the relationship last, but she had never stopped to ask herself why she cared so much about being Liz Duncan's best friend.

Last night, in bed, Amy had wondered if she'd subconsciously *wanted* Jerry Galloway to knock her up just to spite her mother. That had been a startling thought. Now she wondered if she was maintaining a friendship with Liz Duncan for the same misguided reason. Liz had (and relished) the worst reputation in school; she was foulmouthed and irreverent and promiscuous. Hanging out with her might be, for Amy, just one more act of rebellion against Mama's traditional values and morals.

As before, Amy was unsettled by the thought that she might be screwing up her future just to cause her mother pain. If that was true, then the resentment and anger she felt toward her mother was much deeper, much darker, than she had realized. It also meant that she wasn't in control of her life; it meant she was motivated by a black hatred and a corrupting bitterness she couldn't control. She was so unnerved by those ideas that she refused to consider them; she quickly pushed them out of her mind.

"So?" Liz said. "Are you going to tell me what's happening?"

Amy blinked. "Uh . . . well . . . I broke off with Jerry."

"When?"

"Last night."

"After you left the prom? Why?"

"He's a stupid, mean son of a bitch."

"He's always been," Liz said. "But that didn't bother you before. Why all of a sudden? And what's this got to do with needing three or four hundred bucks?"

Amy glanced around, afraid that someone might overhear what she was about to say. They were in the last booth, so there was no one behind her. On the other side, behind Liz, four football jocks were arm-wrestling bois-

terously. At the nearest table two couples, self-styled intel-
lectuals, were intently discussing current movies; they
called them "films" and spoke of "auteurs" as if they'd all
worked in Hollywood for years and knew what it was
about. No one was eavesdropping.

Amy looked at Liz. "Recently I've been getting sick in
the morning."

Liz understood immediately. "Oh, no. What about
your period?"

"Missed it."

"Holy shit."

"So you see why I need the money."

"An abortion," Liz said softly. "Did you tell Jerry?"

"That's why we broke up. He says it isn't his. He won't
help."

"He's a rotten little shit."

"I don't know what I'm going to do."

"Damn!" Liz said. "I wish you'd gone to the doctor I
recommended. I wish you'd gotten that prescription for
the pill."

"I was scared of the pill. You hear all these stories about
cancer and blood clots . . ."

"As soon as I turn twenty-one," Liz said, "I'm going to
get the Band-Aid operation. But the pill's essential in the
meantime. What's worse—the risk of blood clot or getting
knocked up?"

"You're right," Amy said miserably. "I don't know why
I didn't do what you told me to do."

*Except maybe I wanted to get pregnant and didn't even
know it.*

Liz leaned toward her. "Jesus, kid, I'm sorry. I'm sorry

as hell. I feel sick. I really do. I just feel sick that you're in this bind."

"Imagine how I feel."

"Jesus, what a bad break."

"I don't know what I'm going to do," Amy said again.

"I'll tell you what you're going to do," Liz said. "You're going to go home and tell your old man and your old lady."

"Oh, no. I couldn't. It'd be awful."

"Look, I know it won't be pretty. There'll be all sorts of screaming and hollering and name-calling. They'll dump a hell of a load of guilt on you. It'll be an ordeal, for sure. But they aren't going to beat you up or kill you."

"My mother might."

"Don't be silly. The old bitch will rant and rave and make you feel miserable for a while. But let's not lose track of what's important here. The important thing is getting your ass into a clinic and getting that baby scraped out of you as soon as possible."

Amy winced at the other girl's choice of words.

"All you have to do," Liz said, "is grit your teeth and sit through all the shouting, and then *they'll* pay for the abortion."

"No. You're forgetting that my family is Catholic. They think abortion is a sin."

"They might think it's a sin, but they won't force a young girl like you to ruin her whole life. Catholics get abortions all the time, no matter what they say."

"I'm sure you're right," Amy said. "But my mother is too devout. She won't ever agree to it."

"You really think she'd be willing to live with the shame of an illegitimate grandchild right there in her own house?"

"To hurt me . . . and mainly to teach me a lesson . . . yes."

"You're sure?"

"Positive."

They sat in glum silence for a while.

On the jukebox, Donna Summer was singing about the price she had to pay for love.

Suddenly Liz snapped her fingers. "I've got it!"

"What?"

"Even Catholics approve of abortion if the mother's life is in danger, don't they?"

"Not all Catholics. Just the most liberal ones approve of it even under those circumstances."

"And your old lady isn't liberal."

"Hardly."

"But your father's better, isn't he? At least about the religious stuff?"

"He's not so fanatical as Mama. He might agree to let me have an abortion if he truly thought the baby would destroy my health."

"All right. So you make him think it's destroying your *mental* health. Dig it? You get suicidal. You threaten to kill yourself if you can't have an abortion. Act like you're half crazy. Be hysterical. Be irrational. Scream, cry, then laugh without having any reason to laugh, then cry again, break things . . . If all of *that* doesn't convince them, then you can make a phony attempt to slash your wrists, just a big enough cut to smear some blood around. They won't be sure whether you botched it on purpose or by accident, and they won't want to take any chances."

Amy slowly shook her head. "It wouldn't work."

"Why not?"

"I'm not a good actress."

"I'll bet you'd fool them."

"Carrying on like that, pretending . . . Well, I'd feel stupid."

"Would you rather feel pregnant?"

"There must be another way."

"Like what?"

"I don't know."

"Face it, kid. This is your best shot."

"I don't know."

"I *do* know."

Amy sipped her Coke. After a couple of minutes of thought, she said, "Maybe you're right. Maybe I'll try the suicide bit."

"It'll work. Just as smooth as glass. You'll see. When will you tell them?"

"Well, I had been thinking about breaking the news right after graduation if I couldn't find another way out by then."

"That's two weeks! Listen, kid, the sooner the better."

"Two weeks won't hurt anything. Maybe in that time I'll find some way to come up with the money myself."

"You won't."

"Maybe."

"You won't," Liz said sharply. "Anyway, you're only seventeen. You probably couldn't get an abortion without your parents' consent, not even if you had the money to pay for it. I'll bet you have to be at least eighteen before they let you have one on your own say-so."

Amy hadn't considered that possibility. She simply didn't

think of herself as a minor; she felt a hundred and ten years old.

"Get your head on straight, kid," Liz said. "You wouldn't take my advice about the pill. Now get your shit together this time, will you? Please, please, for Christ's sake, listen to me. The sooner the better."

Amy realized that Liz was right. She leaned back in the booth, away from the table, and a wave of resignation swept through her. She sagged as if she were a marionette whose strings had been cut. "Okay. The sooner the better. I'll tell them tonight or tomorrow."

"Tonight."

"I don't think I have the strength for it tonight. If I'm going to put on a big suicide act, I'll need to have my wits about me. I'll have to be rested."

"Tomorrow, then," Liz said. "No later than tomorrow. Get it over with. Listen, we have a great summer coming up. If I go west at the end of the year, like I'm hoping to, this'll probably be the last summer you and I will have together. So we've got to do it up right. We've got to make a lot of memories to last us a long while. Lots of sun, some good dope to smoke, a couple of new guys . . . It'll be a blast. Except it won't be so terrific if you're walking around all bloated and preggy."

For Joey Harper, Sunday turned out to be a fine day.

The morning started with Mass and Sunday school, of course, which was as boring as usual, but then the day improved rapidly. When his father stopped at Royal City

News for the Sunday papers, Joey found a batch of new comic books on the rack and had enough coins in his pockets to buy the two best issues. Then his mother made chicken and waffles for lunch, which was one of his favorite things in the whole wide world.

After lunch his father gave him money to go to the Rialto. That was a theater, a revival house that played only old movies. It was six blocks from their house, and he was allowed to ride his bicycle that far, but no farther. The Rialto was showing two monster flicks for the Sunday matinee—*The Thing* and *It Came from Outer Space*. Both pictures were super.

Joey liked scary stories. He wasn't exactly sure why he did. Sometimes, sitting in a dark theater, watching some slimy *thing* creep up on the hero, Joey almost peed in his pants. But he loved every minute of it.

After the movies he went home for dinner, and his mother made cheeseburgers and baked beans, which was even better than chicken and waffles, better than just about anything he could think of. He ate until he thought he'd bust.

Amy came home from The Dive at eight o'clock, an hour and a half before Joey's bedtime, so that he was still awake when she found the rubber snake hanging in her closet. She stormed down the hall, calling his name, and she chased him around his room until she caught him. After she had tickled him and had made him promise never to frighten her that way again (a promise they both knew he wouldn't keep), he persuaded her to play a sixty-minute time-limit game of Monopoly, and that was a whole lot of fun. He beat her, as usual; for an almost grown-up person, she sure didn't know much about financial wheeling and dealing.

He loved Amy more than anybody. Maybe that was wrong of him. You were supposed to love your mother and father most of all. Well, after God. God came first. Then your mother and father. But Mama was hard to love. She was all the time praying with you or praying for you or giving you a lecture on the proper way to behave, and she *told* you over and over again that she cared that you grew up the right way, but she somehow never *showed* you that she cared. It was all talk. Daddy was easier to love, but he wasn't around that much. He was busy doing law stuff, probably saving innocent men from the electric chair and things like that, and when he was home he spent a lot of time alone, working on the miniature layouts he built for model trains; he didn't like you messing around in his workshop.

Which left Amy. She was there a lot. And she was always there when you needed her. She was the nicest person Joey knew, the nicest he ever expected to know, and he was glad that he had her for a sister instead of that crabby, nasty Veronica Culp, who his best friend, Tommy Culp, had to share a house with.

Later, after the Monopoly game, when he was in his pajamas, teeth brushed, and ready for bed, he said his prayers with Amy, which was much better than saying them with Mama. Amy said them faster than Mama did, and she sometimes changed a word here and there to make the prayers a little bit funny. Like, instead of saying, "Mary, Mother of God, hear my plea," she might say, "Mary, Mother of God, hear my flea." She always made Joey giggle, but he had to be careful not to laugh too loud because Mama would wonder what was so funny about prayers, and then everyone would be in trouble.

Amy tucked him in and kissed him and finally left him alone in the moonglow of his night-light. He snuggled down in the covers and fell asleep almost instantly.

Sunday had been a fine day indeed.

But Monday began badly.

Not long after midnight, in the first few minutes of the new day, Joey was awakened by the spooky, mush-mouthed sound of his mother's whispered conversation. As on other occasions, he kept his eyes closed and pretended to be sleeping.

"My little angel . . . maybe not an angel at all . . . inside . . ."

She was really sloshed, pickled. According to Tommy Culp, when somebody was falling-down drunk, you said they were "pissed." Mama was sure pissed tonight.

She rambled on about how she couldn't decide whether he was good or bad, pure or evil, about how there might be something ugly hidden inside of him and waiting to break out, about how she didn't want to bring devils into the world, about how it was God's work to rid the world of such evil any way you could; and she talked about how she had killed somebody named Victor and hoped she would never have to do the same thing to her precious angel.

Joey started to shiver and was deathly afraid that she would discover he was awake. He didn't know what she might do if she knew he had heard her weird mumblings.

When he felt on the brink of telling her to shut up and go away, Joey tried desperately to tune her out. He forced himself to think of something else. He concentrated on putting together a detailed mental picture of the big, vicious alien creature in *The Thing*, which he had seen just that afternoon at the Rialto. The thing in the picture was like a man, only much bigger. With gigantic hands that could tear you to pieces in a minute. And sunken eyes full of fire. And yet it was a plant. An alien plant that was almost indestructible and lived on blood. He could vividly recall the scene in which the scientists were looking for the alien behind a series of doors; they didn't find it, and they finally gave up, and then the very next door they opened, when they weren't expecting anything, the monster jumped out at them, growling and spitting and eager to eat somebody. Remembering the unexpected fury of the monster's attack, Joey felt his blood turn to ice as it had in the theater. That scene was so spine-chilling, so tingly-icky-awful that it made his mother's drunken rambling seem harmless by comparison. The things that happen to people in horror movies were so terrible that they made the scary things in life seem tame. Suddenly Joey wondered if *that* was why he liked those spooky stories so much.

6

Mama was always the first up in the morning. She went to Mass every day of the week, even when she was sick, even when she had a really bad hangover. During the summer, when school was out, she would expect Amy and Joey to attend services and take Holy Communion nearly as often as she did.

On this Monday morning in May, however, Amy still lay in bed, listening to her mother move through the house and then into the garage, which was directly under Amy's bedroom. The Toyota started on the second try, and the automatic garage door rumbled up, coming to rest with a solid thud that rattled Amy's windows.

After her mother had gone, Amy got out of bed, showered, dressed for school, and went downstairs to the kitchen. Her father and Joey were finishing a breakfast of toasted English muffins and orange juice.

"You're running late this morning," her father said. "Better grab a bite quick. We're leaving in five minutes."

"It's such a beautiful morning," Amy said. "I think I'll walk to school today."

"Are you sure you have enough time?"

"Oh, yes. Plenty of time."

"Me too," Joey said. "I want to walk with Amy."

"The elementary school is three times as far as the high school," Paul Harper said. "Your legs would be worn down to your knees by the time you got there."

"Nah," Joey said. "I can make it. I'm rough and ready."

"One mean hombre," his father agreed. "But just the same, you'll ride with me."

"Aw, shoot!" Joey said.

"Bang," Amy said, pointing a finger at him.

Joey grinned.

"Come on, hombre," his father said. "Let's get moving."

Amy stood at one of the living room windows, watching the man and the boy drive away in the family's Pontiac.

She had lied to her father. She wasn't going to walk to school. In fact she didn't even intend to go to school at all today.

She returned to the kitchen, made a pot of coffee, poured a steaming mug of it for herself. Then she sat down at the kitchen table to wait for her mother to get back from Mass.

Last night, tossing restlessly in bed, plotting how best to make her confession, she had decided that she should tell her mother first. If Amy sat them down and told them both at the same time, Mama's reaction to the news would be calculated to impress not only her daughter but her husband; she would be even tougher on Amy than she might be if Amy told her in private. And Amy also knew that if she told her father first, it would look as if she were sneaking around behind her mother's back, trying to drive a wedge between her parents, trying to make an ally of her father. If Mama thought that was the case, she would be twice as difficult as she otherwise might have been. By telling Mama first, by according her at least that much special respect, Amy hoped to improve her chances of getting the abortion she wanted.

She finished the mug of coffee. She poured herself another, finished that one, too.

The ticking of the kitchen clock seemed to grow louder and louder, until it was a drumbeat to which her nerves jumped in sympathy.

When Mama finally came home from Mass, entering the kitchen through the connecting door to the garage, Amy had never been more tense. The back and underarms of her blouse were damp with perspiration. In spite of the hot coffee, there seemed to be a lump of ice in her stomach.

"Morning, Mama."

Her mother stopped in surprise, still holding the door open, the shadowy interior of the garage visible behind her. "What are you doing here?"

"I want to—"

"You should be in school."

"I stayed home so I could—"

"Isn't this final exam week?"

"No. That's next week. This week we just review material for the tests."

"That's important, too."

"Yes, but I don't think I'll be going to school today."

As Mama closed and locked the door of the garage, she said, "What's wrong? Are you sick?"

"Not exactly. I—"

"What do you mean—not exactly?" she asked, putting her purse on the counter by the sink. "You're either sick or you're not. And if you aren't, you should be in school."

"I have to talk to you," Amy said.

Her mother came to the table and stared down at her. "Talk? About what?"

Amy couldn't meet the woman's eyes. She looked away, turned her gaze to the muddy residue of cold coffee in the bottom of her mug.

"Well?" Mama asked.

Although Amy had drunk a lot of coffee, her mouth was so dry that her tongue stuck to the roof of her mouth. She swallowed, licked her parched lips, cleared her throat, and at last said, "I have to withdraw some money from my savings account."

"What are you talking about?"

"I need . . . four hundred dollars."

"That's ridiculous."

"No. I really need it, Mama."

"For what?"

"I'd rather not say."

Her mother was astonished. "You'd rather not say?"

"That's right."

The astonishment turned to consternation. "You want to withdraw four hundred dollars that's meant for your college tuition, and you don't want to say what you're going to do with it?"

"Mama, please. After all, I earned it."

The consternation turned to anger. "Now you listen to me and listen good, young lady. Your father does well enough at his law practice, but he doesn't do all *that* well. He's not F. Lee Bailey. You want to go to college, and college is expensive these days. You're going to have to help pay for it. In fact you're going to have to pay for most of it. We'll let you live here, of course, and we'll pay for your food, your clothes, your medical bills, while you're going to the junior college, but you'll have to meet the tuition out of your savings. When you go away to the university in a couple of years, we'll send you some money for living expenses, but you'll have to pay for that tuition, too. We just can't do more than that. We'll be sacrificing as it is."

If you didn't spend so much money trying to impress Father O'Hara with your devotion to St. Mary's Church, if you and Daddy didn't contribute a *tithe and a half* to show what good people you are, maybe you'd be able to do more for your own children, Amy thought. Charity starts at home, Mama. Isn't that what the Bible tells us? Besides, if you hadn't made *me* tithe to St. Mary's, I'd have that extra four hundred bucks now that I need it.

Amy wished she could say all of that, but she didn't dare. She didn't want to completely alienate her mother before she even had a chance to mention the pregnancy. Anyway, no matter how she tried to express what she was thinking, no matter what words she chose, she would sound petty and selfish.

But she *wasn't* selfish, damn it.

She knew it was a good thing to give money to the Church, but there had to be limits. And you had to give for the right reasons. Otherwise it didn't mean anything. Sometimes Amy suspected that her mother hoped to *buy* a place in Heaven, and that was definitely the wrong reason to give to the Church.

Amy forced herself to look up at her mother and smile. "Mama, I've already got that small scholarship for next year. If I work real hard I'll probably get scholarships every year, even if they're all just small ones. And I'll be working at The Dive summers and weekends. With what I'll be earning, plus what I've got in the bank already, I'll have more than enough to pay for my own way. By the time I get to Ohio State, I won't need to ask you and Daddy for help, not even for living expenses. I can spare that four hundred dollars right now, Mama. I can spare it easy."

"No," Mama said. "And don't think you can sneak behind my back and get the money on your own hook. My name's on that account along with yours. You're still a minor, don't forget. As long as I can, I'm going to protect you from yourself. I'm not letting you throw your college money away on trendy new clothes you don't need or on some other silly bauble you've just seen in a store window."

"It isn't new clothes I want, Mama."

"Whatever. I won't let you—"

"It's not a silly bauble I want, either."

"I don't care what sort of foolishness—"

"An abortion," Amy said.

Her mother gaped at her. "*What?*"

Touched off by a fuse of fear, the words exploded from

Amy: "I've had some morning sickness, I missed my period, I'm really pregnant, I know I am, Jerry Galloway got me pregnant, I didn't mean for it to happen, I'm so sorry it happened, so very sorry, I hate myself, I really do, I really hate myself, but I have to get an abortion, I've just got to have one, please, please, I've just got to."

Mama's face suddenly turned white, chalk-white. Even her lips were pale.

"Mama? Do you understand that I can't possibly have this baby? I just can't go ahead and have it, Mama."

Mama closed her eyes. She swayed, and for a moment she looked as if she would faint.

"I know what I did was wrong, Mama," Amy said, beginning to cry. "I feel dirty. I don't know if I'll ever feel clean again. I hate myself. And I know that an abortion is even a worse sin than what I did. I know that, and I'm afraid for my soul. But I'm even more afraid of going ahead and having the baby. I've got my life to live, Mama. *I've got my life!*"

Mama's eyes opened. She stared down at Amy, and she tried to speak, but she was too shocked to be able to get any words out. Her mouth moved without producing a sound.

"Mama?"

With such speed that Amy hardly saw it coming, her mother raised a hand and slapped her face. Once. Twice. Hard.

Amy cried out in pain and surprise, and she raised one arm to protect herself.

Mama grabbed her by the blouse and dragged her to her feet in a disconcerting display of strength.

The chair fell over with a crash.

Her mother shook her as if she were a bundle of rags.

Crying, frightened, Amy said, "Mama, please don't hurt me. Forgive me, Mama. Please."

"You filthy, rotten, ungrateful little bitch!"

"Mama—"

"You're stupid, stupid, so damned stupid!" her mother screamed, spraying her with spittle as hot and stinging as venom. "You're an ignorant child, just a stupid little slut! You don't know what could happen. You don't have the slightest idea. You're ignorant. You don't know what you might give birth to. You don't *know*!"

Amy was unwilling and unable to defend herself. Mama pushed her, pulled her, jerked her from side to side, this way and that, shook her, shook her, shook her ferociously, until her teeth rattled and her blouse tore.

"You don't know what sort of thing might come out of you," Mama screeched maniacally. "God knows what it might be!"

What is she talking about? Amy wondered desperately. She sounds as if she's heard Jerry's curse and believes it'll come true. What's going on here? What's wrong with her?

Second by second her mother was becoming increasingly violent. Amy hadn't really believed that Mama would kill her. That's what she had told Liz, but she had been exaggerating. At least she had *thought* she was exaggerating. But now, as her mother continued to curse her and shake her, Amy began to worry that Mama would seriously hurt her, and she tried to squirm away.

Mama refused to let go.

The two women tottered sideways and bumped solidly against the table.

The nearly empty mug fell over, spun around twice, dropped off the table, scattering droplets of cold coffee, and smashed into a dozen pieces when it hit the floor.

Mama stopped shaking Amy, but her eyes were still demented and wildly lighted. "Pray," she said urgently. "We've got to pray that there's no baby inside you. We've got to pray that it's a mistake, that you're wrong."

She pulled Amy down roughly onto the floor, onto her knees, and they knelt side by side on the cool tiles, and Mama began to pray loudly, and she held Amy by one arm, held her so tightly that Mama's fingers seemed to pierce Amy's flesh and touch the bare bone, and Amy wept and pleaded to be released, and Mama slapped her again and told her to pray, demanded that she pray, and Mama asked the Holy Virgin to be merciful, but Mama wasn't merciful when she saw that Amy's head wasn't bowed far enough, for she grabbed her daughter by the back of the neck and forced her face toward the floor, forced it down and down until Amy's forehead was touching the tiles, until her nose was pressed into a wet splotch of spilled coffee, and Amy kept saying, "Mama, please," over and over again, "Mama, please," but Mama wasn't listening to her, because Mama was busy praying to everyone, to Mary and Jesus and Joseph and God the Father and God the Holy Spirit, and she prayed to various saints as well, and when Amy gasped for breath a couple of drops of coffee slipped up her nose from the small puddle into which she was pressed, and she spluttered and gagged, but Mama held her down, held her even harder than before, squeezing the back of her neck, and Mama wailed and whined and shouted and beat the floor with her free hand and thrashed about and shuddered with religious passion, begged and wheedled and whimpered for mercy, mercy for herself and for her wayward daughter, howled and wept and pleaded in a fashion that Catholics usually disdained, in a devout frenzy that was more suited to the fundamental Christianity for the Church of the Nazarene, flailed and babbled fervently, until she was finally all prayed out, hoarse, exhausted, limp.

The ensuing silence was more dramatic than a thunderclap would have been.

Mama let go of Amy's neck.

At first Amy remained as her mother had left her, face against the floor, but after a few seconds she lifted her head and rocked back on her knees.

Mama's hand had cramped from maintaining such an iron grip on Amy's neck. She stared down at the clawlike fingers, massaging them with her good hand. She was breathing hard.

Amy raised her hands to her face, wiped away the coffee and the tears. She couldn't stop shaking.

Outside, clouds passed over the sun, and the morning light streaming through the kitchen windows rippled like bright water, then grew dimmer.

The clock ticked hollowly.

To Amy, the silence was frightening, like the endless instant between a skipped heartbeat and the next sound of your pulse, when you could not help but wonder if perhaps that vital muscle in your chest would never again expand or contract.

When Mama spoke at last, Amy jerked involuntarily.

"Get up," Mama said coldly. "Go upstairs and wash your face. Comb your hair."

"Yes, Mama."

They both stood.

Amy's legs were weak. Her skirt was rumpled; she pressed it down with her quivering hands, smoothed the wrinkled material.

"Change into fresh clothes," Mama said, her voice flat and emotionless.

"Yes, Mama."

"I'll call Dr. Spangler and see if he has an opening in his appointment book this morning. We'll go in right away if he can take us."

"Dr. Spangler?" Amy asked, confused.

"You'll have to take a pregnancy test, of course. There are other reasons why you might have missed your period. We can't really be sure until we get test results."

"I know I am, Mama," Amy said shakily, softly. "I know I'm going to have a baby."

"If the test is positive," her mother said, "then we'll make arrangements to take care of things as soon as possible."

Amy couldn't believe the implications of that statement. She said, "Take care of things?"

"You'll get the abortion you want," Mama said, glaring at her with eyes that contained no forgiveness.

"You don't really mean it."

"Yes. You *must* have an abortion. It's the only way."

Amy almost cried out with relief. But at the same time she was afraid, for she figured that her mother would extract a terrible price for this amazing concession.

"But . . . abortion . . . isn't it a sin?" Amy asked, struggling to comprehend her mother's reasoning.

"We can't tell your father," Mama said. "It's got to be kept a secret from him. He wouldn't approve."

"But . . . I didn't think *you* would approve, either," Amy said, bewildered.

"I *don't* approve," Mama said sharply, a trace of emotion returning to her voice. "Abortion is murder. It's a mortal sin. I don't approve at all. But as long as you've got to live in this house, I won't have such a thing as this hanging over my head. I simply won't have it. I won't live in fear of what might come. I won't go through that terror again."

"Mama, I don't understand. You talk as if you know for a fact that the baby will be deformed or something."

They stared at each other for a moment, and Amy saw more than anger and reproach in her mother's dark eyes. There was fear in those eyes, too, a stark and powerful fear that transmitted itself to Amy, chilling her.

"Someday," Mama said, "when the time was right, I was going to tell you."

"Tell me what?"

"Someday, when you were ready to be married, when you were properly engaged, I was going to tell you why you must never have a child. But you couldn't wait for the proper time, could you? Oh, no. Not you. You had to give yourself away. You had to pull up your skirts the first chance you got. Still little more than a child yourself, and you had to throw yourself at some high school boy. You had to rush out and fornicate in the backseat of a car like a worthless little slut, like the worst kind of pig. And now maybe *it's* inside of you, growing."

"What are you talking about?" Amy asked, wondering if her mother was completely mad.

"It wouldn't do any good for me to tell you," Mama said. "You wouldn't listen. You'd probably even welcome such a child. You'd embrace it just like *he* did. I've always said there was something evil in you. I've always told you that you had to keep it in check. But now you've loosened the reins, and that dark thing is running free, that evil part of you. You've loosed the evil in you, and sooner or later, one way or the other, you'll have a child; you'll bring one of *them* into the world, no matter what I say to you, no matter how I plead with you. But you won't do it in this house. It won't happen here. I'll see to that. We'll go to Dr. Spangler, and he'll abort it for you. And if there's any sin in *that*, if there's mortal sin for someone to bear the burden of, it will rest entirely on your shoulders, not mine. You understand?"

Amy nodded.

"It won't matter to you, will it?" her mother asked meanly. "One more sin won't matter to you, will it? Because you're already destined for Hell anyway, aren't you?"

"No. No, Mama, don't—"

"Yes, you are. You're destined to be one of the Devil's own women, one of his handmaidens, aren't you? I see that now. I see it. All my efforts have been in vain. You can't be saved. So what's one more sin to you? Nothing. It's nothing to you. You'll just laugh it off."

"Mama, don't talk to me like that."

"I'm talking to you like you deserve to be talked to. A

girl who behaves the way you've behaved—how can she expect to be talked to any differently?"

"Please . . ."

"Get a move on," Mama said. "Clean yourself up. I'll call the doctor."

Confused by the several twists that events had taken, baffled by her mother's certainty that the baby would be deformed, wondering about Mama's sanity, Amy went upstairs. In the bathroom she washed her face. Her eyes were bloodshot from crying.

In her bedroom she took another skirt and a clean blouse from the closet. She stripped off her sweat-streaked, wrinkled clothes. For a moment she stood in bra and panties before the full-length mirror, staring at her belly.

Why is Mama so certain that my baby will be deformed? Amy asked herself worriedly. How can she know such a thing for sure? Is it because she thinks I'm evil and that I deserve this sort of thing—a deformed baby, a sign to the world that I'm the Devil's handmaiden? That's sick. That's twisted thinking. It's ridiculous and crazy and unfair. I'm *not* a bad person. I've made some mistakes. I'll admit that. I've made a lot of mistakes for someone my age, but I'm not evil, damn it. I'm not evil.

Am I?

She stared into the reflection of her own eyes.

Am I?

Shivering, she dressed for the visit to the doctor's office.

7

On Sunday the carnival moved to Clearfield, Pennsylvania, by highway and rail, and on Monday the sprawling midway was erected again with military efficiency. Big American Midway Shows gave its own people and its concessionaires a four o'clock show call for Monday afternoon, which meant that every attraction—from the least imposing grab joint to the most elaborate thrill ride—was expected to be operational by that hour.

Conrad Straker's three enterprises, including the funhouse, were in place and ready to receive the marks by three o'clock Monday afternoon. It was a cloudless, warm day. The evening would be balmy. "Money weather," the carnies called it. Although Fridays and Saturdays were always the best for business, the marks would flood in on a mild, breezy night even if it was at the beginning of the week.

With an hour of free time before the fairground gates

were opened to the public, Conrad did what he always did on the first afternoon of a new engagement. He left the funhouse and walked next door to Yancy Barnet's ten-in-one Freak-o-rama, a name that some carnies found offensive, but that drew the marks with greater efficacy than honey ever drew flies. A luridly illustrated banner stretched across the front of Yancy's tent: HUMAN ODDITIES OF THE WORLD.

Yancy had as much respect for show calls as Conrad did, and except for the fact that the human oddities would not arrive from their trailers until four o'clock, the joint was ready for business well ahead of schedule. That was especially commendable when you knew that Yancy Barnet and a few of his freaks always played poker Sunday night, into the wee hours of Monday morning, accompanying the game with a considerable amount of ice-cold beer and Seagram's, which were combined into murderously potent boilermakers.

Yancy's place was a large tent, divided into four long rooms, with a roped-off walkway that serpentined through all four chambers. In each room there were either two or three stalls, and in each stall there was a platform, and on each platform there was a chair. Behind each chair, running the length of the stall, a big sign, colorfully illustrated, explained about the wondrous and incredible thing at which the mark was gawking. With one exception, those wondrous and incredible things were all living, breathing, human freaks, normal minds and spirits trapped in twisted bodies: the world's fattest woman, the three-eyed alligator man, the man with three arms and three legs, the bearded lady, and (as the barker said twenty or thirty times every hour) more, much more than the human mind could encompass.

Only one of the oddities was not a living person. It was to be found in the center of the tent, halfway along the snaking path, in the narrowest of all the stalls. The thing was in a very large, specially blown, clear glass jar, suspended in a formaldehyde solution; the jar stood on the platform, without benefit of a chair, dramatically lighted from above and behind.

It was to this exhibit that Conrad Straker came that Monday afternoon in Clearfield. He stood at the restraining rope where he had stood hundreds of times before, and he stared regretfully at his long-dead son.

As in the other stalls, there was a sign behind the exhibit. The letters were big, easy to read.

VICTOR

"The Ugly Angel"

This child, named Victor by his father, was born in 1955, of normal parents.

Victor's mental capacity was normal. He had a sweet, charming disposition. He was a laughing baby, an angel.

On the night of August 15, 1955, Victor's mother, Ellen, murdered him. She was repelled by the child's physical deformities and was convinced he was an evil monster.

SHE WAS NOT ABLE TO SEE THE SPIRITUAL
BEAUTY WITHIN HIM.

WHO WAS REALLY THE EVIL ONE?
THE HELPLESS BABY?
—OR THE MOTHER HE TRUSTED,
THE WOMAN WHO MURDERED HIM?

WHO WAS THE REAL MONSTER?
THIS POOR, AFFLICTED CHILD?
—OR THE MOTHER WHO REFUSED
TO LOVE HIM?
JUDGE FOR YOURSELF.

Conrad had written the text of that sign twenty-five years ago, and it had expressed his feelings perfectly at that time. He had wanted to tell the world that Ellen was a baby killer, a ruthless beast; he had wanted them to see what she had done and to revile her for her cruelty.

During the off-season the child in the jar remained with Conrad in his Gibsonton, Florida, home. During the rest of the year, it traveled with Yancy Barnet's show, a public testament to Ellen's perfidy.

At each new stand, when the midway had been erected again and the gates were about to be opened to the marks, Conrad came to this tent to see if the jar had been transported safely. He spent a few minutes in the company of his dead boy, silently reaffirming his oath of revenge.

Victor stared back at his father with wide, sightless eyes. Once the green of those eyes had been bright, glowing. Once they had been quick, inquisitive eyes, filled with bold challenge and self-confidence beyond their years. But now they were flat, dull. The green was not half so vibrant as it had been in life; years of formaldehyde bleaching and the relentless processes of death had made the irises milky.

At last, with a renewed hunger for retribution, Conrad walked out of the tent and returned to the funhouse.

Gunther was already standing up on the platform by the boarding gate, dressed in his Frankenstein monster mask and gloves. He saw Conrad and immediately went into his snarling-pawing-dancing act, the one he put on for the marks.

Ghost was at the ticket booth, breaking rolls of quarters and dimes and nickels into the change drawer; his colorless eyes were filled with the flickering, silvery images of tumbling coins.

"They're going to open the gate half an hour early," Ghost said. "Everyone's set up and eager for business, and they say there's already a crowd of marks waiting outside."

"It's going to be a good week," Conrad said.

"Yeah," Ghost said, pushing one slender hand through his spiderweb hair. "I have the same feeling. Maybe you'll even get a chance to repay that debt."

"What?"

"That woman you owe a debt to," Ghost said. "The one whose children you're always looking for. Maybe you'll be lucky and find her here."

"Yes," Conrad said softly. "Maybe I will."

At eight-thirty Monday night, Ellen Harper was sitting in the living room of the house on Maple Lane, trying to read an article in the latest issue of *Redbook*. She couldn't concentrate. Each time she reached the bottom of a paragraph, she couldn't remember what had been in it, and she had to go back and read it again. Eventually she gave up and just leafed through the magazine, looking at the pictures, while she sipped steadily from a glass of vodka and orange juice.

Although it was not late, she was already under the spell of the booze. She didn't feel *good*. Not by a long shot. Not bad, either. Just numb. But not yet numb enough.

She was alone in the room. Paul was in his workshop, out in the garage. He would come in at eleven o'clock, as usual, to watch the late news on television, and then he would go to bed. Joey was in his room, working on a model of his own—a plastic representation of Lon Chaney as the Phantom of the Opera. Amy was upstairs, too, lying low. Except for a brief, fidgety appearance at the dinner table, the girl had been holed up in her room ever since returning from Dr. Spangler's office this afternoon.

The girl. The damned, defiant, wanton girl! *Pregnant!*

They didn't have the test results yet, of course. That would take a couple of days. But she *knew*. Amy was pregnant.

The magazine rustled in Ellen's tremulous hands. She put *Redbook* aside and went out to the kitchen to mix another drink.

She wasn't able to stop worrying about the bind she was in. She couldn't allow Amy to have the baby. But if Paul found out that she had gone behind his back to arrange an abortion, he would not be pleased. For the most part he was a meek man at home, gentle, easygoing, willing to let her run the house and, generally, their lives as well. But he was capable of anger if pushed far enough, and on those rare occasions when he lost his temper, he could be tough.

If Paul learned of the abortion after the fact, he would want to know why she hadn't told him, and he would *demand* to know why she had approved of such a thing. She would have to be able to provide a cogent explanation, a passionate self-defense. Right now, however, she didn't know what in God's name she would say to him if he ever found out about the abortion.

Twenty years ago, when she had married Paul, she should have told him about her year with the carnival. She should have confessed about Conrad and about the repulsive thing to which she had given birth. But she hadn't done what she should have done. She had been weak. She hid the truth from him. She was afraid he would loathe her and turn away from her if he knew about her mistakes. But if she had told him back then, at the very beginning of their relationship, she wouldn't be in such serious trouble now.

Several times during the course of their marriage, she had almost revealed her secrets to him. When he had talked about having a large family, there were a hundred times when she almost said, "No, Paul. I can't have children. I've already had one, you see, and it was no good. No good at all. It was a horror. It wasn't even human. It wanted to kill me, and I had to kill it first. Maybe that hideous child was solely a product of my first husband's damaged genes. Maybe my own genetic contribution wasn't to blame. But I can't take a chance." Although she had been on the brink of making that confession countless times, she had never given voice to it; she had held her tongue, naively certain that love would conquer all—somehow.

Later, when she was pregnant with Amy, she almost went out of her mind with worry and fear. But the baby had been normal. For a short while, a few blessed weeks at most, she had been relieved, all doubts about her genetic fitness banished by the sight of that pink, giggly, supremely *ordinary* infant.

But before long it occurred to her that all freaks were not necessarily *physically* deformed. The flaw, the twisted thing, the horrible difference from normal people—that could be entirely in the mind. The baby she'd borne for Conrad was not merely deformed. It was wicked; it radiated wickedness; it reeked of malevolent intent, a monster in every sense of the word. But wasn't it conceivable that her new girl-child was just as wicked as Victor, except that there were no outward signs of it? Perhaps a worm of evil nestled deep within the child's mind, out of sight, festering, waiting for the proper time and place to emerge.

Such a disturbing possibility was like an acid. It ate away at Ellen's happiness; it corroded and then destroyed her optimism. She soon ceased to take any pleasure in the baby's gurgling and cooing. She watched the child speculatively, wondering what nasty surprises it would spring on her in the future. Perhaps, one night, when the child was grown tall and strong, it would creep into its parents' bedroom and murder them in their sleep.

Or perhaps she was crazy; perhaps the child was as ordinary as it appeared to be, and the problem was in her own mind. That thought did occur to her rather frequently. But each time she began to question her sanity, she remembered the nightmarish battle with Conrad's vicious, bloodthirsty offspring, and that grisly, vivid memory never failed to convince her that she had good reason to be wary and afraid.

Didn't she?

For seven years she resisted Paul's desire to have another child, but she got pregnant in spite of her precautions. Again, she went through nine months of hell, wondering what sort of strange creature she was carrying in her womb.

Joey, of course, turned out to be a normal little boy.

On the outside.

But inside?

She wondered. She watched, waited, feared the worst.

After all these years, Ellen still wasn't sure what to think of her children.

It was a hell of a way to live.

Sometimes she was filled with a fierce pride and love for them. She wanted to take them in her arms and kiss them, hug them. Sometimes she wanted to give them all the affection that she never had been able to give them in the past; but after so many years of guarded feelings and continuous suspicion, she found it virtually impossible to open her arms to them and to accept such a dangerous emotional commitment with equanimity. There were times when she *burned* with love for Joey and Amy, times when she ached with a surfeit of unexpressed love, times when she wept at night, silently, without waking Paul, soaking her pillow, grieving for her own cold, dead heart.

At other times, however, she still thought she saw something supernaturally wicked in her progeny. There were terrible days when she was convinced they were clever, calculating, infinitely evil beings engaged in an elaborate masquerade.

Seesaw.

Seesaw.

The worst of it was her loneliness. She could not share her fears with Paul, for then she would have to tell him about Conrad, and he would be devastated to learn that she had been hiding a checkered past from him for twenty years. She knew him well enough now to understand that what she'd done in her youth would not upset him a tenth as much as the fact that she'd deceived him about it and had kept on deceiving him for so very long. So she had to deal with her fear by herself.

It was a *hell* of a way to live.

Even if she could make herself believe, once and for all, that they were just two kids like any other two kids, even then her worries wouldn't be at an end. There was still the possibility that one of Amy's or Joey's children would be a monster like Victor. This curse might strike only one out of every two generations—the mother but not the child, the grandchild but not the great-grandchild. It might skip around at random, raising its ugly head when you least expected to see it. Modern medicine had identified a number of genetically transmitted diseases and inherited deficiencies that skipped some generations in a family and struck others, leapfrogging down the decades.

If she could only be sure that her first, monstrous baby had been the product of Conrad's rotten, degenerate spermatozoa, if she could just be certain that her own chromosomes were not corrupted, she would be able to lay her fear to rest forever. But of course there was no way she could determine the truth of the matter.

Sometimes she thought that life was too difficult and much too cruel to be worth the effort of living it.

That was why, now, standing in the kitchen on the night of the day that she had learned of Amy's pregnancy, Ellen tossed down the last of the drink that she had mixed only minutes ago, and she quickly poured another. She had two crutches: liquor and religion. She could not have withstood the past twenty-five years without both of those supports.

Initially, the first year after she left Conrad, religion alone was sufficient to her needs. She had gotten a job as a waitress, had become self-supporting after a rocky start, and had spent most of her spare time in church. She had found that prayer soothed her nerves as well as her spirit, that confession *was* good for the soul, and that a meager Communion wafer taken on the tongue during Mass was far more nourishing than any six-course meal.

At the end of that first year on her own, more   two years after she had run from home to join the carnival and to be with Conrad, she felt fairly good about herself. She still suffered from bad dreams most nights. She was still wrestling with her conscience, trying to make up her mind whether she had sinned terribly or had merely done God's work when she had killed Victor. But at least, as a hard-working waitress, she had gained a measure of self-respect and independence for the first time in her life. Indeed, she had felt sufficiently self-confident to return home for a visit, intending to patch up her differences with her parents as best she could.

That was when she discovered they had died in her absence. Joseph Giavenetto, her father, was felled by a massive stroke just one month after Ellen ran away from home. Gina, her mother, died less than six months later. It happened that way sometimes—wife and husband taking leave of life within a short time of each other, as if unable to tolerate the separation.

Although Ellen had not been close to her parents, and although Gina's excessive strictness and religiosity had created a great deal of tension and bitterness between mother and daughter, Ellen had been devastated by the news of their deaths. She was filled with a cold, empty, unfinished feeling. She blamed herself for what had happened to them. Running away as she had done, leaving nothing more than a terse, unpleasant note for her mother, not even saying good-bye to her father—with those actions she might have precipitated her father's stroke. Perhaps she was too hard on herself, but she wasn't able to shrug off the yoke of guilt.

Thereafter, her religion was not able to provide her with sufficient comfort, and she augmented the mercy of Jesus with the mercy of the bottle. She drank too much—more this year than last, not so much this year as next year. Only her family was aware of her habit. The churchwomen with whom she worked in charitable causes four days each week would be shocked to discover that the quiet, earnest, industrious, devout Ellen Harper was a different person at night, in her own home; after sunset, behind closed doors, the saint became a lush.

She despised herself for her sinfully excessive fondness

for vodka. But without booze she couldn't sleep; it blocked out the nightmares, and it gave her a few hours of blessed relief from the worries and fears that had been eating her alive for twenty-five years.

She put the bottle of vodka and the quart of orange juice on the kitchen table, pulled out a chair, and sat down. Now, when her drink ran low, she wouldn't have to get up to freshen it; she would only have to bestir herself when her ice had melted.

For a while she sat in silence, drinking, but then, as she stared at the chair opposite her own, she had a memory-flash of Amy sitting there this morning, looking up, saying, "*I've had some morning sickness, I missed my period, I'm really pregnant, I know I am . . .*" Ellen remembered, far too vividly, how she had struck the girl, how she had shaken her senseless, how she had cursed her. If she closed her eyes she could see herself pulling Amy onto the floor, pushing the girl's head down to the tiles, screaming like a madwoman, praying at the top of her voice . . .

She shuddered.

My God, she thought miserably, suddenly pierced by a painfully sharp insight, *I'm like my mother!* I'm exactly like Gina. I've cowed my husband just as she cowed hers. I've been so strict with my children and so preoccupied with my religion that I've built a wall between myself and my family—a wall exactly like the one that *my* mother constructed.

Ellen felt dizzy, but not merely from the vodka. The patterns of history, the familiar circles drawn by repetitive events, startled and dazed her.

She covered her face with her hands, shamed by the new light in which she suddenly saw herself. Her hands were cold.

The kitchen clock sounded like a ticking bomb.

Just like Gina.

Ellen grabbed her drink and took a long swallow of it. The glass chattered against her teeth.

Just like Gina.

She shook her head violently, as if she were determined to cast off that unwelcome thought. She wasn't as stern and distant and forbidding as her own mother had been. She *wasn't*. And even if she was, she couldn't deal with that insight now. With Amy's pregnancy, Ellen already had too much to worry about. She could deal with only one thing at a time. Amy's problem had to come first. If some horrible *thing* was growing in the girl's womb, it had to be gotten rid of as quickly as possible. Maybe then, after the abortion, Ellen would be able to consider her life and decide what she thought of the woman she had allowed herself to become; maybe then she would have the time to reflect on what she had done to her family. But not now. God, please, not now.

She tilted her glass and chugged the rest of her drink as if it were only water. With an unsteady hand she poured a little more orange juice and a lot more vodka.

Most nights she wasn't really drunk until eleven or twelve o'clock, but tonight, by nine-thirty, Ellen was thoroughly intoxicated. She felt fuzzy, and her tongue was thick. She was floating dreamily. She had attained the pleasant, mindless state of grace that she had desired so strongly.

When she glanced at the kitchen clock and saw that it was nine-thirty, she realized it was Joey's bedtime. She decided to go upstairs, make sure he said his prayers, tuck him in, kiss him good-night, and tell him a bedtime story. She hadn't told him any stories in a long, long time. He'd probably like that. He wasn't too old for bedtime stories, was he? He was still just a baby. A little angel. He had such a sweet, angelic, baby face. Sometimes she loved him so hard that she thought she'd explode. Like now. She was brimming with love for little Joey. She wanted to kiss his sweet face. She wanted to sit on the edge of the bed and tell him a story about elves and princesses. That would be good, so good, just to sit on the edge of the bed with him smiling up at her.

Ellen finished her drink and got to her feet. She stood up too fast, and the room spun around, and she grabbed the edge of the table in order to keep her balance.

Crossing the living room, she bumped into an end table and knocked over a lovely, hand-carved, wooden statue of Jesus, which she had bought a long time ago, in her waitressing days. The statue fell onto the carpet, and although it was only a foot high and not heavy, she fumbled awkwardly with it, trying to retrieve it and set it back where it belonged; her fingers felt like fat sausages and didn't seem to want to bend the right way.

She wondered fleetingly if the bedtime story was a good idea after all. Maybe she wasn't up to it. But then she thought of Joey's sweet face and his cherubic smile, and she went upstairs. The steps were treacherous, but she reached the second-floor hallway without falling.

When she entered the boy's room, she found that he was already in bed. Only the tiny night-light was burning, a single small bulb in the wall plug, ghostly, moon-pale.

She stopped inside the doorway, listening. He usually snored softly when he slept, but at the moment he was perfectly quiet. Maybe he wasn't asleep yet.

Swaying with each step, she walked gingerly to the bed and looked down at him. She couldn't see much in the dim light.

Deciding that he must be asleep, wanting only to plant a kiss on his head, Ellen leaned close—

And a leering, luminous, inhuman face jumped out of the darkness at her, screeching like an angry bird.

She shrieked and staggered backwards. She collided with the dresser, hurting her hip.

In her mind she saw a kaleidoscopic tumble of dark, horrific images: *a bassinet shaken by the fury of its monstrous burden; enormous, green, animal eyes gleaming with hatred; flared, twisted nostrils sniffing, sniffing; a pale, speckled tongue; long and bony fingers reaching for her in the flutter-flash of lightning; claws tearing at her* . . .

The nightstand light came on, dispelling the awful memories.

Joey was sitting up in bed. "Mama?" he said.

Ellen sagged against the dresser and drew deeply, thirstily of the air that, for a few seconds of eternal duration, she had been unable to draw into her lungs. The thing in the darkness had only been Joey. He was wearing a Halloween mask that had been shaded with phosphorescent paint.

"What the *hell* are you doing?" she demanded, pushing away from the dresser, moving toward the bed.

He quickly pulled off the mask. His eyes were wide. "Mama, I thought you were Amy."

"Give me that," she said, snatching the mask out of his hands.

"I put a rubber worm in Amy's cold cream, and I thought it was her coming to get even with me," Joey said, urgently explaining himself.

"When are you going to outgrow this kind of stupid thing?" Ellen demanded, her heart still beating rapidly.

"I didn't know it was you! I didn't know!"

"This kind of prank is sick," she said angrily. Her pleasant vodka haze had evaporated. Her dreamy laziness was gone, replaced by nightmare tension. She was still drunk, but the quality of her high had changed from bright to somber, from happy to grim. "Sick," she said again, looking at the Halloween mask in her hand. "Sick and twisted."

Joey cowered back against the headboard, gripping the covers with both hands, as if he might throw them aside and leap out of bed and run for all he was worth.

Still quivering from the shock of seeing that grinning, fanged, luminous face leap out of the darkness, Ellen looked around at the other weird items in the boy's room. Spooky posters hung on the walls: Boris Karloff as the Frankenstein monster; Bela Lugosi as Dracula; and another horror-movie creature that she couldn't identify. On the dresser, the desk, and the bookshelves there were monster models—three-dimensional plastic figures that Joey had glued together from kits.

Paul permitted the boy to pursue this macabre hobby, and he insisted it was a common interest among kids Joey's age. Ellen had never strenuously objected. Although the boy's fascination with horror and blood worried her, it had seemed like a relatively minor matter, the sort of thing she always conceded to Paul, so that he would feel comfortable about conceding the larger and far more important issues to her.

Now, infuriated by the scare that Joey had given her, upset by the unwanted memories that the prank had resurrected for her, her judgment still distorted by vodka, Ellen threw the mask into the wastebasket. "It's time I put an end to this nonsense. It's time you stopped playing around with this creepy junk and started behaving like a normal, healthy boy." She plucked a couple of monster models from the dresser and dropped them into the wastebasket. She swept up the miniature ghouls and goblins from his desk and put them with the rest of the trash. "In the morning, before you go to school, take down those awful posters and get rid of them. Be careful not to chip the plaster when you pull the staples out of the wall. I'll get some good, no-nonsense prints to hang in here. You understand?"

He nodded. Fat tears rolled down his cheeks, but he didn't make a sound.

"And no more of these practical jokes of yours," Ellen said harshly. "No more rubber spiders. No more phony snakes. No more rubber worms in cold cream jars. Do you hear me?"

He nodded again. He was rigid, sickly white. He appeared to be overreacting to her admonitions. He didn't look like a boy who was facing his stern mother; he looked more like a boy facing certain death. He looked as if he were convinced that she was going to take him by the throat and kill him.

The terror in Joey's face jolted Ellen.

I'm just like Gina.

No! That was unfair.

She was only doing what must be done. The child needed to be disciplined and given guidance. She was merely fulfilling her duty as a parent.

Just like Gina.

She pushed that thought aside.

"Lie down," she said.

Joey obediently slid under the covers once more.

She went to the nightstand and put her hand on the lamp switch. "Did you say your prayers?"

"Yeah," he said weakly.

"All of them?"

"Yeah."

"Tomorrow night you'll say more prayers than usual."

"Okay."

"I'll say them with you to make sure you don't miss a word of them."

"Okay, Mama."

She switched off the light.

In a small, uncertain voice, he said, "I didn't know it was you, Mama."

"Go to sleep."

"I thought it was Amy."

Suddenly she wanted to reach down and lift him from the bed and clasp him to her bosom. She wanted to hug him tight and kiss him and tell him everything was all right.

But as she began to lean down toward him, she remembered the Halloween mask. When she had seen that fearsome countenance, she had thought that the demon in Joey had surfaced at last. She had been sure—just for a second or two, but long enough to have her complaisance blasted to bits—that the long-expected transformation had occurred. Now she was afraid that she would lean down and hug him and encounter another sneering troll's face—except that this time it would be no mask. Maybe this time he would grab her and pull her close, the better to tear out her stomach with his sharp and gleaming claws. The torrent of love washed through her and out of her, leaving a barren wasteland composed of uncertainty and fear. She was afraid of her own child.

Seesaw.

Seesaw.

Abruptly she was aware, once more, of how drunk she was. Rubber-jointed. Unsteady. Dizzy and *vulnerable*.

Beyond the vague glow of the night-light, the darkness pulsed and shifted and edged nearer, as if it were a living creature.

Ellen turned away from the bed and quickly left the room, weaving through the shadows. She closed Joey's door behind her and stood for a moment in the upstairs hallway. Her heart was slamming like a loose, windblown shutter in a storm.

Am I mad? she asked herself. Am I just like my own mother—seeing the work of the Devil in everyone, in everything, in places where it doesn't really exist? Am I *worse* than Gina?

No, she told herself adamantly. I'm not crazy, and I'm not like Gina. I've got good reason. And at the moment . . .

well . . . maybe I've had too much to drink, and I'm not thinking straight.

Her mouth was dry and sour from the booze, but she wanted another drink. She longed to recapture that feeling of floating, that bright, pleasant mood she had enjoyed before Joey had scared her with his Halloween mask.

She already felt the omens of a hangover: a faintly queasy stomach that would gradually succumb to a growing, roiling nausea; a dull throbbing in her temples that would become a splitting headache. What she needed, before she felt any worse, was some hair of the dog that had bit her. A whole lot of hair. Several glassfuls of hair from that funny old dog, the dog that came in a clear bottle, the dog that was distilled from potatoes. Wasn't vodka made from potatoes? Potato juice—that was what would make her feel right again. Lubricated by some potato juice, she would be able to slip back into that comfortable mood just as easily as slipping into a soft, fluffy old robe.

She knew she was a sinner. Pouring down the booze like she did was unquestionably sinful, and when she was sober she could see the spiritual stain that alcohol had left on her.

God help me, she thought. God help me because I just can't seem to help myself.

She went downstairs to get another drink.

Joey stayed in bed for ten minutes after his mother left the room. Then, when he felt it was safe to move, he snapped on the lamp and got up.

He went to the wastebasket by the dresser and stared down at the pile of monster models. They overflowed the can, a tangle of snarling, reaching plastic creatures. Dracula's head had been knocked off. A couple of the others also appeared to be damaged.

I won't cry, Joey told himself firmly. I won't start bawling like a baby. She would enjoy that. I'm not going to do anything she would enjoy.

Tears continued to slide down his cheeks, but he didn't call that crying. Crying was when you wailed your head off and got a runny nose and blubbered and got red in the face and just totally lost control of yourself.

He turned away from the wastebasket and went to his desk, from which Mama had removed all of the miniature monsters he had collected. The only thing left was his bank. He picked that up and carried it to the bed.

He saved his money in a one-gallon Mason jar. Most of it was in coins, squeezed bit by bit from his small weekly allowance, which he earned by keeping his room neat and by helping around the house. He also earned quarters by running to the 7-Eleven for Mrs. Jannison, the old lady who lived next door. There were several dollar bills in the jar, too; most of those were birthday gifts from his Grandma Harper, his Uncle John Harper, and his Aunt Emma Williams, who was Daddy's sister.

Joey emptied the contents of the jar onto the bed and counted it. Twenty-nine dollars. And a nickel. He was old enough to know that it wasn't a fortune, but it still seemed like a lot of money to him.

You could go a long way on twenty-nine dollars. He

wasn't sure exactly how far you could go, but he figured at least two hundred miles.

He was going to pack up and run away from home. He *had* to run away. If he stayed around much longer, Mama was going to come into his room one night, really drunk, really pissed, and she was going to kill him.

Just like she had killed Victor.

Whoever Victor was.

He thought about what it would be like, going off on his own to some strange town, far away. It would be lonely, for one thing. He wouldn't miss Mama. He wouldn't even miss his father very much. But he sure would miss Amy. When he thought of leaving Amy and never seeing her again, he felt his throat tighten, and he thought he was going to bawl.

Stop it! Be tough!

He bit his tongue until the urge to cry subsided and he was sure he was in control of himself.

Running away from home didn't mean he would never see Amy for the rest of his life. She would be leaving home, too, in a couple of years, going away to live on her own, and he could join up with her then. They could live together in an apartment in New York City or someplace great like that, and Amy would become a famous painter, and he would finish growing up. If he showed up on Amy's doorstep a couple of years from now, she wouldn't turn him in to Mama; not Amy.

He felt better already.

He put his money back in the big Mason jar and screwed the lid on tight. He returned the jar to his desk.

He would have to get coin wrappers from the bank and package his nickels, dimes, and quarters into rolls, then trade them in for folding money. He couldn't run away from home with his pockets stuffed full of loose, jangling change; that would be childish.

He slipped into bed again and turned off the light.

The only thing bad about running away was that he would miss the county fair in July. He had been looking forward to it for nearly a year.

Mama didn't approve of going to the fair and mixing with those carnival people. She said they were dirty and dangerous, a bunch of crooks.

Joey didn't put much faith in what Mama said about anyone. So far as Mama was concerned, there was hardly a person in the whole world who was free of sin.

Some years his father took him to the carnival on Saturday, the last day of the fair. But other years there was too much work at the law office, and Daddy couldn't get away.

This year Joey had intended to sneak off to the carnival on his own. The fairgrounds were less than two miles away from the Harper house, and he had to travel only two streets to get there. It was an easy place to find, high up on the hill. Joey had planned to tell his mother that he was going to the library for the day, which he occasionally did; but then he was going to take his bicycle out to the fairgrounds and have himself a real ball all morning and afternoon, getting home just in time for supper, without Mama being any the wiser.

He especially hated to miss the fair this year because it was going to be bigger and better than ever. The midway would be run by a different outfit from the one that had always come to Royal City in the past. This carnival was supposed to be humongous, the second largest in the world, two or three times bigger than the rinky-dink carnival that usually came to town. There would be a lot more rides than there had been in other years, a great many new things to see and do.

But he wouldn't see or do any of them if he was two hundred miles away, starting a new life in a strange city.

For almost a full minute Joey lay in the darkness, feeling sorry for himself—and then he sat bolt upright, electrified by a brilliant idea. He could leave home and still get to see the fair. He could do both. It was simple. Perfect. *He would run away with the carnival!*

8

Wednesday morning the test results came back from the lab. Amy was officially pregnant.

Wednesday afternoon she and Mama went to the bank and withdrew enough money from Amy's savings account to pay cash for the abortion.

Saturday morning they told Amy's father that they were going shopping for a few hours. Instead, they went to Dr. Spangler's clinic.

At the admissions desk Amy felt like a criminal. Neither Dr. Spangler nor his associates, Dr. West and Dr. Lewis, nor any of his nurses was Catholic; they performed abortions every week, month in and month out, without attaching any moral judgment to the act. Nevertheless, after so many years of intense religious instruction, Amy felt almost as if she were about to become an accomplice to a murder, and she knew that at least a residue of guilt would remain with her for a long, long time, staining any happiness she might be able to achieve.

She still found it difficult to believe that Mama had agreed to let her abort the fetus. She wondered about the fear in her mother's eyes.

The operation was done on an outpatient basis, and a nurse took Amy to a room where she could undress and put her clothes in a locker. Mama remained in the waiting room.

In the prep room, after a nurse had taken a blood sample, Dr. Spangler came in to chat with her for a moment. He tried to put her at ease. He was a jovial, chubby man with a bald head and bushy gray sideburns.

"You're not very far gone," he said. "This will be a simple procedure. No serious chance of complications. Don't worry about it, okay? It'll be over before you realize it's begun."

In the small operating room, Amy was given a mild anesthetic. She began to drift out of her body as if she were a balloon rising into a high, blue sky.

In the distance, beyond a haze of light and a curtain of whispering air, Amy heard a nurse talking softly. The woman said, "She's a very pretty girl, isn't she?"

"Yes, very pretty," Dr. Spangler said, his voice fading syllable by syllable, almost inaudible. "And a nice girl, too. I've been her doctor since she was a little tot. She's always been so polite, self-effacing . . ."

Soaring up and away from them, Amy tried to tell the doctor that he was wrong. She wasn't a nice girl. She was a very bad girl. He should ask Mama. Mama would tell him the truth. Amy Harper was a bad girl, evil inside, loose, wild, untrustworthy, just no damned good. She tried to tell Dr. Spangler how worthless she was, but her lips and tongue wouldn't respond to her urging. She couldn't make a sound—

—until she said, "Uh," and opened her eyes in the recovery room. She was on a wheeled cart with railed sides, flat on her back, staring at an acoustic-tiled ceiling. For a moment she couldn't figure out where she was.

Then she remembered everything, and she was amazed that the abortion had been such a quick and easy procedure.

They kept her in the recovery room for an hour, just to be sure she wasn't going to hemorrhage.

By three-thirty she was in the Pontiac with her mother, on the way home. During the first half of the short drive, neither of them spoke. Mama's face looked like a stone carving.

Finally Amy said, "Mama, I know you'll want me to keep a curfew for a couple of months, but I hope you'll let me work evenings down at The Dive, if that's the shift Mr. Donnatelli gives me."

"You can work whenever you want to work," her mother said coldly.

"I'll come home straight from work."

"You don't have to," Mama said. "I don't care what you do. I just don't care anymore. You won't listen to me anyway. You won't behave yourself. You've loosened the reins on that thing inside of you, and now there's no holding it back. There's not a thing I can do. I wash my hands of you. I wash my hands."

"Mama, please. Please. Don't hate me."

"I don't hate you. I just feel numb, blank. I don't feel much of anything for you right now."

"Don't give up on me."

"There's only one road to Heaven," Mama said. "But if you want to go to Hell, you'll find a thousand roads that'll take you there. I can't block all of them."

"I don't want to go to Hell," Amy said.

"It's your own choice," Mama said. "From here on it's your own doing. Do whatever you want. You'll never listen to me anyway, so I wash my hands." As she spoke she pulled the car into the driveway of the house on Maple Lane. "I'm not coming in with you. I've got to do some grocery shopping. If your father's back from the office, tell him the reason you look so pale is because you ate a hamburger for lunch, while we were shopping at the mall, and it didn't agree with you. Go to your room and stay out of his way. The less he sees of you, the less likely he is to get suspicious."

"All right, Mama."

When Amy went in the house she found that her father hadn't returned from the office yet. Joey was still playing at Tommy Culp's house. She was alone.

She changed into pajamas and a bathrobe, then called Liz Duncan. "It's over."

"Really?" Liz asked.

"I just got home."

"You're all scraped out?"

"Do you have to put it so crudely?" Amy asked.

"That's what they do," Liz said blithely. "They scrape you out. How do you feel?"

"Scraped out," Amy admitted miserably.

"Sick in the tummy?"

"A little. And I ache . . . down there."

"You mean you've got a sore cunt?" Liz asked.

"Do you have to talk that way?"

"What way?"

"Gross."

"That's one of my most charming qualities—my complete lack of inhibitions. Listen, other than your tummy and your cunt, how are you feeling?"

"Very, very tired."

"That's all?"

"Yes. It was easier than I thought it would be."

"Gee, I'm relieved. I was worried about you, kid. I was really, really worried."

"Thanks, Liz."

"Are you grounded for the summer?"

"No. I thought there'd be a curfew for a while, but Mama says she doesn't care what I do. She's washed her hands of me."

"She said that?"

"Yes."

"My God, that's terrific!"

"Is it?" Amy wondered.

"Of course it is, you silly ass. You make your own rules now. You're *free*, kid!" Liz put on a phony Southern Negro dialect: "Yo' massah have done turned yo' loose, chile!"

Amy didn't laugh. She said, "Right now, all I care about is getting some sleep. I was awake all last night and most of the night before. And with this business today . . . well, I'm dead on my feet."

"Sure," Liz said. "I understand. I won't keep you on the phone for an hour. Get some rest. Call me tomorrow. We'll make plans for the summer. It's going to be a blast, kid. We'll make some memories and blow out all the candles for our last summer together. I've already got a couple of guys in mind for you."

"I don't think a guy is exactly what I need right now," Amy said.

"Oh, not in the next ten minutes," Liz agreed. "But after you've had a couple of weeks to recover, you'll be ready to get back in the swing of things."

"I don't think so, Liz."

"Sure you will. You're not going to become a nun, for God's sake. You need to get some of that old salami once in a while, kid. You need it the same way I need it. We're two of a kind in that respect. Neither of us can do without a guy for long."

"We'll see," Amy said.

"Only this time," Liz said, "you're going to do what I tell you. You're going to get a prescription for the pill."

"I really don't think I'll need it," Amy said.

"That's what you thought the last time, dope."

A few minutes later, in her room, Amy knelt at the side of her bed and started to say her prayers. But after a minute or two she stopped because, for the first time in her life, she had the feeling that God wasn't listening. She wondered if He would ever listen to her again.

In bed she cried herself to sleep, and no one woke her for dinner or for Mass the next morning. When she opened her eyes again, it was eleven o'clock Sunday morning, and scattered, white clouds were racing like great sailing ships across the sea-blue sky beyond her window. She had slept eighteen hours straight through.

As far as she could remember, this was only the second time she had missed Sunday Mass since she was a few months old. The other time had been when she was nine and in the hospital, recovering from an emergency appendectomy. She had been scheduled to be discharged on Monday, and her mother had argued with the doctor about letting her out one day early so she could be taken to church, but the doctor had said that church wasn't the best place for a child recuperating from surgery.

She was relieved that Mama hadn't forced her to go to church this morning. Apparently Mama didn't think that her wicked daughter belonged in a church anymore.

And maybe Mama was right.

The following day, Monday, May 26, two sign painters went to work on the large billboard at the entrance to the county fairgrounds, just outside the Royal City limits. By midafternoon they were finished.

COMING COMING COMING
** JUNE 30 THROUGH JULY 5 **

THE ANNUAL ROYAL COUNTY FAIR

---

*HARNESS RACING
*ARTS & CRAFTS SHOW
*LIVESTOCK AUCTIONS
*GAMES, THRILL RIDES

MIDWAY ATTRACTIONS BY:

BIG AMERICAN MIDWAY SHOWS

TWO

The Carnival Is Coming . . .

9

A month after the abortion, the last week of June, Amy was working at The Dive, nine-to-five Monday through Friday, and noon-to-six on Saturday. The place was jumping every minute with a tanned and energetic crowd of teenagers.

At six o'clock Saturday evening, as Amy was getting ready to go home, Liz Duncan came in, looking like a million bucks in tight red shorts and a white T-shirt, no bra. "I've got a date with Richie tonight. He's going to meet me here at six-thirty. Want to wait with me so I don't get lonely?"

"You wouldn't get lonely," Amy said. "If you sat down alone, every guy in the place would be hanging on you in two minutes."

Liz looked speculatively at the kids in The Dive, then shook her head. "Nope. Once I've dated a guy and then dropped him, he knows it's over for good; he knows it isn't worth his time to pitch me for a rematch."

"So?"

"So most of the guys in here wouldn't bother me if I sat down alone because I've already screwed most of them."

"Gross," Amy said.

"But almost true," Liz said.

"You're bad."

"That's why the boys like me. Listen, are you going to keep me company till Richie gets here?"

"Sure," Amy said.

She went to the fountain and drew down two Cokes, and she and Liz took the first booth at the front of the room, where they had a view of Main Street. Liz's car was parked out front. It was a yellow Toyota Celica. Her parents had given it to her as a surprise graduation gift.

"No matter how hard I try," Amy said, "I can't picture you and Richie Atterbury as a couple."

"Why not? We were both unique in school," Liz said. "He was the class genius with an IQ of one-eighty, and I was the class slut with a hundred and eighty names on my scorecard."

"I don't know why you keep putting yourself down like that," Amy said. "You haven't had anywhere near a hundred and eighty guys, for God's sake."

"I'm not putting myself down," Liz said. "Honey, I revel in it. I love what I am. It's the only way to fly."

"Richie was always so shy."

"He's not so shy anymore," Liz said. She winked. "Listen, it's been a ball teaching Richie what the game is all about. He was so gangly and clumsy and naive! A real challenge. But he's coming along. He's coming along real nice. He has a real taste for corruption."

"And you're corrupting him?"

"Exactly."

"Isn't that a bit melodramatic?"

"No. Because that's exactly what I'm doing. I'm corrupting Richie Atterbury, boy genius."

"Elizabeth Ann Duncan, sultry temptress, the all-knowing wanton woman of exotic Royal City," Amy said sarcastically.

Liz grinned. "That's me. You know, just three weeks ago, when I first started going out with him, Richie had never smoked grass? Can you imagine? Now he's a regular pothead."

"That's the only reason you're dating him? Just so you can corrupt him?"

"No," Liz said. "It's a hell of a lot of fun to open him up to new things, new experiences. But even if he already knew his way around, he'd be fun to be with. He's clever, witty. And he seems to know something interesting about almost everything. I've never dated a genius before. It's different."

"Sounds like maybe this one will last a little longer than the others," Amy said.

"No way," Liz said quickly. "I figure another month, six weeks at the outside. Then bye-bye, Richie. No matter how clever he is, I'll be bored with him by then. Besides, even if I wanted something permanent with someone, which I *don't* want, but even if for some weird reason I did, I wouldn't want anything permanent with anyone here in this jerkwater town. I don't want anyone holding me back when I'm ready to split for the west."

"You're still planning on going?"

"Hell, yes. I'll work in my father's office until the middle of December, build up a nest egg, and then knock off a couple of weeks before Christmas. After the holiday, I'll pack my clothes into my little yellow car, and I'll be off like a shot to the land of sun and opportunity."

"California?"

"I've decided on Vegas," Liz said.

"Las Vegas?"

"That's the only Vegas I know."

"What will you do there?"

"Sell it," Liz said, grinning again.

"Sell what?"

"Don't be dopey."

"I'm not being dopey."

"As dense as a post."

"I don't understand. What are you going to sell?"

"My *ass*."

"Huh?"

"I'm going to do some heavy hooking."

"Hooking?"

"Jesus!" Liz said. "Listen, kid, don't you realize how much money a high-priced call girl can make in Vegas? A six-figure income, that's how much."

Amy stared at her in disbelief. "You're trying to make me believe that you're going to Vegas to be a whore?"

"I'm not trying to make you believe anything," Liz said. "I'm merely telling you the facts, kid. Besides, I'm not going to be an ordinary whore. 'Whore' is a low-class word. Whores are cheap. I'm going to be a personal escort, an intimate companion to a new gentleman every evening.

Intimate companions are quite expensive, you know. And I'm going to be more expensive than most of them."

"You aren't serious."

"Of course I am. I've got a good personality, a damned nice face, long legs, a cute little butt, almost no waist at all, and *these*." She thrust her chest out, and her large, uptilted breasts strained against the thin T-shirt. "If I can learn not to spend every dime I make, and if I can find a few good investments, I'll be worth at least a million by the time I'm twenty-five."

"You won't do it."

"Yep."

"You're putting me on."

"Nope. Listen, I'm a regular nympho. I know that. You know that. Practically everyone knows that. I can't keep my hands off the guys, and I like variety. So if I'm going to be screwing around every day of the week, I might as well get paid for it."

Amy stared at her searchingly, and Liz met her eyes, and at last Amy said, "My God, you really mean it."

"Why not?"

"Liz, a prostitute's life isn't pleasant. It isn't fun and games. It's lonely and grim."

"Who says?"

"Well . . . everyone says."

"Everyone is full of shit."

"If you go away and do something like this . . . Liz, it'll be such a . . . such a tragedy. That's what it'll be. You'll be throwing your whole life away, ruining everything."

"You sound like your mother," Liz said scornfully.

"I don't, either."

"Oh, yes you do," Liz said. "You sound exactly like her."

Amy frowned. "I do?"

"Smug, moralistic, self-righteous."

"I'm just worried about you."

"I know what I'm doing," Liz said. "Listen, when you're a high-priced call girl, you party all the time. What's so lonely and grim about that? It *is* fun and games. Especially in Vegas, where there's never a dull minute."

Amy was stunned. She had never imagined that she would one day have a friend who was a prostitute. For a while they sat in silence, sipping their Cokes and listening to a Bob Seger number that was blasting out of the juke-box with the force of a jackhammer.

When the music stopped, Liz said, "You know what would be great?"

"What?"

"If you came along with me to Vegas."

"*Me?*"

"Sure. Why not?"

"My God," Amy said, shocked by the idea.

"Listen, I know I'm a damned desirable little package," Liz said. "But I'm not one bit sexier than you are. You've got just what it takes to be a huge success in Vegas."

Amy laughed with embarrassment.

"You really do," Liz insisted.

"Not me."

"They'd be standing in line for a chance to get in your pants. Listen, kid, in that town you'd outdraw Liberace and Frank Sinatra *combined*."

"Oh, Liz, I couldn't do that sort of thing. Not in a million years."

"You did it with Jerry."

"Not for money."

"Which is foolish."

"Anyway, that was different. Jerry was my steady boyfriend."

"What's so great about steady?" Liz demanded. "Did going steady mean anything to Jerry? He dumped you the second he heard you were knocked up. He wasn't considerate or sympathetic or loyal or anything else a steady is supposed to be. I guarantee you, none of the men you'd be escorting in Vegas would treat you that shabbily."

"With my luck," Amy said, "my first client would turn out to be a homicidal maniac with a butcher knife."

"No, no, no," Liz said. "Your clients would all come with seals of approval from hotel pit bosses and other casino executives. They'd send you only the high rollers— doctors, lawyers, famous entertainers, millionaire businessmen . . . You'd only take on the best people."

"This may come as a surprise to you," Amy said, "but even a millionaire businessman can turn out to be a homicidal maniac with a butcher knife. It's rare. I'll grant you that. But it's not impossible."

"So you carry your own knife in your purse," Liz said. "If he starts acting creepy, *you* make the first cut."

"You have an answer for everything, don't you?"

"I'm just a girl from little old Royal City, Ohio," Liz said, "but I'm not a hick."

"Well, I don't think I'll be going to Vegas with you at

the end of the year," Amy said. "It's going to be a long, long time before I'm even ready to go on a nice, quiet, no-sex date. I've sworn off men for a while."

"Bullshit," Liz said.

"It's true."

"You *have* been a stick-in-the-mud so far this summer," Liz said. "But that'll pass."

"No. I mean it."

"Last week you went to the doctor I recommended," Liz said smugly.

"So?"

"So you got a prescription for the pill. Would you get a prescription for the pill if you really intended to be a wallflower?"

"You talked me into that," Amy said.

"For your own good."

"I wish I hadn't gone to that doctor. I won't be needing the pill or anything else until I'm out of college. I'm going to sit back, with my knees together, and be virginal."

"Like hell you are," Liz said. "Two weeks from now, you'll be flat on your back, pinned under one stud or another. Two weeks at most. I know it. I know you backwards and forwards, up and down, inside and out. You know how it is that I'm able to read you so clearly? It's because you're exactly like me. We're two of a kind. Peas in a pod. Oh, not on the surface, necessarily. But deep down, deep in your heart where it counts, you're exactly like me, honey. That's why we'd be great together in Vegas. We'd have a ball."

Richie Atterbury walked up to the table. He was a tall, thin boy, not handsome but not unattractive, either. He had thick, dark hair, and he wore horn-rimmed glasses that made him look a little bit like Clark Kent. "Hi, Liz. Hi, Amy."

Amy said, "Hello, Richie. That's a pretty shirt you're wearing."

"You really think so?" he asked.

"Yes. I like it a lot."

"Thanks," Richie said awkwardly. He looked at Liz with his big, lovesick, puppy eyes, and he said, "Ready for the movie?"

"Can't wait," Liz said. She stood up. To Amy, she said, "We're going to the drive-in. That's really fitting, too." She grinned wickedly. "Because Richie sure knows how to drive it in."

Richie blushed.

Liz laughed and said, "The only way I'm going to see much of this movie is if we set up a series of mirrors to reflect it onto the ceiling of the car."

"Liz, you're terrible," Amy said.

"Do you think I'm terrible?" Liz asked Richie.

"I think you're terrific," Richie said, daring to put an arm around her waist. He still seemed somewhat bashful, even if Liz *had* made him more than passingly familiar with sex and drugs.

Liz looked at Amy. "See? He thinks I'm terrific, and *he* was the class genius, so what do *you* know about it?"

Amy smiled in spite of herself.

"Listen," Liz said, "when you're ready to start living again, when you're sick and tired of playing Sister Purity, give me a call. I'll line someone up for you. We'll double-date."

Amy watched Liz and Richie as they walked outside and got into the yellow Celica. Liz drove. She pulled away from the curb with a torturous squeal of tires that made everyone in The Dive look toward the front windows.

After Amy left The Dive at twenty minutes till seven, she didn't go straight home. She walked aimlessly for more than an hour, not really window-shopping in the stores she passed, not really noticing the houses she passed, not really enjoying the clean spring evening, just walking and thinking about the future.

When she got home at eight o'clock, her father was in his workshop. Her mother was sitting at the kitchen table, leafing through a magazine, listening to a radio call-in program, and sucking on vodka and orange juice.

"If you didn't have dinner at work," Mama said, "there's some cold roast beef in the refrigerator."

"Thank you," Amy said, "but I'm not hungry. I ate a big lunch."

"Suit yourself," Mama said. She turned up the volume on the radio.

Amy interpreted that as a sign of dismissal. She went upstairs.

She spent an hour with Joey, playing five-hundred rummy, his favorite card game. The boy didn't seem himself. He hadn't been the old, effervescent Joey since Mama had made him get rid of his monster models and posters. Amy worked hard at making him laugh, and he *did* laugh, but his good humor seemed like a facade to her. He was tense underneath, and she hated to see him that way, but she couldn't figure out how to reach him and cheer him up.

Later, in her room, she stood nude again in front of the

full-length mirror. She appraised her body with a critical eye, trying to decide if she did, indeed, measure up to Liz. Her legs were long and quite well shaped. Her thighs were taut; the muscle tone in her whole body was very good. Her bottom was round and sort of perky, very firm. Her belly was not just flat but slightly concave. Her breasts weren't as large as Liz's, but they weren't small by any definition, and they were extremely well shaped, upthrust, with large, dark nipples.

It was definitely a body well designed for sex, for easily attracting and satisfying a man. The body of a courtesan? The body of, as Liz put it, an intimate companion? The legs and hips and buttocks and breasts of a whore? Was that what she had been born for? To sell herself? Was a future as a prostitute unavoidable? Was it somehow her destiny to spend thousands of sweaty nights clutching total strangers in hotel rooms?

Liz said she saw corruption in Amy's eyes. Mama said the same thing. To Mama, that corruption was a monstrous, evil thing that must be suppressed at all costs; but to Liz, it was nothing to be afraid of, something to be embraced. There couldn't be two people more different than Liz and Mama, yet they agreed on what was to be seen in Amy's eyes.

Now Amy stared at her reflection in the mirror, peered into the windows of her soul; but although she looked very hard, she wasn't able to see anything more than the characterless surfaces of two dark and rather pretty eyes; she couldn't see either the rot of Hell or the grace of Heaven.

She was lonely, frustrated, and terribly, terribly confused. She wanted to understand herself. More than anything she wanted to find the right role for herself in the world, so that for the first time in her life she would not feel tense and hopelessly out of place.

If her hope of going to college and her dream of becoming an artist were unrealistic, then she didn't want to spend years struggling for what she was not meant to have. Her life had been too much of a struggle already.

She touched her breasts, and her nipples sprang up at once, stiff, proud, as large as the tips of her little fingers. Yes, this was a bad thing, a sinful thing, just as Mama said, yet it felt so good, so sweet.

If she could be sure that God would listen to her, she would get down on her knees and ask Him for a sign, an irrefutably holy sign that would tell her, once and for all, whether she was a good person or a bad person. But she didn't think God would listen to her after what she'd done to the baby.

Mama said she was bad, that Something lurked inside of her, that she had let go of the reins that had been holding that Something back. Mama said she had the potential to be evil. And a mother should know that kind of thing about a daughter.

Shouldn't she?

Shouldn't she?

Before he went to bed, Joey counted the money in his bank again. During the past month he had added two dollars and ninety-five cents to the contents of the jar, and now he had exactly thirty-two dollars.

He wondered if he would have to bribe someone at the

carnival to let him run away with them when they left town. He figured he would need twenty dollars as a minimum bankroll, which would keep him in grub until he started earning money as a carny, sweeping up after the elephants and doing whatever else a ten-year-old boy could find to do on a midway. So that left only twelve bucks that he could spare for a bribe.

Would that be enough?

He decided to ask his father for two dollars to go to the Sunday matinee at the Rialto theater. But he wouldn't actually spend the money on the movies. He would go over to Tommy Culp's house and play tomorrow afternoon, pretend that he'd seen the movies when his father asked about them, and add the two bucks to his escape fund.

He returned the bank to the desk.

When he said his prayers before going to bed, he asked God to please keep Mama from getting pissed and coming into his room again.

The next day, Sunday, Amy called Liz.

"Hello," Liz said.

"This is Sister Purity," Amy said.

"Oh, hello, Sister."

"I've decided to leave the nunnery."

"Hallelujah!"

"It's cold and drafty here in the nunnery."

"Not to mention boring," Liz said.

"What have you got for me that I won't find boring?"

"How about Buzz Klemmet?"

"I don't know him," Amy said.

"He's eighteen, soon nineteen I think. He was in the class ahead of ours—"

"Ah, an older man!"

"—but he dropped out of school in eleventh grade. He works at the Arco station on the corner of Main and Broadway."

"You sure know how to pick them," Amy said sarcastically.

"He may not sound like much," Liz said, "but wait till you see him. He's a hunk."

"A hunk of what?"

"Pretty muscle."

"Can he speak?"

"Just well enough."

"Can he tie his own shoelaces?"

"I'm not sure," Liz said. "But he usually wears loafers, so you won't have to worry about that."

"I hope you know what you're doing."

"Trust me," Liz said. "You'll love him. What night should I set it up for?"

"Doesn't matter," Amy said. "I work days."

"Tomorrow night?"

"Fine."

"We'll double," Liz said. "Me and Richie, you and Buzz."

"Where do you want to go?"

"How about my place? We'll play some records, watch a movie on my folks' videocassette machine, roll a few joints. I got some bitchin' grass that'll mellow us out real fast."

"What about your parents?" Amy asked.

"They're leaving on a two-week vacation today. New Orleans. I'll have the house all to myself."

"They trust you alone there for two weeks?"

"They trust me not to burn the place to the ground," Liz said. "And that's really all they care about. Listen, kid, I'm glad you finally came to your senses. I was afraid the summer was going to be a bummer. We'll sure raise hell now that you're back in the swing of things."

"I'm not sure I want to get back in the swing of things, at least not all the way, if you know what I mean. I want to have some fun. I want to date. But I don't think I'm going to screw around anymore. Not until college is behind me."

"Sure, sure," Liz said.

"I mean it."

"Take it at your own pace, honey. Anyway, we'll sure have some fun with my old man and old lady out of town."

"And the county fair is next week," Amy said.

"Hey, yeah! I really get off on smoking some good dope and then hopping on those thrill rides."

"I suspect you would."

"And did you ever get high and then go through the funhouse, with all those fake monsters jumping out at you?"

"Never did," Amy said.

"It's hilarious."

"I'll look forward to it," Amy said.

10

Janet Middlemeir was a safety engineer for the county. Her job was to make certain that all public buildings—courthouses, firehouses, libraries, schools, sheriff's substations, government-subsidized sports arenas and stadiums, and so forth—were at all times clean, well lighted, and safe for both visitors and workers. She was responsible for the inspection of the structural integrity of those buildings as well as for the condition and suitability of all machinery and all major nonmechanical equipment within their walls. Janet was young, only a few years out of college, only two years on the job, and she was still as dedicated to her work as she had been when she had first started; her duties seemed almost holy to her, and the words "public trust" still held some meaning for her, even if they didn't mean much to some of the people with whom she worked in the county and state bureaucracies. She had not yet been a public employee long enough to be tainted by the inevitable corrupting influences that were attendant to any government program. She *cared*.

On Monday, June 23, when the carnival came to Rockville, Maryland, Janet Middlemeir presented herself at the office-trailer that provided working space for Mr. Frederick Frederickson, the silver-haired owner and operator of Big American Midway Shows. With characteristic directness and crispness, Janet stated her intention of going through the lot from one end to the other, until she was fully satisfied that the thrill rides and the other large attractions were safely erected. She would not approve the opening of the carnival if she felt that it represented a threat to the well-being of the citizens of her county.

She was pushing her authority a little bit, perhaps even exceeding it. She wasn't entirely sure that the carnival's equipment came under her jurisdiction, even though it stood on the county-owned fairgrounds. The law was vague on that point. No one from the county Office of Public Safety had ever inspected the carnival before, but Janet felt she couldn't shirk that responsibility. Just a few weeks ago a young woman had died when a carnival ride had collapsed in Virginia; and although that tragic accident hadn't happened on the lot of Big American Midway Shows, Janet was determined to put Big American under a microscope before the fairground gates swung open.

When she stated her intentions to Mr. Frederickson, she was afraid that he would think she was trying to shake him down, and she didn't know quite how she would handle him if he tried to bribe her. She knew that carnivals employed a man whose job it was to bribe public officials; they called him the "patch" because he went into town ahead of the show and patched things up with the police and certain other key government employees, lining their pockets with folding money and books of free tickets for their friends and families. If a patch didn't do his job, the police usually raided the midway, closing down all the games, even if it was a straight carnival that didn't dupe the marks out of their money; unpaid and angry about it, the police could shutter even the cleanest girly shows and legally declare the thrill rides hazardous, quickly and effectively bringing the carnival to its knees. She didn't want the people at Big American to think she was after a fast buck.

Fortunately, Mr. Frederickson was a well-educated, well-spoken, courtly gentleman, not at all what she had expected, and he both recognized and admired her sincerity. No bribe was offered. He assured her that his people were as concerned about the health and safety of their customers as she was, and he gave her permission to poke around in every corner of the midway for as long as she liked. Frederickson's superintendent of transportation, Max Freed, issued her a badge with the letters "VIP" on it, so that all the carnies would cooperate with her.

For most of the morning and afternoon, wearing a hard hat, carrying a big flashlight and a notebook, Janet prowled the grounds, watching the midway rise like a phoenix, inspecting bolts and rivets and spring-locked joints, crawling into dark, tight places when that was necessary, overlooking nothing. She discovered that Frederick Frederickson had been telling the truth; Big American was conscientious about maintenance and more than conscientious, down-right *fussy*, about the erection of rides and sideshows.

At a quarter past three she came to the funhouse, which appeared to be ready for business a full hour and fifteen minutes before the gates were scheduled to open. The area around the attraction was deserted, quiet. She wanted someone to give her a guided tour of the funhouse, but she couldn't locate anyone associated with it, and for a moment she considered skipping the place. She hadn't found even one major safety problem anywhere else on the midway, and it wasn't likely that she would uncover a dangerous construction-code violation here. She'd probably just be wasting her time. Nevertheless . . .

She had a strong sense of duty.

She walked up the boarding ramp, past the ticket booth, and stepped down into the sunken channel in which the gondolas would move when the ride was started up. From the boarding gate the channel led to a set of large plywood doors that were painted to resemble the massive, timbered, iron-hinged doors of a forbidding castle. When the ride was in service, the doors would swing back to admit each oncoming car, then fall shut behind it. At the moment, as she approached the entrance, one door was propped open. She peered inside.

The interior of the funhouse wasn't as dark now as it would be when the ride was in operation. A string of work lights ran the length of the track and disappeared around a bend fifty feet away; when the place was open for business, those lights would be extinguished. Yet even with that chain of softly glowing bulbs, the funhouse was gloomy.

Janet leaned through the doorway. "Hello?"

No one answered.

"Is anyone there?" she asked.

Silence.

She switched on her flashlight, hesitated only a second, and stepped inside.

The funhouse smelled damp and oily.

She knelt and inspected the pins that joined two sections of track. They were securely fastened.

She got up and moved deeper into the building.

On both sides of the track, slightly elevated from it, life-sized mechanical figures stood in secret niches in the walls: an ugly, leering pirate with a sword in his hand; a werewolf, claws coated with silvery, day-glow paint that would make them look like glinting blades in the dark, phony but realistic blood on his wolfish snout and on his two-inch-long fangs; a grinning, blood-drenched ax-murderer standing over the hideously wounded corpse of one of his victims; and many others, some more gruesome than those first few. In this light Janet could see that they were only clever, lifelike mannequins, but she felt uneasy around them. Although none of them was animated, as all of them would be when the funhouse was in operation, they looked as if they were about to pounce on her; to her chagrin, the damned things spooked her. But her dislike of them didn't prevent her from inspecting the anchor bolts on a few of them to make sure they wouldn't topple down into a passing gondola and injure a rider.

Walking along the passageway, looking up at the monsters, Janet wondered why people insisted on referring to a place like this as a *fun*house.

She turned the bend at the end of the first length of track, moved farther into the funhouse, turned another corner, then another, marveling at the richness of invention that had been employed in the design of the place. It was huge, as large as a medium-sized warehouse, and it was crammed full of genuinely frightening things. It wasn't the sort of amusement that appealed to her, but she had to admire the work, the craftsmanship, and the creativity that had gone into it.

She was in the center of the enormous structure, standing on the track, looking up at a man-sized spider hanging overhead, when someone put a hand on her shoulder. She gasped, jumped, jerked away from the unexpected contact, turned, and would have screamed if her throat hadn't frozen.

A man was standing on the tracks behind her. He was extremely tall, at least six and a half feet, broad-shouldered, barrel-chested, and he was wearing a Frankenstein outfit: a black suit, a black turtleneck, monster gloves, and a rubber mask that covered his entire head.

"Scared?" he asked. His voice was exceptionally deep and hoarse.

She swallowed hard, finally breathed, and said, "Yes, my God! You scared me half to death."

"My job," he said.

"What?"

"Scare the marks. My job."

"Oh. You work here at the funhouse?"

"My job," he said.

She decided that he must be dull-witted. His simple,

halting declarations resembled the speech patterns of a severely retarded child. Trying to be friendly, hoping to keep *him* friendly, she said, "My name's Janet. What's yours?"

"Huh?"

"What's your name?"

"Gunther."

"That's a nice name."

"Don't like."

"You don't like your name?"

"No."

"What would you like to be called?"

"Victor."

"That's a nice name, too."

"Victor his favorite."

"Whose favorite?"

"His."

She realized that she was in a bad spot—in a strange and poorly lighted place, out of sight and perhaps out of earshot of anyone who might be inclined to help her, alone except for a badly retarded man big enough to break her in half the way she might break a breadstick.

He took a step toward her.

She backed up.

He stopped.

She stopped, too, shaking, aware that she couldn't outrun him. His legs were longer than hers, and he was probably more familiar with the terrain than she was.

He made an odd sound behind the mask; it was like a dog sniffing busily at a scent.

"I'm a government official," she said slowly, hoping he would understand. "A very important government official."

Gunther said nothing.

"Very important," Janet said nervously. She tapped the VIP badge that Max Freed had given her. "Mr. Frederickson told me I could go anywhere I wanted on the midway. Do you know who he is? Do you know Mr. Frederickson?"

Gunther didn't reply. He just stood there, big as a truck, looking down at her, his face hidden behind that mask, his arms dangling limply at his sides.

"Mr. Frederickson owns this carnival," she said patiently. "You must know him. He's probably your boss. He told me I could go wherever I wanted."

Finally Gunther spoke again. "Smell woman."

"What?"

"Smell woman. Smell good. Pretty."

"Oh, no," she said, starting to sweat.

"Want pretty."

"No, no," she said. "No, Gunther. That wouldn't be right. That would only get you in trouble."

He was sniffing again. The mask seemed to interfere with the scent he was trying to catch, and he reached up and pulled the Frankenstein monster face off, revealing his own face.

When Janet saw what had been hidden by the mask, she stumbled backwards on the track and screamed.

Before anyone could possibly have heard her cry, Gunther sprang at her and cut the scream short with one blow of his big hand.

She fell.

He dropped on top of her.

*   *   *

Fifteen minutes before the fairground gates opened to the public, Conrad made a final inspection tour of the funhouse. He walked the length of the track to be sure there were no obstructions on it, no forgotten tools or misplaced pieces of lumber that might derail one of the gondolas.

In the Hall of the Giant Spiders he found the dead woman. She was on the tracks, below one of the big, phony tarantulas. She was sprawled on top of her bloody clothes—naked, bruised, slashed. Her head had been torn off; it rested, faceup, a yard away from her body.

At first he thought Gunther had killed a carnival woman. That was unquestionably the worst thing that could happen. The bodies of outsiders could be disposed of in such a fashion as to direct the police away from everyone connected with Big American Midway Shows. But if one of the carnival's own was found raped and mutilated, the police would be summoned onto the lot, and Gunther would interest them sooner or later. The carnies accepted the boy now, as they accepted all freaks, because they didn't have any knowledge of his uncontrollable need to rape, kill, and taste blood. He hadn't always been this violent. The carnies knew he was different, but they didn't realize how *dangerously* different he had become during the past three years, when he had belatedly acquired a sex drive. No one ever paid much attention to Gunther; he was almost a shadow in their midst, a marginally perceived presence. But if a carny woman was killed, someone would take a much closer look at Gunther than ever before, and there would be no way to hide the truth.

After an initial rush of panic, Conrad saw that the dead woman was not from the carnival. He had never seen her face before. There was still a chance that he could save Gunther and himself.

Aware that he didn't have much time to conceal the evidence, Conrad stepped around the bloody remains and hurried toward the end of the Hall of the Giant Spiders. Just before he reached the next turn in the tracks, he climbed out of the gondola channel and stepped into a tableau featuring two animated figures: a man and a man-sized spider locked in mortal combat, unmoving now that there were no marks to witness their struggle. The battling man and tarantula were posed in front of a jumbled pile of papier-mâché boulders. Conrad went around behind the false rocks and knelt down.

The glow from the string of work lights above the tracks did not reach back here. He put a hand out in the darkness in front of him and felt the rough board floor. After a few seconds he located the ringbolt for which he had been searching. He pulled on the ring, lifting a trap-door, one of six that were scattered around the funhouse for maintenance purposes.

He slid on his belly, backwards through the trap, feeling with his feet for the rungs of a slanted ladder that he knew was there. He found the ladder and descended into pitch blackness. Just after his head was below the funhouse floor, his feet touched the plank flooring of the bottom level, and he pushed away from the ladder and stood up straight.

He reached into the darkness on his right side, passed his hand through the air, found the light chain, and pulled it. Two dozen bulbs came on all over the basement, but the place was still shadowy. He was in a low-ceilinged room full of machinery, cogwheels, cables, belts, pulleys, chain-driven mechanisms of odd design; these were the mechanical guts of the funhouse.

Turning away from the ladder, Conrad sidled between two machines and stepped into a narrow aisle between banks of long, notched cables that stretched across a series of large metal wheels. He hurried to the northwest corner of the chamber, where there was a workbench, a tool cabinet, a metal rack full of spare parts, a pile of tarps, and a couple of suits of coveralls.

Conrad quickly pulled off his barker's jacket, stepped out of his trousers, and wriggled into a pair of coveralls. He didn't want to explain bloodstained clothes to Ghost.

He picked up one of the tarps and rushed back to the ladder. Upstairs in the funhouse again, he returned to the dead woman on the tracks.

He glanced at his wristwatch. Today's show call was for four-thirty, and that was precisely the time his watch showed him. At this very moment the fairground gates were swinging open, and the marks were pouring through. Within ten minutes the first of them would be buying tickets for the funhouse.

Ghost wouldn't start the system until he'd gotten a final report on the condition of the track. He must be wondering what was taking Conrad so long. In two or three minutes, he would come looking.

Conrad spread the tarp out in the gondola channel. He picked up the still-warm body and dropped it in the middle of the sheet of canvas. He grabbed the long, trailing hair and lifted the woman's severed head—its mouth open, its eyes wide—and put that on the tarp as well. He added her shredded, bloody clothes to the pile, then a flashlight, a small notebook, and a hard hat. What sort of woman wore a hard hat? What had she been doing in the funhouse? He looked for a purse. A woman ought to be carrying a purse; but he couldn't find one. At last, panting from the exertion, he pulled the ends of the tarp together, lifted it, and hefted it out of the gondola channel, onto the ledge where the man and the spider were temporarily frozen in combat.

As he scrambled onto the ledge after the tarp, he heard someone call his name. "Conrad?"

With a sinking heart, Conrad looked back along the tracks, down the gloomy gondola tunnel.

It was Ghost. The albino was standing fifty feet away, at the far end of the straightaway, just inside the entrance to the Hall of the Giant Spiders. He was only a pale silhouette; Conrad wasn't able to see the albino's face.

And if I can't see him clearly, he can't see me any better, Conrad thought, relieved. He can't see the tarp, and even if he *can* see it, he can't possibly know what's in it.

"Conrad?"

"Yeah. Here."

"Is something wrong?"

"No, no. Nothing."

"The gates are open. We'll have marks swarming all over us in a couple of minutes."

Conrad crouched beside the tarp, using his body to further block Ghost's view of it. "There was some junk on the track. But it's okay now. I've taken care of it."

"You need some help?" Ghost asked, starting toward him.

"No! No, no. I've got everything under control. You better get out front, throw the switch, and start selling tickets. We're ready to roll."

"Are you sure?"

"Of course I'm sure!" Conrad snapped. "Get moving. I'll be out in a few minutes."

Ghost hesitated for just a second, then turned and walked back the way he had come.

As soon as the albino was out of sight, Conrad dragged the tarp behind the papier-mâché boulders. He had a bit of trouble squeezing the grisly bundle through the trapdoor. He leaned in after it, lowered it the length of his arms, then let it drop the rest of the way. It landed at the foot of the ladder. The tarp flopped open, and the ghastly, disembodied head looked up at him, mouth stretched in a silent scream.

Conrad went down the ladder again. He closed the trapdoor above him. He bent, gathered up the corners of the tarp, and dragged the corpse to the maintenance area in the northwest corner of the funhouse basement.

Overhead, the building was abruptly filled with eerie, tape-recorded music as Ghost started switching on the system.

Grimacing, Conrad picked up the dead woman's gore-spattered clothes, one piece at a time. He checked the pockets of her jeans, jacket, and blouse, looking for some scrap of identification.

He found her car keys right away. Attached to the key ring was one of those miniature license plates that were sold by some veterans' organizations. The number on it was the number on her real plates.

Even before he had finished his search of her clothes, he saw the Big American Midway VIP badge pinned to her blouse. That discovery rocked him. If she was someone with important carnival connections, Gunther's secret could no longer be concealed.

Conrad found the sort of thing he was looking for in the last pocket he turned out. It was a laminated ID card that said she was Janet Leigh Middlemeir; she worked for the county Office of Public Safety; she was a safety engineer, whatever the hell that was, and she was accredited by the State of Maryland.

A government official. That was bad. But not as bad as he had feared. At least she wasn't a sister or a cousin of one of the carnies. She didn't have any friends or relatives on the lot, no one who would be looking out for her. Evidently she had been on the midway strictly in a professional capacity, making spot safety checks. No one would have realized that she had disappeared in the middle of one of those inspections because no one would have been paying special attention to her. There was a good chance that Conrad could move the body and plant it far away from the carnival, in such a way that the police would think she had been killed after she quit working.

But he couldn't do anything more until it was dark; it would be a risky bit of business even then. Now he had to get out front, on the barker's platform, before Ghost started wondering what had happened to him and came looking again.

Conrad took a coil of rope from one of the storage shelves and threaded it through the eyelets around the edges of the tarpaulin. Then he pulled the rope like a drawstring and made a bag out of the tarp, with the dead woman and her belongings inside. He put the bag in the corner. He stripped out of the bloody coveralls and put them with the bag. His hands were bloody, and he wiped them off as best he could on a couple of dirty rags that were on the workbench; then he put the rags with his coveralls. Finally he stacked the other tarps on top of all that incriminating evidence, until there was nothing to see but a mound of rumpled canvas. No one would stumble across the dead woman, at least not during the few hours she would be there.

Conrad put on his street clothes and left the funhouse by a rear door. Because the basement wasn't underground, the door opened onto the warm, late-afternoon sunshine behind the building.

He walked to the nearest comfort station. Because the gates had opened only minutes ago, there weren't yet any marks in the restrooms. Conrad scrubbed his hands until they were as clean as a surgeon's.

He returned to the funhouse and walked around to the front of it. The giant clown's face was laughing. Elton, one of Conrad's employees, was selling tickets. Ghost was working at the boarding gate. Gunther was dressed like the Frankenstein monster and was growling enthusiastically at the marks; he saw Conrad, and they stared at each other for a moment, and although they were too far apart to see each other's eyes, an understanding passed between them.

—*I did it again.*

—*I know. I found her.*
—*What now?*
—*I'll protect you.*

Until night fell over the fairgrounds, Conrad worked on the pitchman's platform, ballying the marks, drawing them in with his polished spiel. As soon as darkness came, he complained of a migraine headache and told Ghost that he was going back to his motor home to lie down.

Instead, he went to the large parking area adjacent to the fairgrounds, and he searched for Janet Middlemeir's car. He had the miniature license plate on her key ring to guide him, and even though there were a great many cars to check through, he located her Dodge Omni in just half an hour.

He drove the Omni onto the lot through a service gate, well aware that he was leaving an evidential trail in other people's memories, but there was nothing else he could do. He parked in the shadows behind the funhouse. The service alley was deserted at the moment. He hoped no one would stroll past on the way to the comfort station.

He entered the funhouse basement through the rear door and carried out the tarp that contained the corpse, while the marks screamed at mechanical monsters in the dark tunnels overhead. He put the gruesome bundle in the Omni's trunk, and then he drove away from the fairgrounds.

Although he had never been so bold before, he decided the best place to leave the dead woman was in her own home. If the police thought she had been murdered in her own house by an intruder, they wouldn't be likely to link the killing with the carnival. It would look like just another random act of senseless violence, the sort of thing the cops saw all the time.

Two miles from the fairgrounds, in a supermarket parking lot, he looked through the car, trying to find some indication of where Janet Middlemeir lived. He discovered her purse under the front seat, where she had left it while making her inspection tour of the carnival. He went through the contents of the purse and found her address on her driver's license.

With the help of a map that he picked up at an Exxon station, Conrad managed to find the pleasant apartment complex in which the woman lived. There were a number of long, two- and three-story, colonial-style buildings angled through and around the parklike grounds. Janet Middlemeir's unit was on the ground floor, at the corner of one of the buildings, and there was an empty parking slot behind her place, not more than fifteen feet from her back door.

The apartment was dark, and Conrad hoped that she lived alone. He hadn't found anything to indicate that she was married. There were no rings on her hands; nothing in her purse bore the word "Mrs." Of course she might have a girlfriend rooming with her, or there might be a live-in boyfriend. That could mean trouble. Conrad was prepared to kill anyone who walked in on him while he was disposing of the body.

He got out of the car, leaving the dead woman in the Omni's trunk, and he let himself into her apartment. A

quick check of the closet in the single bedroom was sufficient to convince him that Janet Middlemeir lived by
herself.

He stood at the kitchen window and watched as a car
drove into the parking area. Two people got out of it and
went into an apartment two doors away. At the same time
a man left yet another apartment, got into a Volkswagen
Rabbit, and drove off. When all was quiet again, Conrad
went out to the Omni, took the tarp from the trunk, and
carried it inside, hoping that no one was watching him
from a window in one of the other apartments.

He took the tarp into the small bathroom and opened
it there. Taking care to keep himself clean, he lifted the
canvas and dumped the contents into the bathtub. There
was still a great deal of blood trapped in the torn body
cavity, and he spread some of the viscous stuff around,
smearing it on the walls and the floor.

He took a macabre pride in the cleverness of his plan. If
he had left the dead woman in the bedroom, the police
pathologists would have realized at once that she hadn't
been killed there, for they wouldn't have found enough
blood on the carpet to support that theory. (Most of her
blood had been spilled in the funhouse, on the gondola
tracks, and had soaked into the boards there.) But when
the cops found her here, in the bathroom, maybe they
would think that the missing pints of blood had simply
gone down the bathtub drain.

Conrad remembered the VIP badge on her blouse. He
fished that out of the tub and stuck it in his jacket pocket.

He also retrieved her hard hat, flashlight, and notebook, which were spotted with blood. He cleaned those

off at the sink, then took them out to the foyer closet and put them on the shelf above the coatrack. He didn't know whether that was where she usually kept those items, but the police wouldn't know, either, and it seemed a likely enough place.

He folded the empty tarp.

In the kitchen, in the harsh glow of the fluorescent lights, he inspected his hands carefully. He had washed them in the bathroom, when he had cleaned the articles that he'd taken to the foyer closet, but there was still some blood caked under his fingernails. He went to the kitchen sink and washed his hands once more, vigorously.

He found the drawer in which the dead woman had kept her dish towels. He wrapped one of the towels around his right hand and took another one to the kitchen door. He opened the door, which had three small, decorative windows arranged in the center of it. He looked out at the parking lot; under the stark light of the sodium-vapor lamps, there was no sound or motion. He put the folded dish towel against the exterior surface of one of the door's little panes, and then he struck the interior surface with his wrapped right hand, trying to make as little noise as possible. The glass broke with only a dull crack, and he used the folded towel to push the fragments inward onto the kitchen floor, so that it would look as if the killer had smashed the pane from the outside in the process of forcing entry. Conrad quietly closed the door, shook the dish towels to be certain there were no slivers of glass clinging to the fabric, refolded them, and returned them to the drawer in which he had found them.

He suddenly realized that threads from the dish towels might be snagged on the shards of glass. He stared down at the bright fragments. He didn't have time to examine each of them. Likewise, he didn't have time to study the trunk of her car with a magnifying glass to see if there were spots of blood in it. There were probably other loose ends, too. He would just have to do the best he could and trust in the protection of the dark god who guided him.

He left Janet Middlemeir's car keys on the kitchen counter and picked up the folded tarp. As he stepped out of the apartment he wiped the doorknobs with his handkerchief. He didn't have an arrest record; his fingerprints weren't on file anywhere, but nevertheless he was cautious.

He walked away from the apartment complex. The fairgrounds lay nine miles to the west, but he wasn't going to cover the entire distance on foot. He intended to call a taxi to take him back to the carnival, but he didn't want to risk summoning a ride from anywhere near the Middlemeir apartment; the cabdriver would keep a record of the trip and might even remember his passenger's face. A mile from the woman's place, he disposed of the tarp in a big trash bin behind another apartment building. After walking another mile, he came to a Holiday Inn. He stopped in the hotel bar, had two double Scotches, and then took a cab to the fairgrounds.

In the taxi he thought back over what he had done from the moment he had found the corpse on the gondola tracks, and as far as he could see, he hadn't made any serious mistakes. The cover-up probably would work. Gunther would remain free—at least a while longer.

Conrad couldn't let them take Gunther from him. Gunther was his son, his very special child, his own blood.

But more than that, Gunther was a gift from Hell; he was Conrad's instrument of revenge. When Conrad finally found Ellen's children, he would kidnap them, take them to an isolated place where their screams couldn't be heard, and turn them over to Gunther. He would encourage Gunther to play with them in cat-and-mouse fashion. He would urge Gunther to torture them for several days, use them sexually again and again, no matter if they were girls or boys, and then, only then, tear them apart.

Sitting in the darkness in the back of the taxi, Conrad smiled. He seldom smiled these days. He hadn't laughed in a long, long time. He wasn't amused by those things that amused other people; only death, destruction, cruelty, and damnation—the dark handiwork of the god of evil, whom he worshipped—could bring a smile to his lips. Ever since he was twelve years old, he had been unable to obtain joy or satisfaction from innocent, wholesome pleasures.

Not since *that* night.

Christmas Eve.

Forty years ago . . .

The Straker family always decorated their house from top to bottom for the Christmas season. They had a tree as tall as the ceiling would allow. Every room was festooned with evergreen wreaths, nut wreaths, candles, Nativity scenes, tinsel, Christmas cards received from friends and relatives, and much more.

The year that Conrad turned twelve, his mother added a new piece to the family's enormous collection of holiday decorations. It was an all-glass oil lantern; the flame was reflected and refracted within the angled walls of the lamp, so that there were a hundred images of fire instead of just one, and the eye was amazed and dazzled.

Young Conrad was fascinated by the lantern but wasn't permitted to touch it because he might burn himself. He knew he could handle the lantern safely, but he couldn't convince his mother of that. So when everyone else was asleep, he crept downstairs, struck a match, lit the lantern— and accidentally knocked it over. Burning oil spilled across the living room floor. At first he was sure he could put the fire out by beating it with a sofa cushion; but just a minute later, when he realized his folly, it was too late.

He was the only one to escape unscathed. His mother died in the blaze. His three sisters died. His two brothers died. Papa didn't die, but he was scarred for life—his chest, his left arm, his neck, the left side of his face.

The loss of his family left Papa with mental and emotional scars every bit as horrendous as his physical injuries. He wasn't able to accept the idea that God, in whom Papa devoutly believed, would let such a tragic accident happen on Christmas Eve, of all nights. He refused to believe it had been accidental. He made up his mind that Conrad was evil and had set the fire on purpose.

From that day until Conrad finally ran away several years later, his life was hell. Papa constantly badgered and accused him. He was not allowed to forget what he had done. Papa reminded him of it a hundred times a day. Conrad breathed guilt and wallowed in self-hatred.

He had never been able to run away from his shame. It came back to him every night, in his dreams, even now that he was fifty-two years old. His nightmares were full of fire and screams and the scarred, twisted face of his father.

When Ellen became pregnant, Conrad had been certain that, at last, God was giving him a chance to redeem himself. By raising a family, by giving his own children a wonderful life filled with love and happiness, perhaps he would be able to atone for the death of his mother, his sisters, and his brothers. Month by month, as Ellen became heavier with child, Conrad became increasingly sure that the baby was the beginning of his salvation.

Then Victor was born. Initially, for just a few hours, Conrad thought that God was heaping more punishment on him. Rather than give him a chance to atone for his sins, God seemed to be rubbing his face in them, telling him in no uncertain terms that he would never know grace and spiritual comfort.

After the first bitter shock had passed, Conrad began to see his mutant son in a different light. Victor hadn't come from Heaven. He had come from Hell. The baby was not a punishment from God; it was a great blessing from Satan. God had turned His back on Conrad Straker, but Satan had sent him a baby as a gesture of welcome.

That might have seemed like tortuous reasoning to a normal man, but to Conrad, desperate to find release from his guilt and shame, it made perfect sense. If the gates of Heaven were forever closed to him, he might as well face the gates of Hell with eagerness and accept his destiny without remorse. He longed to belong somewhere, anywhere, even in Hell. If the god of light and beauty would not give him absolution, then he would obtain it from the god of darkness and evil.

He read dozens of books about satanic religions, and he quickly discovered that Hell was not the place of brimstone and suffering that Christians said it was. Hell was a place, said the satanists, where sinners were rewarded for their sins; it was, in every respect, the place of their dreams. Best of all, in Hell there was no such thing as guilt. In Hell there was no shame.

As soon as he accepted Satan as his savior, Conrad knew that he had made the right decision. The nightly dreams of fire and pain did not stop; however, he found a greater measure of peace and more contentment in his daily life than he had known since before that fateful Christmas Eve; and for the first time in memory, his life had meaning. He was on earth to do the devil's work, and if the devil could offer him self-respect, he was prepared to labor long and hard for the cause of the Antichrist.

When Ellen killed Victor, Conrad knew she was doing God's work, and he was furious. He almost killed her. But he realized that he might be imprisoned or executed for murdering her, and that would keep him from fulfilling the role that Satan had written for him. It occurred to him that if he got married again, Satan might send him another sign, another demonic child who would grow up to be the scourge of the earth.

Conrad married Zena, and in time Zena bore him Gunther. She was the devil's Mary, but she didn't realize it. Conrad never told her the truth. Conrad saw himself as Joseph to the Antichrist, father and protector. Zena thought the child was just a freak, and although she didn't feel comfortable with it, she accepted it with the equanimity with which carnies always accepted freaks.

But Gunther wasn't merely a freak.

He was more than that. Much more.

He was holy.

He was the coming. The dark coming.

As the taxicab sped toward the fairgrounds, Conrad looked out at the quiet, suburban houses and wondered if even one person out there realized they were living in the last days of God's world. He wondered if even one of them sensed that Satan's child was on earth and had recently reached his brutal maturity.

Gunther was just beginning his reign of terror. A thousand years of darkness would descend.

Oh, yes, Gunther was much more than just a freak.

If he were merely a freak, that would mean that Conrad was wrong in everything that he had done during the past twenty-five years. It would mean more than that; it would mean that Conrad was not just wrong but stark, raving mad.

So Gunther was more than a freak. Gunther was that legendary dark beast slouching toward Bethlehem.

Gunther was the destruction of the world.

Gunther was the herald of a new Dark Age.

Gunther was the Antichrist.

He *had* to be. For Conrad's sake, he *had* to be.

11

For Joey, the week prior to the county fair crept by like a snail. He was eager to become a carny and leave Royal City behind forever, but it seemed to him that the time for his escape would come only after his mother had murdered him in his bed.

There wasn't anyone around to help make the time pass more quickly. He avoided Mama, of course. Daddy was, as always, preoccupied with his law practice and his railroad models. Tommy Culp, Joey's best friend from school, was away on vacation with his family.

Even Amy was hardly ever around these days. She worked at The Dive every day but Sunday. And during the past week she had been out every night, dating some guy named Buzz. Joey didn't know what Buzz's last name was. Maybe it was Saw.

Joey hadn't intended to go to the fairgrounds until

Saturday, the last day, so that no one would figure out where he had gone until the carnival was far, far away in another state. But by the time Monday, June 30, rolled around, he was so keyed up that he couldn't keep his resolve. He told his mother he was going to the library, but he got on his bicycle and pedaled two miles to the county fairgrounds. He still wasn't going to run away from home until Saturday. But Monday was the day that the carnival set up, and he figured he ought to learn how that was done if he was ever going to be a carny himself.

For two hours he wandered around the midway, keeping out from underfoot but getting a good look at everything, fascinated by the speed with which the Ferris wheel and the other rides took shape. A couple of carnies, big men with lots of muscles and lots of funny tattoos, kidded him, and he joked right back at them, and everyone he met seemed to be just swell.

By the time he reached the site on which the funhouse was being erected, they were hoisting a giant clown's face to the top of the structure. One of the workers was a man in a Frankenstein mask, and that made Joey giggle. One of the others was an albino; he glanced at Joey, pinning him with colorless, rainwater eyes as cold as winter windows.

Those eyes were the first things in the carnival that Joey didn't like. They seemed to look straight through him, and he half-remembered an old story about a woman whose eyes turned men to stone.

He shivered, turned away from the albino, and walked toward a place in the middle of the midway, where they were putting up the Octopus, one of his favorite rides. He had taken only a few steps when someone called to him.

"Hey, there!"

He kept walking, even though he knew it was himself the man was calling to.

"Hey, son! Wait a minute."

Sighing, expecting to be thrown off the midway, Joey looked back and saw a man jumping down from the front platform of the funhouse. The stranger was tall and lean, maybe ten years older than Joey's father. He had coal-black hair, except at the temples, where it was pure white. His eyes were so blue that they reminded Joey of the gas flames on the kitchen stove at home.

As the man approached he said, "You aren't with the carnival, are you, son?"

"No," Joey admitted glumly. "But I'm not getting in anyone's way. I'm really not. Someday . . . maybe . . . I'd like to work in the carnival. I just want to see how things are done. If you'll let me stay and watch for a while—"

"Whoa, whoa," the stranger said. He stopped in front of the boy and stooped down. "You think I'm going to throw you out?"

"Aren't you?"

"My heavens, no!"

"Oh," Joey said.

"I could tell you weren't just a gawker," the man said. "I could see you were a young man with a genuine interest in the carnival way of life."

"You could?"

"Oh, yes. It just shines through," the stranger said.

"Do you think I could be . . . a carny someday?" Joey asked.

"You? Oh, sure. You've got the stuff," the stranger said.

"You could be a carny or just about anything you wanted. That's why I called out to you. I could see the right stuff shining in you. I sure could. Even from up there on the platform."

"Well . . . gee," Joey said, embarrassed.

"Here," the stranger said. "Let me give you these." He reached into a pocket and withdrew two rectangles of thin, pink cardboard.

"What are those?" Joey asked.

"Two free passes to the fairgrounds."

"You're kidding."

"Do I look like I'm kidding?"

"Why give them to me?"

"I told you," the stranger said. "You have the right stuff. As the carnies say, you're with it and for it. Whenever I see someone who's with it and for it, someone who's a carny at heart, I always give them a couple of free passes. Come any night and bring a friend. Or maybe your brother. Do you have a brother?"

"No," Joey said.

"A sister?"

"Yeah."

"What's her name?"

"Amy."

"What's your name?"

"Joey."

"Joey what?"

"Joey Alan Harper."

"My name's Conrad. I'll have to sign the back of the passes." He produced a ballpoint pen from another pocket and signed his two names with a flourish that Joey admired. Then he handed over the free passes.

"Thanks a lot," Joey said, beaming. "This is terrific!"

"Enjoy yourself," the stranger said, grinning. He had very white teeth. "Maybe someday *you* will be a carny, and you'll hand out free passes to people who are obviously with it and for it."

"Uh . . . how old do you have to be?" Joey asked.

"To be a carny?"

"Yeah."

"Any age, just about."

"Could a kid join up if he was just ten?"

"He could easy enough, if he was an orphan," Conrad said. "Or if his parents just didn't care about him at all. But if he had a family who gave a hoot, they'd come looking for him, and they'd take him home."

"Wouldn't you . . . you carnival people . . . wouldn't you hide the kid?" Joey asked. "If the worst thing in the world for him was to be taken home, wouldn't you hide him when his folks came looking?"

"Oh, couldn't do that," the man said. "Against the law. But if nobody cared about him, if nobody wanted him, the carnival would take him in. It always has, and it always will. What about you? I'll bet your folks care about you a lot."

"Not a lot," Joey said.

"Sure. I'll bet they care a whole bunch. What about your mother?"

"No," Joey said.

"Oh, I'll bet she cares a lot. I'll bet she's really proud of a handsome, intelligent boy like you."

Joey blushed.

"Do you get your good looks from your mother?" Conrad asked.

"Well . . . yeah . . . I look more like her than like my dad."

"Those dark eyes, that dark hair?"

"Yeah," Joey said. "Like Mama's."

"You know," Conrad said, "I knew someone once who looked quite a bit like you."

"Who?" Joey asked.

"A very nice lady."

"I don't look like a lady!" Joey said.

"No, no," Conrad said quickly. "Of course you don't. But you have her dark eyes and hair. And there's something in the lines of your face . . . You know, it's just possible she could have a boy your age now. Yes. Yes, it's quite possible. Wouldn't that be something—if you were the son of my long-lost friend?" He leaned closer to Joey. The whites of his eyes were yellowish. There was dandruff on his shoulders. A single breadcrumb was stuck in his mustache. His voice became even heartier than before when he said, "What *is* your mother's name?"

Suddenly Joey saw something in the stranger's eyes that he liked even less than what he had seen in the albino's eyes. He stared into those two crystalline blue dots, and it seemed to him that the man's friendliness was an act. Like on that TV show *The Rockford Files*, the way Jim Rockford, the private detective, could be so charming and so friendly, but he was just putting it on in order to get some vital information out of a stranger without the stranger knowing that he was being pumped. All of a sudden Joey felt that this guy was putting on the charm just like Jim Rockford did. Joey felt as if he were being pumped for information. Except that under his phony friendliness, Jim Rockford really *was* a nice guy. But underneath Conrad's smile, there wasn't a nice guy at all. Deep down in his blue eyes there wasn't anything warm or friendly; there was just . . . darkness.

"Joey?"

"Huh?"

"I asked you what your mother's name is."

"Leona," Joey lied, without really understanding why he must not tell the truth. He sensed that telling the truth right now would be the worst thing he could ever do in his whole life. Leona was Tommy Culp's mother.

Conrad stared hard at him.

Joey wanted to look away but couldn't.

"Leona?" Conrad asked.

"Yeah."

"Well . . . maybe my friend changed her name. She never did like the one she was born with. Your mother might still be her. About how old would you say your mother is?"

"Twenty-nine," Joey said quickly, remembering that Tommy Culp's mother had recently had a twenty-ninth birthday party at which, according to Tommy, all the guests had gotten pissed.

"Twenty-nine?" Conrad asked. "You're sure?"

"I know exactly," Joey said, "because Mama's birthday is one day before my sister's, so we always get two parties close together every year. This last time my sister was eight, and my mother was twenty-nine." He was surprised that he could lie so easily and smoothly. Usually he was a lousy liar; he couldn't fool anyone. But now he was different. Now it was almost as if someone older and wiser were speaking through him.

He didn't know why he was so positive that he had to lie to this man. Mama couldn't be the woman that Conrad was looking for. Mama wouldn't ever have been friends with a carny; she thought they were all dirty and crooked. Yet Joey lied to Conrad, and he had the feeling that someone else was guiding his tongue, someone who was looking out for him, someone like . . . God. Of course that was a dumb thought. To please God, you always had to tell the truth. Why would God take control of you just to make you lie?

The carny's blue eyes softened, and the tension went out of his voice when Joey said his mother was twenty-nine. "Well," the carny said, "I guess your mother couldn't be my old friend. The woman I'm thinking of would have to be around forty-five."

They looked at each other for a moment, the boy just standing there and the man stooping down, and finally Joey said, "Well . . . thanks a lot for the free passes."

"Sure, sure," the man said, standing up, obviously no longer the least bit interested in the boy. "Enjoy them, son." He turned and walked back to the funhouse.

Joey went across the midway to watch the workers erect the Octopus.

Later, the encounter with the blue-eyed carny seemed almost like a dream. The two pink passes—with the name Conrad Straker neatly written on the backs of them, below the printed words, "this pass authorized by"—were the only things that kept the incident real and solid in Joey's memory. He remembered being afraid of the stranger and lying to him, but he couldn't recapture the gut feeling that had made him so certain that lies were necessary; and he felt somewhat ashamed of himself for not telling the truth.

That night, at six-thirty, Buzz Klemmet picked up Amy at the Harper house. He was a ruggedly handsome guy with a lot of hair, muscles, a cocky attitude, and a carefully cultivated tough-guy image. Mama had met him once, the second night he'd come for Amy, and she hadn't liked him one bit. In keeping with her statement that she no longer cared what happened to Amy, Mama hadn't said a word for or against Buzz, but Amy could see the loathing in her mother's eyes. Tonight, Mama stayed in the kitchen and didn't even bother to come out to glare at Buzz.

Richie and Liz were already in the backseat of Buzz's vintage GTO convertible. The roof was down, and as soon as Buzz and Amy got in, Richie said, "Hey, put the top up so we can pass a joint around on the way to the fairgrounds without everyone seeing us."

"Good old Royal City, Ohio," Liz said. "Still frozen in the Middle Ages. Would you believe there are some places in this country where you can smoke grass right out in the open without getting thrown in jail?"

Buzz put up the top, but he said, "Hold the joint until after we've stopped for gas."

Half a mile from the Harper house, they stopped at a Union 76 station. Buzz got out to check the oil, and Richie got out to pump the gas.

As soon as Liz and Amy were alone in the car, Liz leaned forward from the backseat and said, "Buzz thinks you're the hottest thing he's ever seen."

"Oh, sure," Amy said.

"No, he really does."

"He tell you that?"

"Yeah."

"We haven't *done* anything," Amy said.

"That's one reason he thinks you're so hot. He's such a dreamboat that he's used to girls just falling on their backs for him. But you tease him along, let him feel a little, and then stop him right on the brink. He's not used to that. It's different for him. He's got the idea that when you finally give in you'll be absolutely wild."

"*If* I give in," Amy said.

"You'll give in," Liz said confidently. "You still don't want to admit it, but you're just like me."

"Maybe."

"You've been dating him every night for a week, and each night you let him get a little farther than the night before," Liz said. "You're coming out of your shell an inch at a time."

"Buzz told you exactly how far I've let him go?" Amy asked.

"Yep," Liz said, grinning.

"Jeez," Amy said. "He's got such class."

"Oh, hell," Liz said, "he wasn't tattling on you. It's not like he told a stranger. I'm your best friend. And Buzz and I go way, way back. I used to screw around with him, and we're still the best of buddies. Listen, kid, when we leave the carnival tonight, let's go back to my house. My folks are still away. You and Buzz can use their bedroom. Stop teasing the guy. Give him a break. Give *yourself* a break. You want the old salami just as much as I do."

Buzz and Richie got back in the car, and Richie fired up a joint. While Buzz drove to the fairgrounds, they passed around the dope, and each of them took a couple of deep drags, holding the smoke in their lungs as long as they could. In the parking lot at the fairgrounds, they lit another joint and sat in the car until they had done that one, too.

By the time they reached the ticket booth, Amy was feeling warm, airy, and a bit giggly. As she drifted onto the carnival lot, into that roar of sound and whirlpool of motion, she had the peculiar feeling that tonight was going to be one of the most important nights of her life. Tonight she would make decisions about herself; tonight she would either accept the role in life that both Liz and Mama believed she was suited for, or she would make up her mind to be the good, responsible person that she had always wanted to be. She was standing on a thin line, and it was time to jump one way or the other, time to make up her mind about herself. She didn't know how she knew that, but she did know it. The feeling was unshakable. At first it sobered her and made her a little bit afraid, but then Liz made a very funny crack about a fat woman who was walking up the midway in front of them, and Amy laughed, and the grass had its effect, and the laugh turned into an uncontrollable giggle, and she was floating again.

THREE

The Funhouse

12

Amy discovered that Liz was right about a little grass making the thrill rides even more fun than usual. They rode the Octopus, the Tilt-a-Whirl, the Dive Bomber, the Whip, the Loop-de-Loop, the Colossus, and others. The ramps seemed higher than those on thrill rides that Amy had ridden in previous carnivals; the dips seemed deeper; the whipping action, the spinning, soaring, diving, twisting, and turning, all seemed wilder and faster than ever before. Amy held on to Buzz and screamed with delight and with a quiver of genuine terror as well. Buzz pulled her close; he used her fear and the sudden lurchings of the rides as excuses to cop some quick, cheap feels. Like Liz, Amy was wearing shorts, a T-shirt, but no bra. Buzz couldn't resist touching her breasts and her long, bare, nicely tanned legs. Each time she got off a ride, Amy was disoriented for a minute or two and had to cling to Buzz, and he liked that, and she liked it, too, because Buzz had such big, hard, muscular arms and shoulders.

Only forty minutes after they arrived at the fairgrounds, they slipped off the midway, between a couple of sideshows, to the back lot, where rows of carnival trucks were parked. They went around behind the trucks, into a deserted cul-de-sac that ended at the fairgrounds' ivy-covered fence. They stood in shadow-dappled, summer-evening sunlight and passed around a third joint that Liz took out of her purse; they sucked in the sweet smoke, held it down as long as they possibly could, then let it out with urgent gasps of pleasure.

"This one's a little different," Richie said as the hand-rolled cigarette made its second circle around their huddle.

"This one what?" Amy asked.

"This joint," Richie said.

"Yeah," Liz said. "It's spiced up."

"With what?" Buzz asked.

"Trust me."

"Angel dust?" Richie asked.

"Trust me," Liz said.

"Hey," Buzz said, "I'm not sure I like smoking something that I don't know what it is."

"Trust me," Liz said.

"I trust you about as far as I can throw you," Buzz said.

"Doesn't matter," Liz said. "We've almost finished the joint anyway."

Buzz was holding the stub. He hesitated, then said, "Oh, hell, why not live dangerously." He took one last drag on it.

Richie started to kiss Liz on the neck, and Buzz kissed Amy, and without quite realizing how it happened, Amy found herself pinned against the side of one of the trucks, and Buzz was running his hands up and down her body, kissing her hard, pushing his tongue into her mouth, and then he tugged her T-shirt out of her shorts and got one hand under it and squeezed her bare breasts, thumbed her nipples, and she moaned softly, concerned that someone might walk around behind the trucks and see them, but unable to express her concern, responding even to Buzz's crude caresses.

Suddenly Liz said, "Enough, you guys. Save it for later. I'm sure as hell not going to lie down right here, in broad daylight, and take it in the dirt."

"The dirt is the best place," Richie said.

"Yeah," Buzz said. "Let's do it in the dirt."

"It's the natural thing," Richie said.

"Yeah," Buzz said.

"All the animals do it in the dirt," Richie said.

"Yeah," Buzz said. "Let's be natural, just hang loose and be real natural."

"Stifle yourselves," Liz said. "There's a lot more carnival to see. Come on. Let's go."

Amy tucked in her T-shirt, and Buzz gave her one more wet kiss.

Back on the midway, Amy thought the rides seemed to be spinning faster than before. All the colors were more vivid, too. The dozens of different sources of music seemed louder than they had been ten minutes ago, and each song possessed a subtleness of melody of which she hadn't been previously aware.

I'm not totally in control of myself, Amy thought worriedly, dizzily. I'm not out of control yet, but I'm liable to

wind up that way. I've got to be careful. Sensible. Watch
out for that dope. That damned, spiced-up dope. If I don't
watch myself, I'm going to end up in a bedroom at Liz's
house, with Buzz on top of me, whether that's what I
really want or not. And I don't think that's what I want.
I don't want to be the kind of person Liz and Mama say
I am. I don't. *Do I?*

They rode the Loop-de-Loop again.

Amy clung to Buzz.

After spending Monday morning and part of the afternoon
at the fairgrounds, watching the carnies set up their equipment, Joey hadn't intended to return to the carnival until
Saturday night, when he would run away forever. But
Monday evening he changed his mind.

Actually, his mother changed it for him.

He was sitting in the family room, watching television,
drinking Pepsi, when he accidentally knocked over his
glass. The soda splashed on his chair and spilled all over the
carpet. He got a bunch of paper towels from the kitchen
and cleaned up the mess as best he could, and he was sure
that he hadn't permanently stained either the carpet or the
chair's upholstery.

In spite of the fact that the damage wasn't serious,
Mama was furious when she walked in and saw him with
handfuls of Pepsi-soaked paper towels. Although it was
only seven-thirty, she was half drunk already. She grabbed
him and shook him and told him that he behaved like a
little animal, and she sent him to bed more than two hours
early.

He felt miserable. He couldn't even turn to Amy for sympathy because she was out somewhere, on another date with Buzz. Joey didn't know where she and Buzz had gone, and even if he did he couldn't run after her, whimpering about how Mama had shaken and scared him.

In his room Joey sprawled on the bed for a while, crying, utterly disconsolate, angered by the injustice of it all—and then he thought of the two pink passes that the carny had given him earlier in the day. *Two* passes. He would use one to get into the fairgrounds on Saturday evening, when he would try to join up with the carnies by telling them that he was an orphan and had nowhere else to go. But that left one pass, and if he didn't use it between now and Saturday, it would only go to waste.

He sat up on the edge of the bed and thought about it for a few minutes, and he decided that he could sneak off to the carnival, have a lot of fun, and sneak back into the house without his mother knowing that he'd been gone. He got up and pulled the drapes shut, so that hardly any of the fading, summer-evening sunlight reached into the room. He took a spare blanket and an extra pillow from his closet and used those to form a dummy under the covers. He switched on his dim night-light, stepped back from the bed, and studied his handiwork critically. Even with the splinters of light showing at the edges of the drapes, he thought the dummy would pass Mama's inspection. Usually she didn't come to his room until eleven o'clock at the very earliest, and if she waited that long tonight, until well after dark, when the room would be illuminated by only the night-light, the trick would surely work; she would be fooled by the dummy.

The hard part was going to be getting out of the house without drawing her attention. He took a few dollar bills from his thirty-two-dollar kitty and tucked the money into a pocket of his jeans. He also pocketed one of the carnival passes and stuck the other one under the glass-jar bank that stood on his desk. He carefully opened his bedroom door, looked both ways along the upstairs hall, stepped out of the room, and closed the door behind him. He crept to the stairs and began the long, tense journey down toward the first floor.

Amy, Liz, Buzz, and Richie stopped in front of a sideshow that advertised a magician called Marco the Magnificent. The come-on was a large poster that showed a screaming woman being decapitated by a guillotine, while a grinning magician stood with his hand on the executioner's lever.

"I love magicians," Amy said.

"I love anyone I can get my hands on," Liz said, giggling.

"My Uncle Arnold used to be a stage magician," Richie said, pushing his glasses up on his nose to take a closer look at Marco's lurid poster.

"Did he make stuff disappear and everything?" Buzz asked.

Liz said, "He was so bad that he made *audiences* disappear."

Amy was giddy from the spiced-up pot that she had smoked, and Liz's little joke seemed hysterically funny. She laughed, and her laughter infected the others.

"No, now, really, honestly," Buzz said when they finally got control of themselves. "Did your Uncle Arnold make his living that way? It wasn't just a hobby or something?"

"No hobby," Richie said. "Uncle Arnold was the real thing. He called himself the Amazing Arnoldo. But I guess he didn't make *much* of a living at it, and he got to hate it after a while. He's been selling insurance for the past twenty years."

"I think being a magician would be neat," Amy said. "Why did your uncle hate it?"

"Well," Richie said, "every successful magician has to have a trick that's all his own, a special illusion that makes him stand out in a crowd of other magicians. Uncle Arnold had this gimmick where he made twelve white doves appear, one after the other, out of thin air, in bursts of flame. The audience would applaud politely when the first dove appeared, and then they'd gasp when the second and third ones popped up, and by the time half a dozen birds had materialized, the audience was cheering. When the entire dozen had been brought out of their hiding places in my uncle's clothes, each presented in a little puff of fire, you can imagine the ovation the audience gave him."

"I don't understand," Buzz said, frowning.

"Yeah," Amy said. "If your uncle was so great, why'd he quit and start selling insurance?"

"Sometimes," Richie said, "not often, but about once in every thirty or forty performances, one of the doves would catch fire and burn up alive, right there on stage. It bummed out the audience, and they booed Uncle Arnold."

Liz laughed, and Amy laughed, too, and Liz did an imitation of a burning dove trying to slap the flames off its wings, and Amy knew that it wasn't really funny, knew that it was a horrible thing to happen to the poor birds, and she knew she shouldn't laugh, but she couldn't help herself, because it seemed like the most hilarious story she had ever heard.

"It wasn't very funny to Uncle Arnold," Richie said between whoops of laughter. "Like I said, it didn't happen often, but he never knew when it *was* going to happen, so he was always tense. The tension gave him an ulcer. And even when the birds didn't burn up, they shit in his suit pockets."

They all laughed again, with renewed vigor, holding on to each other. People passing them on the midway gave them strange looks, which only made them laugh even harder.

Richie treated everyone to tickets for Marco's next show.

The ground inside the magician's tent was covered with sawdust, and the air was musty. Brightly colored plastic flags and posters of Marco decorated the dimly lighted, canvas-walled space.

Amy, Liz, Buzz, and Richie joined two dozen spectators who were crowded around a small, raised stage at one end of the tent.

A moment later Marco appeared in a cloud of blue smoke, taking a bow as a tape-recorded fanfare filled the room. It was painfully obvious that he had merely stepped through a slit in the rear wall of the tent, using the smoke for cover. In fact he hadn't even stepped onto the stage; he had stumbled.

Liz glanced at Amy. They both giggled.

"Thank God he's a magician and not a tightrope walker," Richie whispered.

Amy felt as if she were standing on balloons, balancing precariously, about to perform some splendid magic act of her own.

What had Liz added to that joint?

Marco's appearance was as pathetic as his entrance. He was a middle-aged man with bloodshot eyes, and he was heavily made up to resemble the Devil. His lips were red; his face was frost-pale; his eyes were outlined with thick black mascara; and his widow's peak was also accentuated with mascara. He wore a shabby tuxedo and a pair of white gloves that were marred by several large yellow stains.

"He shouldn't wear those gloves when he jerks off," Liz whispered.

They all laughed.

"Gross," Richie said.

"He looks gross enough to do it," Buzz whispered.

Marco glanced nervously at them, unable to hear what they were saying. He smiled at them and doffed his top hat in a feeble attempt to win their silent attention.

"Whatever you do," Liz told the others, "for God's sake don't let him shake hands with you."

They all laughed again.

A few of the other spectators were glancing at Amy, some just curious, some disapproving, but she didn't care what they thought. She was having so much fun.

Marco decided to ignore them, and he picked up a deck of cards that was on the small table in the center of the stage. He shuffled the cards and wrapped them in a silk handkerchief, with only one edge of the deck exposed. He placed that bundle in a clear glass goblet, every movement performed with a flourish. When he stepped back and pointed at the goblet, cards began to rise individually from the silk-swathed deck: first the ace of diamonds . . . then the ace of clubs . . . the ace of hearts . . . and finally, mistakenly, the jack of diamonds. Marco looked embarrassed, quickly swept the cards away, and went on to his next trick.

"Boy, does he stink," Buzz said softly.

"It's those gloves you smell," Liz said.

"Richie, is this guy really your Uncle Arnold?" Amy asked.

Marco blew up a balloon and knotted it. When he touched a burning cigarette to the balloon, the sphere popped noisily, and a live dove appeared in the heart of the explosion. It was a better illusion than the card trick, but Amy still saw the bird dart out from beneath the magician's tuxedo jacket.

Marco performed two more tricks that drew only half-hearted applause from the audience, and then Liz said, "Are you guys about ready to split?"

"Not yet," Richie said.

"This is a fuckin' bore," Liz said.

"I want to see the finale," Richie said. "The guillotine."

"What guillotine?" Buzz asked.

"The one on the poster outside," Richie said. "He chops off some broad's head."

"That's the only way he's ever going to get head from a woman," Liz said, giggling.

Marco spoke for the first time. His voice was surprisingly rich and commanding. "And now, for those of you who are connoisseurs of the bizarre, the macabre, the gruesome, the grotesque . . . I will close my show with what I fondly refer to as 'The Impaler.'"

"What about the guillotine?" Richie said to Buzz.

"Asshole," Liz said. "That's just a come-on."

Marco rolled a large upright box to the center of the stage. It was a foot or so shorter than a coffin, but otherwise it looked exactly like the centerpiece of a funeral.

"I hear you mumbling out there," Marco said. "I hear you saying . . . the guillotine . . . the guillotine. Unfortunately, that device belonged to my predecessor. Both it and he are being held by the police due to an unfortunate accident. The last lady who assisted him lost her head and caused a messy scene."

The audience laughed uneasily.

"What a cornball act," Liz said. "Jesus."

But on the contrary, to Amy, Marco appeared to have undergone an eerie metamorphosis. He was not shabby and silly-looking now, as he had been when he first stumbled onto the platform. His crude makeup no longer seemed like a joke; second by second he looked increasingly demonic, and there was a new, terrifying, evil gleam in his eyes. His nervous smile had become a knowing, wicked leer. When his eyes met Amy's, she felt as if she were staring at twin windows that offered a glimpse of Hell, and she was cold all the way through to the marrow.

Don't be ridiculous, Amy told herself, shuddering. Marco the Magnificent hasn't changed. It's only my perception of him that's been altered. I'm having a mild hallucination. Tripping. Flying. It's that damned joint. The drugs. What spice did Liz add to that grass?

Marco held up a two-foot-long, pointed wooden stake. "Ladies and gentlemen, I promise you'll enjoy this illusion more than you would have enjoyed the guillotine. It's really much, much better." He grinned, and there was something dark and unwholesome in that Cheshire-cat expression. "I need a volunteer from the audience. A young woman." His malevolent eyes slowly swept the faces below him. He raised one hand and pointed ominously at each woman, one after the other, and for a breathtaking moment he seemed to stop at Amy; then he moved his hand again and stopped even longer at Liz; but finally he chose an attractive redhead.

"Oh, no," the redhead told him. "I couldn't. Not me."

"Of course you can," Marco said. "Come on, folks, let's give this charming, brave young lady a hand."

The audience applauded on cue, and the woman reluctantly walked up the steps to the stage.

Marco took hold of her arm as she reached the platform. "What's your name?"

"Jenny," she said, smiling shyly at the audience.

"You're not afraid, are you, Jenny?"

"Yes," she said, blushing.

Marco grinned. "Smart girl!" He escorted her to the coffin. It was standing on end, tilted back slightly on large metal braces. Marco pulled open the lid, which was hinged at the left side. "Please step into the box, Jenny. I promise that you will feel absolutely no pain whatsoever."

With the magician's help, the redhead stepped backwards into the box; facing the audience. Her neck fit into a U-shaped cutout in the top of the box. Because the coffin was short, her head stuck out of it when Marco closed the lid.

"Comfortable?" Marco asked.

"No," the woman said nervously.

"Good," Marco said. He grinned at the audience, then secured the front of the box with a large padlock.

A premonition of disaster, a feeling that she was in the presence of Death, seized Amy in its invisible, icy hands.

Just the damned drugs, she told herself.

Marco the Magnificent spoke to the audience. "In the fifteenth century, Vlad the Fifth of Wallachia, known as Vlad the Impaler to his frightened subjects, tortured tens of thousands of male and female prisoners, mostly foreign invaders. Once, the Turkish army turned back from a planned invasion when it encountered a field where thousands of men were propped on spikes that had been driven all the way through their bodies by Vlad's hand-picked death squads. Tiring of his name, Vlad selected a new one, that of his father, an equally nasty man known as Dracul, meaning 'the Devil.' Adding the letter 'A,' he became Dracula, the son of the Devil. And so, my friends, are legends born."

"Cornball," Liz said again.

But Amy was mesmerized by the strange, new, and dangerous creature that appeared (at least to her eyes) to have taken possession of Marco's body. The bottomless, all-knowing, evil eyes of the magician met Amy's eyes again and seemed to see all the way through her before they looked away.

Marco displayed the two-foot-long, pointed wooden

stake once more. "Ladies and gentlemen, I present . . . 'The Impaler.'"

"About fuckin' time," Liz said.

Marco picked up a small but heavy mallet. "If you will look at the front of the box, you will see that a small hole has been drilled through the lid."

Amy saw the hole. A bright red heart had been painted around it.

"The hole lies directly over the volunteer's heart," Marco said. He licked his lips, turned, and carefully inserted the stake into the hole. "Do you feel the point of the stake, Jenny?"

She giggled nervously. "Yes."

"Good," the magician said. "Remember . . . there will be no pain at all." Holding the stake in his left hand, he raised the mallet in his right. "Absolute silence! Those of you who are squeamish, avert your eyes. She will feel no pain . . . but that does not mean there will be no blood!"

"Huh?" Jenny said. "Hey, wait, I—"

"Silence!" Marco shouted, and he swung the mallet hard against the stake.

No! Amy thought.

With a sickening, wet, tearing sound, the stake sank deep into the woman's chest.

Jenny screamed, and blood gushed from her twisted mouth.

The audience gasped. A couple of people cried out in horror.

Jenny's head slumped to one side. Her tongue lolled. Her eyes stared sightlessly over the heads of the people in the tent.

Death miraculously transformed the face of the volunteer. The red hair turned to blond. The eyes changed from green to blue. The face was no longer that of Jenny, the woman who had walked onto the stage from the audience. It was now Liz Duncan's face. Every plane, every hollow, every feature, every detail, belonged to Liz. It wasn't just a trick of the light and shadows. It was Liz in that coffin. It was *Liz* who had been impaled. It was *Liz* who was dead, blood still oozing from between her ripe lips.

Having trouble drawing her breath, Amy looked at the girl beside her and was amazed to see that her friend was still there. Liz was in the audience—yet somehow she was also on the stage, in the box, dead. Confused, disoriented, Amy said, "But it's you. It's you . . . up there."

Liz-in-the-audience said, "What?"

Liz-in-the-coffin stared into eternity and drooled blood.

Liz-in-the-audience said, "Amy? Are you all right?"

Liz is going to die, Amy thought. Soon. This is some sort of premonition . . . clairvoyance . . . whatever you call it. Could that be true? Could it? Will Liz be killed? Soon? Tonight?

Marco's look of shock and horror, which he had assumed the instant that blood began to spurt from his volunteer's mouth, now melted into a grin. The magician snapped his fingers, and the woman in the box suddenly came to life; the pain vanished from her face; she smiled dazzlingly— and she no longer resembled Liz Duncan.

She never did look like Liz, Amy thought. It was just me. The drugs. Hallucinations. It wasn't a premonition; Liz isn't going to die soon. God, am I out of it!

The audience sighed with relief as Marco pulled the

stake out of the hole in the lid of the box. The magician
had ceased to look sinister. He was the same shabby, pudgy,
inept man who had stumbled through the canvas flap ten
or fifteen minutes ago. The omniscient, evil personality no
longer looked out through Marco's eyes; his resemblance
to the Devil was gone.

Imagination, Amy told herself. Delusions. It meant nothing. Nothing at all. Liz isn't about to die. None of us is
going to die. I've got to get hold of myself.

Marco helped Jenny out of the box and introduced her
to the audience. She was his daughter.

"Another cheap trick," Liz said, disgusted.

As she left Marco's tent, Amy sensed the disappointment
in her three companions. It was almost as if they had hoped
that a woman really would be pierced through the heart or
have her head chopped off by a guillotine. The spice that
Liz had added to the last joint of grass was something
extremely powerful, for already it was making them fidgety,
restless; they required more and bigger thrills to dissipate
their newfound, nervous energy. A decapitation and some
spilled blood were apparently just the sort of things that
Buzz and Liz, if not Richie, needed to see in order to burn
off the chemicals bubbling in their bloodstreams, the sort
of thing they needed to experience in order to mellow out
again.

No more dope tonight, Amy vowed. No more dope
ever. I don't need drugs to be happy. Why do I use them?

They went to a sideshow called Animal Oddities, and
the bizarre creatures in that attraction gave Amy the willies.
There was a goat with two heads; a bull with a three-eyed,
triple cranium; a disgusting pig with eyes on either side of

its snout plus two more eyes higher in its head, greenish drool trickling over its cracked and leathery lips, two extra legs coming out of its left side. They finally came to a pen that contained a normal-looking lamb, and Amy reached out to pet it; but when it turned toward her, she saw it had an extra nose and a bulging, sightless, third eye on the side of its head, and she pulled her hand away. The nightmarish animals were a beer chaser to the whiskey-like effect of the spiced grass she had smoked; when she left Animal Oddities, she felt higher, more thoroughly detached from reality than when she had entered.

They rode the Rocket-Go-Round. Amy sat in front of Buzz on the motorcycle-like seat, in one of the two-passenger, bullet-shaped cars. In the relative privacy of that rapidly spinning container, he put his hands on her braless breasts. The centrifugal force pushed her back against him, and she felt the heat and size of his erection as his crotch was jammed hard against her buttocks.

"I want you," he said, putting his mouth against her ear, making himself heard above the roar of the Rocket-Go-Round and the fierce whining of the wind.

It felt good to be wanted so badly, to be needed as Buzz needed her, and Amy wondered if maybe it was a good thing to be like Liz. At least you always had someone around who needed you for *something*.

At Bozo the Clown's booth, both Buzz and Richie managed to hit the bull's-eye and dunk the jeering clown in a huge tub of water. Buzz went about it doggedly, buying three baseballs, then three more, then three more, until at last he connected and sent Bozo into the tub. Richie, on the other hand, disdained that approach. He considered the situation with a mathematician's eye and sensibilities, threw two bad pitches, learned from each of them, and banged the bull's-eye on his third try.

Later, when their car stopped for a moment at the top of the Ferris wheel, with the diamond-bright midway spread out below them, Buzz kissed Amy, kissed her deeply, hungrily, his tongue probing her mouth. His hands were all over her. She knew that tonight had to be the turning point in their relationship. Tonight she would either have to drop him or give him what he wanted. She couldn't stall any longer. She had to decide who and what she was.

However, she was so high, so loose, that she didn't want to think—*couldn't* think—about complex problems like that. She just wanted to float along, enjoying the lights, the sounds, the blur of motion, constant action.

After the Ferris wheel, they boarded the bumper cars and bashed each other mercilessly. Sparks crackled and flew from the exposed-wire grid overhead. The air smelled of ozone. Each noisy, shattering collision sent a jolt of sensual pleasure through Amy.

On one side of the bumper-car pavilion, the carousel turned in a blur of brilliant lights. On the other side, the Tilt-a-Whirl spun, rose, fell. Calliope music mixed with the roar of the crowd and the constant chatter of the pitchmen and the crashing of the bumper cars.

Amy loved the carnival. As she pursued Richie's car and slammed into it broadside, as she was spun around by the impact, she thought that the carnival, with all of its lights and excitement, might be a little bit like Las Vegas, and she wondered if perhaps she would enjoy going to Nevada with Liz.

From the bumper cars they went to Freak-o-rama, and Amy's disorientation was made worse by what she saw in that place: the three-eyed man whose skin was like the skin of an alligator; the fattest woman in the world, sitting on a gigantic couch, dwarfing that piece of furniture, her body nothing more than a lump, her facial features lost in doughy fat; a man with a second pair of arms growing out of his stomach; and a man with two noses and a lipless mouth.

Liz, Buzz, and Richie thought Freak-o-rama was the best thing on the midway. They pointed and laughed at the creatures on exhibit, as if the people at whom they were laughing could neither see nor hear them. Amy didn't feel the least bit like laughing, even though she was still very high on grass. She remembered Jerry Galloway's curse and Mama's certainty that the baby would be deformed; and such sights as those in Freak-o-rama struck too close to home to amuse her. Amy was embarrassed, both for herself and for the pathetic freaks who posed for a living in the stalls. She wished there were some way she could help them, but of course she couldn't, so she listened to her friends making wisecracks, and she smiled dutifully, and she tried to hurry them along.

Strangely, the most frightening exhibit in Freak-o-rama was the baby in the enormous jar. All of the other human oddities were alive and of such size that they might potentially pose a threat, but the dead, harmless thing in the jar, no possible threat to anyone, was the most unsettling of all. Its large green eyes stared blindly out of its glass prison; its twisted, flared nostrils seemed to be sniffing at Amy, Liz, Buzz, and Richie; its black lips were parted, and its pale, speckled tongue was visible, and it looked as if it were snarling at them, at nobody else but them, as if it would close its mouth after they walked away.

"Creepy," Liz said. "Jesus!"

"It isn't real," Richie said. "It wasn't ever alive. It's just *too* freaky. No human being could give birth to that."

"Maybe no human being did," Liz said.

"That's what the sign says," Buzz observed. " 'Born in 1955, of normal parents.'"

They all looked up at the sign on the wall behind the jar, and Liz said, "Hey, Amy, its mother's name was Ellen. Maybe it's your brother!"

Everyone laughed—except Amy. She stared at the sign, at the five large letters that spelled her mother's name, and yet another tremor of premonition passed through her. She felt as if her presence at the carnival was not happenstance but destiny. She had the uncanny and distinctly unpleasant feeling that her seventeen years of life could have led her nowhere else but here on this night of all nights. She was being maneuvered, constantly manipulated; if she reached overhead, she would feel the strings of the puppetmaster.

Was it possible that this thing in the bottle actually had been Mama's child? Was *this* the reason Mama had insisted that Amy have an abortion immediately?

No. That's crazy. Absurd, Amy thought desperately.

She didn't like the idea that her life had been funneled inexorably to this tiny spot on the surface of the earth, at this minute among the trillions of minutes that composed the flow of history. That concept left her feeling helpless, adrift.

It was just the drugs. She couldn't trust her perceptions because of the drugs. No more grass, ever again.

"I don't blame its mother for killing it," Liz said, peering at the thing in the jar.

"It's just a rubber model," Richie insisted.

"I'm going to get a closer look," Buzz said, slipping under the restraining rope.

"Buzz, don't!" Amy said.

Buzz approached the platform where the jar stood and leaned close to it. He reached out, put a hand to the glass, slowly ran his fingers down across the front of the jar, beyond which rested the face of the monster. Abruptly he jerked his hand away. "Son of a bitch!"

"What's the matter?" Richie asked.

"Buzz, come back here, please," Amy said.

Buzz returned, holding his hand up for them to see. There was blood on one of his fingers.

"What happened?" Liz asked.

"Must have been a sharp seam on the jar," Buzz said.

"You better go to the first-aid station," Amy said. "The cut might be infected."

"Nah," Buzz said, determined not to let a crack show in his macho image. "It's only a scratch. Funny, though, I didn't *see* any sharp edges."

"Maybe you didn't cut it on the glass," Richie said. "Maybe the thing in there bit you."

"It's dead."

"Its body is dead," Richie said, "but maybe its spirit is still alive."

"A minute ago you told us the goddamned thing was just a rubber fake," Amy said.

"I've been known to be wrong," Richie said.

"How do you explain it biting through the jar?" Buzz asked sarcastically.

"A psychic bite," Richie said. "A ghost bite."

"Don't give me the spooks," Liz said, hitting Richie on the shoulder.

"Ghost bite?" Buzz asked. "That's stupid."

The thing in the bottle watched them with its clouded, emerald, moon-lamp eyes.

The name Ellen seemed to burn brighter on the sign than any of the other words.

Coincidence, Amy told herself.

It *had* to be a coincidence. Because if it wasn't, if this really was Mama's child, if Amy *had* been brought to the carnival by some supernatural force, then the other premonitions might also be true. Liz actually might die here. And that was unthinkable, unacceptable. So it was coincidence.

Ellen.

Coincidence, damn it!

Amy was relieved when they left Freak-o-rama.

They rode the Shazam and took another turn on the Loop-de-Loop, and then suddenly they were all starving. It was a drug-induced hunger, the insatiable appetite familiar to all serious pot smokers. They ate hot dogs, ice cream, and candy apples.

Eventually they found themselves in front of the funhouse.

A big man in a Frankenstein costume capered on a low platform, threatening the people who were boarding the cars to go into the funhouse. He waved his arms and snarled and jumped up and down in a terrible imitation of Boris Karloff.

"He's a real ham," Richie said.

They moved a few feet to the barker's platform, where a tall, distinguished-looking man was ballying the passing crowd. He looked down at them as he talked, and he had the bluest eyes Amy had ever seen. After a few seconds, she realized that the giant clown's face atop the building had been painted in the barker's image.

"Terror-fying! Terror-fying!" the barker shouted. "Goblins, ghosts, and ghouls! Spiders larger than men! Monsters from other worlds and from the darkest bowels of this one! Are all of the creatures that stalk the funhouse merely make-believe . . . or is one of them real? See for yourself! Learn the truth at your own peril! Can you stand the test, the tension, the fear? Are you man enough? Ladies, are your men strong enough to comfort you inside . . . or will you have to comfort them? Terror-fying!"

"I *love* to go through the funhouse when I'm high as a kite," Liz said. "When you're really, truly wrecked, it's a gas. All those dumb plastic monsters jumping out at you."

"So let's go," Richie said.

"No, no," Liz said. "We've got to save it until we're really high."

"I'm really high now," Amy said.

"Me too," Buzz said.

"Oh, we'll get more wasted than *this*," Liz said. "This is nothing."

"If I get more wasted than this," Richie said, "I'll have to be institutionalized."

"Make it a cell for two," Buzz said.

"That's the idea," Liz said excitedly. "You've got to be *really* wrecked to fully appreciate the funhouse."

Not me, Amy reminded herself. No more dope tonight. No more dope *ever*.

They bought tickets for a ride called the Slithering Snake. The man at the controls was a dwarf, and while Liz waited for the ride to start, she teased the little man, made jokes about his height. He glared at Liz, and Amy wished her friend would shut up. When the Slithering Snake finally began to move, the dwarf got his revenge; he gave it much more speed than usual, and the chain of cars flashed around the looping, rising, falling track so fast that Amy was terrified it was going to fly off the rails. What should have been a thrilling ride became a knuckle-whitening, stomach-clenching ordeal, a sweat-popping torture that seemed like it would never end. Incredibly, even under those conditions, when the automatic canvas cover closed over the fast-moving train, Buzz took advantage of the darkness to take advantage of Amy; his hands were all over her.

This whole night is like the Slithering Snake, Amy thought. It's out of control.

After they rode the Octopus again, after they gleefully bashed each other around in the bumper cars once more, they returned to the cul-de-sac behind the carnival trucks, at the perimeter of the fairgrounds, and Liz stoked up another of her specially spiced joints. Darkness had come to the fairgrounds now, and they weren't able to see each other clearly as they passed the reefer around. They made jokes about some stranger stepping out of the darkness and taking a toke without anyone being the wiser, and they kidded each other about seeing freaks hiding under the trucks around them.

Amy tried to fake it when the joint came to her. She

took a drag on it, but she didn't inhale. She held the smoke in her mouth for a moment, then blew it out.

Even in the darkness, with only the glowing tip of the cigarette and the sound of indrawn breath to judge by, Liz realized that Amy hadn't really taken a good pull on the weed. "Don't hold back on us, kid," she said sharply. "Don't be a party pooper."

"I don't know what you mean," Amy said.

"Like hell you don't. Take another hit on that joint. When I'm wasted I like a lot of company in the same condition."

Rather than irritate Liz, Amy took another drag on the joint and sucked the smoke deep this time. She hated herself for her lack of willpower.

But I don't want to lose Liz, she thought. I need Liz. Who else do I have?

When they walked back onto the midway, they nearly collided with an albino. His thin, cottony white hair streamed behind him in the warm June breeze. He turned transparent eyes on them, eyes like cold smoke, and he said, "Free tickets to Madame Zena's. Free tickets to get your fortunes told. One for each lady, compliments of the carnival management. Tell all your friends that Big American is the *friendly* carnival."

Surprised, Amy and Liz accepted the tickets from the worm-white hands that offered them.

The albino vanished in the crowd.

13

The four of them crowded into the fortune-teller's small tent. Liz and Amy sat in the two available chairs, at the table where the crystal ball was filled with lambent light. Richie and Buzz stood behind the chairs.

Amy didn't think that Madame Zena looked much like the Gypsy she was supposed to be, even dressed up in all the colored scarves and pleated skirts and gaudy jewelry. But the woman was very pretty, and she was suitably mysterious.

Liz got her fortune told first. Madame Zena asked her all sorts of questions about herself and her family, information that she needed (so she said) in order to focus her psychic perceptions. When she had no more questions to ask, she peered into the crystal ball; she leaned so close to it that the eerie light and the shadows it cast made her features look different, hawklike.

In four glass chimneys, in the four corners of the tent, four candles guttered.

In its large cage to the right of the table, the raven shifted on its perch and made a cooing sound in the back of its throat.

Liz glanced at Amy and rolled her eyes.

Amy giggled, giddier than ever from the dope.

Madame Zena stared into the crystal ball with a theatrical scowl, as if she were struggling to pierce the veils that concealed the world of tomorrow. But then the expression on her face changed and became a look of genuine puzzlement. She blinked, shook her head, and leaned even closer to the glowing sphere on the table.

"What is it?" Liz asked.

Madame Zena didn't respond. Her face held a ghastly look, so *real* that Amy was unnerved by it.

"No . . ." Madame Zena said.

To Liz, apparently, Madame Zena still seemed to be putting on an act. Liz evidently didn't see the uncontrived horror in the fortune-teller's face, which Amy was sure she saw there.

"I don't . . ." Madame Zena began, then stopped and licked her lips. "I never . . ."

"What am I going to be?" Liz asked. "Rich or famous or both?"

Madame Zena closed her eyes for a moment, slowly shaking her head, then looked again into the crystal. "My God . . . I . . . I . . ."

We should get out of here, Amy thought uneasily. We should go before this woman tells us something we don't want to hear. We should get up and leave and run for our lives.

Madame Zena looked up from the crystal ball. All the blood had drained from her face.

"What an actress!" Richie said softly.

"Bunch of mumbo-jumbo," Buzz said sullenly.

Madame Zena ignored them and spoke to Liz. "I . . . I would rather not . . . tell your fortune . . . just yet. I need . . . time. Time to interpret what I've just seen in the crystal. I'll read your friend's future first, and then . . . I'll come back to yours, if that's all right."

"Sure," Liz said, enjoying what she thought was a con game of some sort, a way to prime the customer for a joke or a request for money to pay for a more detailed reading. "Take as long as you want."

Madame Zena turned to Amy. The fortune-teller's eyes were not what they had been a few minutes ago; now they were haunted.

Amy wanted to get up and leave the tent. She was experiencing the same kind of psychic energy that had electrified her at Marco the Magnificent's show. A chill, clammy sensation swept through her, and she saw stroboscopic images of graves and rotting corpses and grinning skeletons, nightmare flashes as if clips of film were being projected on a screen behind her eyes.

She tried to stand up. She couldn't.

Her heart was hammering.

It was the drugs again. That was all. Just the drugs. The spice Liz had added to the pot. She wished she hadn't smoked any more of it; she wished she'd stood up to Liz and refused.

"I'll have to ask you some questions . . . about yourself . . . and your family," Madame Zena said haltingly, without any of the theatrical pizazz that she had shown while plying Liz with her spiel. "It is just as I told your friend here . . . I need the information in order to focus my psychic perceptions." She sounded as if she wanted to jump up and run out of the tent every bit as much as Amy did.

"Go ahead," Amy whispered. "I don't want to know . . . but I've got to."

"Hey, what's going on here?" Richie asked, picking up on the new, evil vibrations that now filled the tent.

Still blissfully unaware of the sudden seriousness in the fortune-teller's demeanor, Liz said, "Ssshh, Richie! Don't spoil the show."

To Amy, Madame Zena said, "Your name?"

"Amy Harper."

"Your age?"

"Seventeen."

"Where do you live?"

"Here in Royal City."

"Do you have any sisters?"

"No."

"Brothers?"

"One."

"His name?"

"Joey Harper."

"His age?"

"Ten."

"Is your mother alive?"

"Yes."

"What is her age?"

"Forty-five, I think."

Madame Zena blinked, licked her lips.

"What color hair does your mother have?"

"Dark brown, almost black, like mine."

"What color are her eyes?"

"Very dark, like mine."

"What is . . ." Madame Zena cleared her throat.

The raven flapped its wings.

Finally Madame Zena spoke again. "What is your mother's name?"

"Ellen Harper."

The name clearly jolted the fortune-teller. Fine beads of sweat broke out along her hairline.

"Do you know your mother's maiden name?"

"Giavenetto," Amy said.

Madame Zena's face became even whiter, and she began to tremble visibly.

"What the hell . . . ?" Richie said, perceiving the very real fear in the phony Gypsy, baffled by it.

"Ssshh!" Liz said.

"What a bunch of crap," Buzz said.

Madame Zena was obviously reluctant to look into the crystal ball, but at last she forced her eyes to it. She blinked and gasped and cried out. She pushed her chair back from the table and stood up. She swept the glass sphere off the table; it crashed to the earthen floor, but it was too heavy to break that easily. "You've got to get out of here," she said urgently. "You've got to go. Get away from the carnival. Go home and lock your doors and stay there until the carnival leaves town."

Liz and Amy stood up, and Liz said, "What's all the malarkey? We were supposed to get our fortunes told for free. You haven't told us how we're going to be rich and famous."

From the other side of the table, Madame Zena stared at them with wide, frightened eyes. "Listen to me. I'm a fake.

A phony. I don't have any psychic ability. I just con the marks. I've never seen into the future. I've never seen anything in that crystal ball except the light from the flashlight bulb in the wooden base. But tonight . . . just a minute ago . . . my God, I *did* see something. I don't understand it. I don't *want* to understand it. My God, Jesus, Jesus Christ, who would *want* to be able to see the future? That would be a curse, not a gift. But I *saw*. You've got to leave the carnival now, right away. Don't stop for anything. Don't look back."

They stared at her, amazed by her outburst.

Madame Zena swayed, and her legs seemed to turn to mush, and she collapsed into her chair again. "Go, damn you! Get the hell out of here before it's too late! Go, you goddamned fools! Hurry!"

Out on the midway, standing in a pool of flashing lights, with people streaming past, with waves of calliope music breaking over them, they looked at each other, waiting for someone to say something.

Richie spoke first. "What was *that* all about?"

"She's nuts," Buzz said.

"I don't think so," Amy said.

"A real looney-tune," Buzz insisted.

"Hey, don't you guys understand what happened?" Liz asked. She laughed happily and clapped her hands with delight.

"If you've got an explanation, tell us," Amy said, still chilled to the bone by the look that had come over Madame Zena's face when she had peered into the crystal ball.

"It's a scam," Liz said. "The carnival security men spotted us smoking dope. They don't want that kind of trouble on their lot, but they also don't want to call the cops.

Carnies don't truck with the cops. So they arranged for the albino to give us free tickets to Zena's, so she could try to *scare* us off."

"Yeah!" Buzz said. "I'll be damned. That's it, all right."

"I don't know," Richie said. "It doesn't make a lot of sense. I mean, why wouldn't they just have their goons throw us out?"

"Because there's too many of us, dummy," Liz said. "They'd need at least three bouncers. They wouldn't want to make a big scene like that."

"Could she have been sincere?" Amy asked.

"Madame Zena?" Liz said. "You mean to tell me you believe she really saw something in her crystal ball? Horseshit!"

They talked about it some more, and gradually they came to accept Liz's theory. It seemed to make more sense by the minute.

But Amy wondered if it would make any sense at all if they weren't half wasted on dope. She thought of Marco the Magnificent; Liz's face on the woman in the coffin; Buzz cutting his finger on the jar that contained the monster. It was too much to think about; too scary. Even if Liz's explanation was thin, it was at least conveniently simple, and Amy gladly accepted it.

"I have to pee," Liz said. "Then I want some ice cream and a ride through the funhouse. After that we can split for home." She tickled Richie under the chin. "When we get home, I'll take you on a thrill ride better than anything they have here." She turned to Amy. "Come to the restroom with me."

"I don't really have to," Amy said.

Liz took her hand. "Come on. Keep me company. Anyway, we have to talk, kid."

"Meet you at the ice-cream stand over there," Richie said, pointing to a joint beyond the carousel.

"Back in a jiffy," Liz assured him. Then she pulled Amy through the crowd, toward the edge of the midway.

Conrad was standing in the shadows beside Zena's tent when the four teenagers came out and stopped in the pool of flashing red and yellow light that was cast by the nearby Tilt-a-Whirl. He heard the blond girl say that she wanted to use the restroom, get an ice cream, and then take a tour of the funhouse. As soon as the group split up and moved away, Conrad slipped into Zena's tent. As he went inside, he pulled down a canvas flap that covered the entire entrance; on the outside of it, there were six words— CLOSED/WILL RETURN IN TEN MINUTES.

Zena was sitting in her chair. Even in the flickering light of the candles, Conrad could see that she was ashen.

"Well?" he said.

"Another dead end," Zena said nervously.

"This one looks more like Ellen than most of the others that I've sent to you."

"Just coincidence," Zena said.

"What's her name?"

"Amy Harper."

Those four syllables electrified Conrad. He remembered the small boy to whom he had given two free passes just this afternoon. That child's name had been Joey Harper, and he had said that his sister's name was Amy. He, too, had resembled Ellen.

"What did you learn about her?" he asked Zena.

"Not much."

"Tell me."

"She's not the one."

"Tell me anyway. Brothers? Sisters?"

Zena hesitated, then said, "One brother."

"What's his name?"

"What does it matter? She isn't the one you're looking for."

"Just curious," Conrad said evenly, sensing that she was hiding the truth from him, but afraid to believe that he had found his prey after all this time. "What's her brother's name?"

"Joey."

"What's her mother's name."

"Nancy," Zena said.

Conrad knew she was lying. He stared down at her and said, "Are you sure it isn't Leona?"

Zena blinked. "What? Why Leona?"

"Because this afternoon, when I happened to have a friendly little chat with Joey Harper while he was watching us erect the funhouse, he told me that his mother's name was Leona."

Zena gaped at him, amazed and perplexed.

Conrad walked around the table and put a hand on her shoulder.

She looked up at him.

He said, "You know what I think? I think the boy lied

to me. I think he sensed danger somehow, and he lied about his mother's name and age. And now you're lying to me."

"Conrad . . . let them go."

Her words were an admission that he had found Ellen's children, and a shattering, explosive elation tore through him.

"I saw something in the crystal ball," she said in a voice that contained fear and awe. "It's not even crystal. It's just a cheap piece of crap. There's nothing magical about it. Yet . . . tonight . . . when those girls were here . . . I saw images in the ball. It was awful, horrible. I saw the blond screaming, her hands thrown up in front of her face as if she were trying to ward off something hideous that was reaching for her. And I saw the other one . . . Amy . . . in torn clothes, all covered with blood." She shuddered violently. "And I think . . . the boys, too . . . in the background of the vision . . . the boys who were with those girls . . . all bloody."

"It's a sign," Conrad said. "I told you, I've been sent signs. This is another one. It tells me not to wait. It tells me to get Amy tonight, even if I have to take care of the others as well."

Zena shook her head. "No. No, Conrad, I can't let you do that. You can't have your revenge. It's sick. You can't just go out there and kill those four kids."

"Oh, I probably won't kill any of them with my own hands," he said.

"What do you mean?"

"Gunther will take care of them."

"Gunther? He wouldn't hurt anyone."

"Our son has changed," Conrad said. "I'm the only one who knows how much he's changed. He's come of age at last. He needs women now, and he takes what he needs.

He doesn't just screw them, either. He leaves quite a mess behind. I've been covering up for him the last few years. And now I'll be repaid. He'll give me the vengeance I've dreamed about for so long."

"What do you mean when you say he takes women?"

"Uses them and then rips them apart," Conrad said, knowing that she was the type who would feel morally responsible for the actions of her freakish offspring, smiling as he saw the pain flicker across her face.

"How many?" she asked.

"I've lost count. A few dozen."

"My God," Zena said, shaken to her roots. "What have I done? What have I brought into the world?"

"The Antichrist," Conrad said.

"No," she said. "You're not in your right mind. You have delusions of grandeur. It's nothing as special as the Antichrist. It's just a vicious, mad beast. I should have had Ellen's good sense. I should have killed it like she killed Victor. Now . . . I'm responsible for everyone who has died and for everyone who will die before it's finished."

Standing over her, Conrad reached down, put his hands on her throat, and said, "I can't let you spoil everything."

Zena struggled. But she didn't have a strong enough desire to live, while Conrad had an exceedingly strong desire to kill her. He had never known such power and purpose as that which coursed through him now. He felt supercharged, crackling with a demonic energy. Zena thrashed and kicked and scratched his face, but she died much more easily than he had expected. He dragged her body into the darkest corner of the tent; later, he would figure out some way to get rid of it.

The raven squawked hysterically.

Afraid that the bird would draw someone to the body before it could be disposed of, Conrad opened the cage, thrust his hands inside, seized the raven, and broke its neck.

He left Zena's tent and hurried back to the funhouse. Amy Harper and her friends would be arriving shortly, and he wanted to be prepared for them.

Tonight Joey was a winner. He won sixty-five cents pitching pennies. He won a small teddy bear by throwing darts at balloons. And he won a free ride on the carousel when he managed to grab a brass ring the first time around.

He was on the carousel, riding a black stallion like the one in the movie of the same name, when he saw Amy. He hadn't considered the possibility that her date had brought her to the carnival, but there she was, in dark green shorts and a pale green T-shirt. She wasn't with Buzz, though. She was with Liz, and the two girls were headed toward the edge of the midway. Joey lost sight of them as the carousel revolved, and when he came around again, they had disappeared in the crowd.

When he got off the merry-go-round a couple of minutes later, he went looking for his sister. He knew she would enjoy hearing how he had fooled Mama. She would think he was clever and brave for coming all the way to the fairgrounds on his own. He valued Amy's approval more than anything else, and he was eager to hear what she would say when she saw him here all by himself.

14

The comfort station was brightly lighted. It smelled of damp concrete, mildew, and stale urine. The sinks were stained by years of dripping, mineral-rich water.

After Amy and Liz washed their hands, as they were leaning toward the mirrors, fixing their makeup, two older women left the restroom, and the girls were alone.

"You feeling high?" Liz asked.

"Yes."

"Me too. All the way up. I'm fuckin' wired, for sure. Are you just high, or are you really wired?"

"I'm totally wasted," Amy said, squinting into the mirror, applying lipstick with a shaky hand.

"Good," Liz said. "I'm glad you're really wrecked. Maybe you'll finally loosen up."

"I'm loose as a goose," Amy said.

"Great," Liz said. "Then I won't have to sell you on it."

"Sell me on what?"

"The orgy," Liz said.

Amy looked at her, and Liz grinned almost drunkenly, and Amy said, "Orgy?"

"I've already sold the idea to those two pussy-hounds out there," Liz said.

"Buzz and Richie?"

"They're both game."

"You mean . . . the four of us in one bed?"

"Sure," Liz said, putting away her own lipstick, snapping her purse shut. "It'll be *fan*tastic!"

"Oh, Liz, I don't know about that. I don't—"

"Let it slide, kid."

"I've got college and—"

"You've got the pill. You won't get knocked up again. Don't be so damned prim. Go with the flow, kid. Be what you are. Stop pretending you're Sister Purity."

"I couldn't—"

"Of course you could," Liz said. "You *will*. You want it. You're just like me. Face facts and enjoy yourself."

Amy put one hand on the sink to steady herself. It wasn't just the dope that made her feel woozy. She was dizzied by the prospect of just letting go, being like Liz, forgetting about the future, living just for the moment, incapable of guilt or remorse. It must be nice to live that way. It must be so relaxing, so *free*.

Liz moved close to her and said, "My place. As soon as we leave the fairgrounds. The four of us. My parents have a king-size bed. Think of it, honey. You can have both those guys at the same time. They're both dying to slip the old salami to you. It'll be great. You'll have a ball. I know you will because *I'll* have a ball, and you're just like me."

Liz's melodic, rhythmic voice was draining all the energy and all the will out of Amy. Amy leaned against the sink and closed her eyes and felt that warm, seductive voice pulling her down, down into a place she wasn't sure she wanted to go.

Then Amy felt a hand on her breast. She opened her eyes with a start.

Liz was touching her intimately, smiling.

Amy wanted to push the other girl's lewd hand away, but she couldn't find sufficient strength to present Liz with even that small token of resistance.

"I've always wondered what it would be like, you and me, just us two girls," Liz said.

"You're wasted," Amy said. "You're so high you don't know what you're saying."

"I know exactly what I'm saying, kid. I've always wondered . . . and tonight I can find out. We can make some real memories, kid." She leaned close, kissed Amy lightly on the mouth, tongue flicking like the quick tongue of a snake, and then she left the restroom, twitching her bottom as she went.

Amy felt dirty, but she also experienced a tremor of pleasure that oscillated through every inch of her.

She looked in the mirror again, squinting because the bright fluorescent lights stung her bleary eyes. Her face looked soft, as if it were melting off her bones. Searching once more for that wickedness that others could see in her, she stared into her own eyes. All of Amy's life, her mother had told her that she was filled with a terrible evil that must be repressed at all costs. After years and years of listening to that hateful line, Amy didn't like herself very much. Her self-respect had been whittled down to a fragile stick; Mama had wielded the whittling knife. Now Amy thought she finally could see a hint of the evil that Mama and Liz saw in her; it was a peculiar shadow, a writhing darkness deep in her eyes.

No! she thought desperately, frightened by the speed with which her resolution was dissolving. I'm not that kind of person. I have plans, ambitions, dreams. I want to paint beautiful pictures and bring happiness to people.

But she could vividly recall the thrill that had snapped through her like an electric current when Liz's tongue had licked her lips.

She thought of being in bed with Richie and Buzz, both of them using her at the same time, and suddenly it wasn't impossible for her to picture herself in that situation.

Standing there in the harshly lighted comfort station, acutely uncomfortable in the stink of mildew and urine and rotting hope, Amy felt as if she were waiting in the anteroom of Hell.

At last she walked to the door and opened it.

Liz was waiting outside, in the night. She smiled at Amy and held out her hand.

Conrad sent Ghost off to work at the grab joint, which was busier than the funhouse tonight. As soon as the albino was gone, Conrad shut the ticket booth and sent Elton to assist at the pitch-and-dunk, which formed the third corner of Straker's three-cornered carnival empire.

Elton gave him an odd look. The funhouse was much too busy to justify closing it down for the night. But unlike Ghost, Elton never asked questions; he simply did as he was told.

When those marks who were already in the funhouse came out through the big, swinging exit doors and disembarked from their gondolas, Conrad shut down the power to the track. He didn't switch off the lights or the music; in fact he turned up the volume on the music and on the voice of the laughing clown as well.

Gunther watched Conrad with puzzlement. But when the situation was explained to him, he understood at once, and he went into the funhouse to wait.

Conrad took up a position by the shuttered ticket booth. He turned away the marks when they asked if they could buy tickets. For the rest of the night, the funhouse would be open for only four very special people.

After they ate ice-cream bars covered with chocolate and nuts, Liz and Amy and Richie and Buzz went to the funhouse.

The barker, the man with the brilliantly blue eyes who had been on the elevated platform earlier, was no longer haranguing the people who passed by. He was standing at the ticket booth, which appeared to be closed.

"Oh, no," Liz said disappointedly. "Mister, you aren't going to shut down for the night already?"

"No," the barker said. "We just had a minor mechanical problem."

"When will it be fixed?" Liz asked.

"It's fixed already," the barker said. "But I've got to wait for the boss to get back before I start up."

"How long will that be?" Richie asked.

The barker shrugged. "Hard to tell. The boss likes, shall we say, to tipple. If he's tippled too much while we were fixing the motors, he might not be back at all."

"Ah, shit!" Liz said. "We saved this for last because it's my favorite."

The barker looked at Amy, and she didn't like what she saw in his eyes. His gaze was so intent and somehow menacing, *hungry*.

I should have worn a bra, Amy thought. I shouldn't have tried to be like Liz. I shouldn't have gone out in short shorts, a flimsy T-shirt, and no bra. I'm just advertising myself. No wonder he's staring at me like that.

"Well," the barker said, sweeping them all with his gas-flame eyes, "I'll tell you what. You don't look like an ordinary group of marks to me. You look like you're with it and for it."

"You bet your ass we are," Liz said.

"Whatever that means—with it and for it," Buzz said.

"It's a carny expression," the barker told them. "It means what it says and says what it means."

Liz laughed. "Which makes everything perfectly clear."

The barker grinned and winked at her.

"You're a pretty sharp dude," Liz said.

"Thank you," the barker said. "And you're a very sharp lady. But I'll take your money just the same."

Richie and Buzz dug in their pockets for money.

The barker glanced at Amy again. That same hunger.

Amy crossed her arms over her breasts, so he couldn't see her nipples through the pale green T-shirt she wore.

Joey had just about given up trying to find Amy in the crowd that surged around the midway—and then he saw her. She was with Liz, Buzz, and another boy. The carny who had given Joey the free passes was helping them into a gondola at the funhouse boarding gate.

Joey hesitated, remembering how weird the carny had acted this afternoon. But he was so eager to tell Amy about how he had fooled Mama that he shrugged off his misgivings and headed toward the funhouse.

The gondola seated four: two forward, two behind. Liz and Richie took the front seats; Amy and Buzz sat in back of them.

They started with a jolt that made Liz yelp and laugh. The phony castle doors opened, swallowed them, and closed again.

At first the gondola moved rapidly into the pitch blackness, but then it slowed. A light popped on to the left of the track and above it, and a leering, grizzled pirate laughed and thrust a sword at them.

Liz squealed, and Buzz took the opportunity to put his arm around Amy.

On their right, just past the pirate, a very realistic-looking werewolf was crouched on a ledge, suddenly illuminated by a moon that lit up behind him. His eyes glowed red; there was blood on his huge teeth; and his claws, which he raked at the gondola, gleamed like splinters of a mirror.

"Oh, protect me, Richie!" Liz shouted in make-believe terror. "Protect my virgin body from that horrid beast!" She laughed at her own performance.

The car slowed even more, and they came to a display in which an ax-murderer was standing over one of his victims. The ax was buried in the dead man's skull, cleaving his forehead in two.

The gondola came to a complete stop.

"What's wrong?" Liz asked.

"Must have broken down again," Richie said.

They were sitting in purple-brown shadows. The only light came from the ax-murderer exhibit beside them, and that was an eerie, greenish glow.

"Hey!" Liz shouted into the darkness and into the waves of creepy music that crashed over them. "Hey, let's get this show on the road!"

"Yeah!" Buzz shouted. "Hey, out there!"

For a minute or two they all called to the barker, who was on the platform outside, beyond the closed doors of the attraction, no more than thirty of forty feet away. No one responded to them, and at last they gave up.

"Shit," Liz said.

"What should we do?" Amy asked.

"Stay put," Richie said. "It'll start moving again eventually."

"Maybe we should get out and walk back to the doors," Buzz said.

"Absolutely not," Richie said. "If we did, and then the

ride started up again, our gondola would go off without us. And if another car came through the entrance doors, it would run us down."

"I hope we don't have to wait in here too long," Amy said, remembering the way the barker had looked at her. "It's spooky."

"What a pain in the ass," Liz said.

"Be patient," Richie said. "We'll be rolling soon."

"If we've got to just sit here," Liz said, "I wish they'd shut off that fuckin' music. It's way too loud."

Something creaked loudly overhead.

"What was that?" Amy asked.

They all looked up in the darkness.

"Nothing," Buzz said. "Just the wind outside."

"There isn't any wind tonight," Amy said.

The creaking noise came again. This time there were other loud sounds with it: a scraping, a thud, an animal-like grunting.

"I don't think we—" Richie began.

Something flashed out of the darkness and seized him by the throat. An arm thrust down from the low, unlighted ceiling over the gondola, an arm that ended in a large, long-fingered, fur-covered hand that was tipped with murderously sharp claws. Though the arm moved fast, they all saw it in the backwash of green light from the ax-murderer exhibit, but they couldn't see what was in the blackness above, at the other end of the arm. Whatever it was, its claws pierced Richie's throat, hooked deep into his flesh; and the thing hauled him up, off his seat. Richie kicked frantically, his shoes drumming on the front of the gondola for a second or two. Then he was out of the car, up, up, dragged through a hole in the ceiling, as if he weighed only a few pounds.

Overhead, a trapdoor banged shut.

The attack had transpired in only three or four seconds.

For a moment Amy was too stunned to move or speak. She stared at the darkness above, where Richie had disappeared, and she couldn't make herself believe what she had seen. It had to be a trick, part of the funhouse tour, an incredibly clever illusion.

Apparently Liz and Buzz thought the same thing, for they, too, were mesmerized.

Gradually, however, Amy realized that Richie was really gone and that no carnival in the world would risk injuring a customer with a trick as dangerous as that one.

Liz said, "Blood."

That single word broke the spell.

Amy and Buzz looked at her.

Liz was turned part of the way around in the front seat. She was holding up her arms. They were spattered with something wet and dark. Even in the green light, it was obvious that Liz was spotted with blood.

Richie's blood.

Amy screamed.

15

As soon as Conrad switched off the power to the tracks, stranding the carload of teenagers, he went down the boarding ramp toward the midway. He intended to walk around to the back of the funhouse, enter by the rear basement door, lock it after him, and locate Gunther. He wanted his son to kill three of those kids, but not Amy Harper. Amy, of course, would have to suffer for several days before she died; she would have to be well used, perhaps by both himself and Gunther; that was the way Conrad wanted it, the way he had dreamed of it for twenty-five years. He had instructed Gunther carefully, but he wasn't sure that Gunther would be able to control himself once the killing began. Gunther needed to be reminded; he needed constant guidance through the next critical hour.

But when Conrad reached the bottom of the ramp, as he was about to head for the walkway between the funhouse and Freak-o-rama, he saw the boy. Joey Harper. Amy's little brother was standing over by the second set of castle doors, through which the gondolas exited the funhouse.

He must have seen his sister go inside, Conrad thought. He's waiting for her. When she doesn't come out, what will he do? Go for help? Seek out a security guard?

Joey glanced at him.

Conrad smiled and waved.

He would have to do something about the damned boy, and quick.

Buzz climbed onto the ledge where the ax-murderer display was bathed in green light, and he pulled the ax out of the skull of the mannequin that was crumpled at the foot of the mechanical madman. Ax in hand, he jumped down into the gondola channel, where Amy and Liz were huddled together, waiting for him.

"It's a real ax," he said. "Not very sharp, but it ought to be of some use."

"I just don't understand," Liz said shakily. "What is going on here? What the fuck is this all about?"

"I don't know for sure," Buzz said. "I can only guess. But you saw that hand . . ."

"It wasn't a *hand*," Liz said.

"Claw, paw, whatever you want to call it," Buzz said. "Anyway, it was just like the hands on the thing in the jar, that dead freak we saw pickled in formaldehyde over at Freak-o-rama. Only this hand was a lot bigger."

Amy had to make an effort to speak. She was surprised she could talk at all. "You mean . . . you think we're trapped in here with a freak that kills people?"

"Yeah," Buzz said.

"It didn't kill Richie!" Liz said, her voice cracking. "Richie isn't dead. He's alive. He's . . . somewhere . . . and he's alive."

"It's possible," Buzz said. "Maybe it's just a kidnapping scheme or something. Maybe they're just going to hold Richie for ransom. It's possible."

He and Amy exchanged looks, and although it wasn't easy to read his expression in the green light, Amy knew that Buzz felt the same way about it as she did. Richie couldn't possibly be alive. There wasn't one chance in a million that he would ever smile at them again. Richie was dead, gone, forever.

"We've got to get out of here and call the cops," Liz said. "We've got to save Richie."

"Come on," Buzz said. "We'll walk back to the entrance doors. If we can't open them, maybe this ax is just sharp enough so that I can chop a way out."

There was no light whatsoever between the green glow of the display on their left side and the front doors, thirty feet away.

Liz looked down the tomb-black tunnel and said, "No. No, I can't walk through all that darkness. What if it's waiting there for us?"

"You have matches in your purse," Amy said. "We can use those to find our way."

"Good idea!" Buzz said.

Liz rummaged through her purse with shaking hands and found two packs of matches, one full and one half-empty.

Buzz took them from her. He walked off, into the darkness, struck a match, and was visible again. "Let's go."

"Wait," Liz said. "Wait a minute. Maybe . . ."

"Maybe what?" Amy asked.

Buzz shook out the match as it came close to burning his fingers, and he stepped back into the green light.

Liz shook her head to clear it. "I'm so damned wasted. I'm really wrecked. I can't think straight. So isn't it possible that maybe this isn't really happening? Isn't it possible that this is just a bad trip? That *was* PCP I mixed in the last two joints. You can have a bad trip on A-dust, you know. Some of the worst trips you ever had. Maybe that's what this is. Just a bad trip."

"We wouldn't all be having the same hallucination," Buzz said.

"How do I know you're even real?" Liz asked. "You might just exist in my mind. Maybe the real Buzz is sitting beside Amy in the back of that gondola, halfway through the funhouse by now. Maybe I'm in that car, too, so spaced out I don't realize where I am."

Amy gently slapped Liz's face. "Listen. Listen to me, Liz. This isn't a bad trip. Not the way you mean it. This is real, and I'm scared out of my wits, so let's stop fooling around and get the hell out of here."

Liz blinked, licked her lips. "Yeah. You're right. Sorry. It's just . . . I wish I didn't feel so wasted."

Buzz lit one match, then another and another, and they

followed him down the dark tunnel toward the funhouse entrance.

Joey stood with the barker in front of the funhouse, trying to remember why he had been frightened of this man earlier in the day. Now the carny was as friendly as a person could be, and he had a smile so nice that Joey couldn't help smiling, too.

"Have you been through my funhouse yet, son?" the barker asked.

"No," Joey said. "I've been on a lot of other things, though."

He had been avoiding the funhouse because he felt uneasy about Conrad Straker, even though Straker had given him two free passes.

"My funhouse is the best attraction on the midway," Conrad said. "Why don't you let me take you on a personally guided tour? How about that? Not just an ordinary ride like all the marks get, but a guided tour with the owner. I can show you the workings of it, the behind-the-scenes stuff that few people are ever fortunate enough to see. I'll show you how the monsters are built, how they're made to move and growl and gnash their teeth. Everything. All of it. I'll show you the kind of things that a with-it-and-for-it person would enjoy learning about."

"Gee," Joey said, "you'd really do that?"

"Certainly," the barker said heartily. "As I'm sure you noticed, I closed the funhouse down for the night. The ticket booth is closed, as you can see. I just sent the last car through, four nice teenagers."

"One of them was my sister," Joey said.

"Oh, really? Let me guess. There *was* one who looked like you. The dark-haired girl in the green shorts."

"That's her," Joey said. "She doesn't know I'm here tonight. I want to wait for her to come out . . . to say hello. Hey, maybe she would like the guided tour, too. Could she come along? I'll bet Amy would really enjoy it."

The front doors of the funhouse were designed to open inward on hydraulic rams. There were no handles on them, nothing by which they could be gripped or moved.

"If I could get hold of an edge," Buzz said, "maybe I could pry them open. But they're closed so damned tight."

"It wouldn't matter if you could get your fingers through a crack," Amy said. "You wouldn't be able to pull the doors open anyway. I'll bet they're just like the automatic door on the garage at home. As long as they're hooked up to the hydraulic system, they can't be opened manually."

"Yeah," Buzz said. "You're right. I should have thought of that."

Amy was surprised that she was holding up so well. She was scared, and she got a sinking feeling—part grief and part disgust—when she thought of what happened to Richie. But she wasn't coming apart at the seams. In spite of the dope she had smoked, she was in control of herself. In fact she was thinking faster and clearer than Buzz. She didn't consider herself to be a strong person; Mama always told her that she was weak, flawed. Now her fortitude amazed her.

Liz, on the other hand, was rapidly breaking down.

Her eyes brimmed with a steady flow of tears. She looked drawn, years older than she had looked minutes ago. She mewled like a scared kitten.

"Don't panic," Buzz said. "I've still got the ax."

Amy lit a series of matches while Buzz swung the ax at the door—six, eight, a dozen blows.

At last he stopped, breathing hard. "No good. There isn't any edge on the damned blade."

"Someone *must* have heard all that pounding," Liz said.

"I doubt it," Amy said. "Remember, the actual funhouse entrance is set back at least fifteen feet from the ticket booth and the midway, beyond the boarding ramp, at the end of the entrance channel. No one passing by is likely to hear the ax, not above all this music and that laughing clown."

"But the barker's out there," Liz said. "He'll hear it."

"For Christ's sake, Liz," Buzz said, "get your head together. The barker's not on *our* side. He's obviously part of it. He lured us in is what he did."

"So some freak could kill us?" Liz asked. "That doesn't make sense. That's ridiculous. The barker doesn't even know us. Why would he choose a bunch of kids at random and throw them to . . . that thing?"

"Don't you listen to the news on TV?" Buzz asked. "Things don't have to make sense anymore. The world's full of crazies."

"But why would he *do* it?" Liz demanded.

"Maybe just for kicks," Amy said.

"We'll scream," Liz said. "We'll scream our fuckin' heads off."

"Yeah," Buzz said.

"No," Amy said. "That's useless, too. The music is louder than usual, and so's the clown's laugh. Nobody's going to hear us—or if someone does, he'll think we're just having fun in here. People are *supposed* to scream in a funhouse."

"So what are we going to do?" Liz asked. "We can't just wait here for that *thing* to come back. We've got to do something, damn it!"

"We'll go around to some of these mechanical monsters and see if we can find anything else like the ax, stuff we can use to defend ourselves," Buzz said.

"The ax isn't even sharp," Liz said petulantly. "What the hell good is it?"

"It's sharp enough to hold that thing off," Buzz said, hefting the ax in both hands. "Maybe it's too dull to cut wood, but it'll sure do some damage to that bastard's face."

"The only way you're going to hold off that freak is with a shotgun," Liz said shakily.

As the flame neared Amy's fingers, she dropped the match she was holding. It was burnt out by the time it reached the floor. For a couple of seconds they stood in a darkness like no other that Amy had ever experienced. The darkness did not merely seem to contain a threat; it *was* the threat. It seemed to be a living, evil, purposeful darkness that pressed close around her, seeking, touching with its cool, black hands.

Liz whimpered softly.

Amy struck another match, and in the welcome burst of light, she said, "Buzz is right. We've got to arm ourselves. But that won't be enough. Even a shotgun might not be enough. That freak could drop out of the ceiling or pop up from the floor so fast that you wouldn't have time to pull the trigger anyway. What we've got to do is find another way out."

"There isn't a way out," Liz said. "The exit door will be just like this one. You won't be able to open it or chop it down. We're trapped."

"There's probably an emergency exit," Amy said.

"That's right!" Buzz said. "There has to be an emergency door somewhere. And maybe a service entrance, too."

"We'll arm ourselves as best we can," Amy said, "and then we'll go looking for a way out."

"You want to go deeper into this place?" Liz asked incredulously. "Are you out of your fuckin' minds? It'll get us if we go in there."

"It's just as likely to get us if we stand here by the doors," Amy said.

"Right," Buzz said. "Let's get moving."

"No, no, no!" Liz said, shaking her head violently.

The flame flickered.

Darkness.

Amy struck another match.

The renewed light revealed Liz crouching very low against the sealed doors, looking up at the ceiling, shivering like a cornered rabbit.

Amy took the girl by the arm and pulled her to her feet. "Listen, kid," Amy said gently, "Buzz and I aren't going to just stand here until that thing comes back for us. So you have to go with us now. If you stay here alone, you're finished for sure. Do you want to stay here all by yourself in the dark?"

Liz put her hands to her eyes, wiped away the tears;

droplets still glistened in her lashes, and her face was wet. "All right," she said unhappily, "I'll go. But I'm sure as hell not going to go first."

"I'll lead the way," Buzz assured her.

"I won't go last, either," Liz said.

"I'll bring up the rear," Amy said. "You'll be safe in the middle, Liz. Now let's go."

They fell into line and took only three cautious steps before Liz stopped and said, "My God, how did she know?"

"How did who know what?" Amy asked impatiently.

"How did that fortune-teller know something like this was going to happen?"

They stood in baffled silence for a moment, and the match went out, and Amy fumbled for a long time with the next one before she finally got it burning; suddenly her hands were shaking. Liz's unanswerable question about the fortune-teller had sparked a strange feeling in Amy—a tingle along her spine, not a shiver of fear but an unnerving quiver of déjà vu. She felt that she had been in this situation before—trapped in a dark place with exactly this same horrible freak. For a few seconds that feeling was so shatteringly powerful, so overwhelming, that she felt as if she might faint; but then it passed.

"Did Madame Zena really see into the future?" Liz asked. "That isn't possible, is it? That's too damned weird. What the hell is going on here?"

"I don't know," Amy said. "But we don't have time to worry about that now. First things first. We've got to find that emergency exit and get out of here."

Outside, the clown laughed.

Amy, Liz, and Buzz moved deeper into the funhouse.

* * *

For a minute after Joey asked for a rain check on the guided tour, Conrad stood behind the boy, staring at the double exit doors, pretending to wait for the sister and her friends to come out of the funhouse.

"What's taking them so long?" Joey asked.

"Oh, it's the longest ride on the midway," Conrad said quickly. He pointed to a poster that proclaimed precisely that virtue of the funhouse.

"I saw that," Joey said. "But it can't be this long."

"Twelve full minutes."

"They've been in there longer than that."

Conrad looked at his watch and frowned.

"And why haven't any other cars come out?" Joey asked. "Weren't there cars ahead of them?"

Conrad stepped up to the gondola channel by the exit ramp and looked down at the tracks. Faking surprise, he said, "The center drive chain isn't moving."

"What's that mean?" Joey asked, stepping up beside him.

"It means the damned machinery has broken down again," Conrad said. "It happens every once in a while. Your sister and her friends are stuck in there. I'll have to go inside and see what's wrong with the equipment." He turned away and started around the side of the funhouse. Then he stopped and looked back as if he had forgotten Joey for a moment. "Come along, son. I might need your help."

The boy hesitated.

"Come on," Conrad said. "Let's not leave your sister sitting in the dark."

The boy followed him to the rear of the funhouse.

Conrad opened the door that led to the room beneath the main floor of the structure. He went inside, felt for the light chain, pulled on it.

Joey entered after him. "Wow!" the boy said. "I didn't realize there'd be so many machines!"

Conrad closed and locked the door behind them. When he turned to Joey, he grinned and said, "You lying little shit. Your mother's name isn't Leona."

Amy, Liz, and Buzz were deep in the funhouse when a string of lights came on above the track. They had turned several sharp bends, had edged nervously down a couple of long, dark straightaways, and had just started up a steep slope, past wax dummies of monsters from various science fiction movies. The lights didn't completely dispel the darkness. Deep shadows lay close by. But any light at all was welcome, for Amy had only one match left.

"What's happening?" Liz asked anxiously. She was frightened of any change in their situation, even if that change meant light instead of darkness.

"I don't know," Amy said uneasily.

"It's turned the lights on so it can look for us more easily," Liz said. "That's what's happening, and you know it."

"Well, if that *is* the case," Amy said, "we'll be a lot harder to find if we keep moving."

"Right," Buzz said. "Let's don't just stand here. Let's find a way out."

"There isn't one," Liz said. But she moved uphill with them.

When they reached the top of the rise, they found a large display featuring six man-sized, tentacled, bug-eyed monsters. The aliens were disembarking from a flying saucer, absurd shapes frozen in the frost-pale backwash from the lights above the tracks.

"That saucer's pretty damned big," Buzz said. "I'll bet we could all three hide in it."

"They'd be sure to look in there," Amy said. "We can't stand still, and we can't hide. We have to get out."

Just as she finished speaking, the drive chain in the center of the tracks started to move.

They all jumped, startled.

In the distance an approaching gondola rattled noisily along the rails—*clatter-clunk-clatter-clunk*—a hard, sharp sound, audible above the music and the recorded laughter, growing louder by the second.

"It's coming for us," Liz said. "Oh, Jesus, Jesus, that freak is coming to get us!"

The dull, rusty knife that Amy had taken off one of the monster models now seemed like a laughable weapon.

Clatter-clunk-clatter-clunk . . .

"Quick," Buzz said. "Get off the tracks."

They clambered onto the wide ledge where the six aliens were coming out of the flying saucer.

Clatter-clunk-clatter-clunk . . .

"You two go over by the spaceship," Buzz said. "Make yourselves visible. Make sure his attention is on you."

"What are you going to do?" Amy asked.

Buzz grinned. It was a strained, frightened, utterly humorless grin. He was struggling to maintain his macho image. He pointed to a papier-mâché boulder and said,

"I'm going to stand over there by that rock. When the car comes up the hill . . . when the bastard in it sees the two of you, I'm going to chop him before he has a chance to jump out onto the tracks."

"It might work," Amy said.

"Sure," Buzz said. "I'll split him wide open."

Clatter-clunk-clatter-clunk . . .

The gondola turned the nearest corner and started up the slope toward them.

Liz tried to run and hide.

Amy grabbed her by the wrist and pulled her over to the flying saucer, where the occupant of the gondola would spot them just as he reached the crest of the hill.

Buzz positioned himself beside the rock, completely visible to Liz and Amy, but hidden from the oncoming car. He held the ax in both hands.

Clatter-clunk . . . clatter-clunk . . . clatter . . . clunk . . .

The car was slowing down as the grade of the tracks increased.

Buzz lifted the ax over his head.

Amy saw the front of the gaily painted car move into sight.

"Jesus, let me go, let me go, Amy," Liz said.

Amy held her wrist even more firmly.

The first seat of the car was visible now. It appeared to be empty.

Clatter . . . clunk . . . clatter . . .

Very slowly now.

Hardly moving now.

Finally the rear seat came into view.

Amy squinted. If the lights had been just a fraction

dimmer than they were, she wouldn't have been able to see the thing in the backseat of the gondola. But she *did* see it. Just a lump. A formless shadow. It was crouched on the floor of the car, trying to deceive them.

Buzz saw it, too. With a karate-like yell of fury, he stepped out from behind the boulder and swung the ax down, below the level of his feet, into the gondola. It connected with such force at the extreme end of its arc that it was jerked out of his hands.

The thing in the car didn't move, and the car itself ground to a complete stop.

"I got him!" Buzz shouted.

Liz and Amy rushed to him.

Buzz got down on his knees, reached into the gondola channel, into the car, and seized the ax handle again. He pulled up, and the thing into which the dull blade had sunk was lifted up with it.

A head.

Not the freak's head.

The freak hadn't been on that rear seat.

The dull blade of the ax was embedded deeply in Richie's skull. Brains oozed from the fissures in the bone and slid down his bloody face.

Liz screamed.

Buzz dropped the ax and turned away from the gondola. He vomited on the papier-mâché boulder.

Amy was so stunned that she let go of Liz's hand.

Liz was screaming at Buzz now. "You stupid son of a bitch! You killed him! You killed Richie!" Both Liz and Amy had armed themselves with dull, rusty knives that they had taken from the funhouse displays, and now Liz raised her knife as if she might attack Buzz with it. "You stupid asshole! You *killed* Richie!"

"No," Amy said. "No, Liz. Baby, listen. Buzz didn't kill him. Listen, Richie was already dead. It was just his corpse in that car."

Sobbing with terror, her fear magnified by the drugs that she had taken all evening, Liz turned and ran before Amy could grab her. She fled across the flying saucer display, between two tentacled aliens whose rubbery appendages wobbled in the air after she brushed past them. She vanished in shadows, behind the papier-mâché rocks.

"Liz, damn it!" Amy said.

The sound of the other girl's panicked flight faded rapidly. She disappeared into the bowels of the funhouse.

Amy turned to Buzz again.

He was on his knees. He had just finished being violently sick. The stink was terrible. He wiped the back of his hand across his soiled mouth.

"Are you okay?" Amy asked.

"Holy Christ, it was Richie," he said weakly.

"He was already dead," Amy said.

"But it was *Richie!*"

"Don't flake out on me," Amy said.

"I . . . I won't."

"You're okay?"

"I guess . . . yeah."

"Get hold of yourself."

"I'm all right."

"We have to keep our cool if we're going to survive."

"But this is *crazy*," Buzz said.

"It's crazy," Amy agreed. "But it's happening."

"Locked in a funhouse with a . . . a monster."

"It's happening, and we have to deal with it," she said patiently.

Buzz nodded, sucked in his stomach, struggled to regain his macho self-confidence. "Yeah. We'll deal with it. We can handle it. I'm not afraid of any freak."

The instant he finished speaking, a blossom of blood appeared in the center of Buzz's forehead. At first Amy didn't even realize it was blood. It looked black, like a spot of ink. But then the wan light caught it at a slightly different angle, and she could see that it was red.

Then there was a follow-up noise that echoed through the cavern an instant after the blood appeared; it was barely louder than the clatter that the moving gondola had made—*crack!*

Buzz's mouth fell open.

Less than a second after that, while Amy was still unaware of what was happening, Buzz's right eye exploded in a spray of blood and ruined tissue and splintered bone, and the dark, empty socket looked like a screaming mouth.

Again: *crack!*

Blood and pieces of flesh spattered the front of Amy's green T-shirt.

She whirled around.

The barker was standing only ten feet away. He was pointing a small handgun at Buzz. It wasn't a very big gun; it looked like a toy.

Behind Amy, Buzz sighed and made an odd gurgling sound and slumped over in his own vomit.

This can't be happening! Amy thought.

But she knew it was. She knew that this night had been

waiting to happen for a long, long time; it was a night written into her life before she was born.

The barker smiled at her.

"Who *are* you?" she asked.

"The new Joseph," he said.

"What?"

"I'm the father of the new God," he said. His smile was sharklike.

Amy held her rusted knife at her side, hoping the barker wouldn't see it and that somehow she would get close enough to him to use the blade.

"Say hello to your little brother," the barker said. He was holding a rope in one hand. He pulled on it. Joey staggered out of the darkness, at the other end of the leash.

"Oh, God," Amy said. "God, help us."

"He can't help you," the barker said. "God is weak. Satan is strong. God can't help you this time, bitch."

16

Liz stumbled into someone in the shadows. He was big. She cried out before she realized that it wasn't the freak. She had walked into another of the mechanical monsters, which were all motionless and silent now.

Liz was sweating, shaking, disoriented. She kept colliding with things in the darkness, and each time her heart nearly stopped. She knew she should either sit down until she was calm again—or go back to the gondola channel, where there was some light, but she was too frightened to do what she ought to.

She staggered forward, hands out in front of her, the knife in one hand, gagging when she thought of Richie with the ax buried in his head, resisting the urge to throw up, her head light from the effects of adrenaline and dope, just trying to save herself, gasping, whimpering, aware that all the noise she was making might be the death of her, but unable to be silent, just trying to save herself any way she could, hoping she would luck into an exit, counting on the fact that she'd always been a very lucky girl, wishing (crazily) that she had time to stop and smoke another joint, and that was when she tripped over something and fell, hard, onto the plank floor, and she reached back to free her foot, and she discovered a metal ring in the floor, a large ring in which she had caught the toe of her shoe, and she cursed the pain in her twisted ankle, but then she saw a thread of light coming up through the floor, light from a room below, and she realized that the ring was a handle on a trapdoor.

A way out.

Laughing excitedly, Liz scrambled off the trap, on which she had been sprawled. She knelt in front of the door and took hold of the ring. The door was warped; it didn't want to open. She grunted, put all her strength into one hard tug, and finally the trap swung up.

Light filled the funhouse around her.

The huge, hideous freak was standing on the ladder directly under the trapdoor. He reached up, fast as a striking snake, seized a handful of Liz's long blond hair, and dragged her, screaming, through the hole in the floor, into the funhouse basement.

"Let my brother go," Amy said.

"Not likely," the barker said.

Joey's hands were tied behind his back. Another rope was tightly knotted around his neck; the barker held the loose end of that leash. Joey's throat was rope-burned, and he was crying.

Amy looked into the brilliantly blue but inhuman eyes of the barker, and for the first time in her life she knew beyond all doubt that she wasn't the evil person her mother had always insisted she was. *This* was evil. This man was evil. This maniac. And the murderous freak that had killed Richie. This was the quintessence of evil, and it was as utterly different from her as she was different from . . . Liz.

Suddenly, incredibly, in spite of the fact that both she and Joey seemed close to death at that moment, Amy was filled with a bright, cascading river of self-confidence, with a great and good feeling about herself that she had never experienced before. That river washed away all the dark, confused, and bitter emotions with which she had been plagued for so long.

Simultaneously, she had another flash of déjà vu. She had the uncanny feeling that this scene had been acted out before, perhaps not in every detail, but in essence. And she felt, too, that she was somehow connected to the barker far less casually than she appeared to be. A tremendous sense of destiny settled like a cloak upon her shoulders, a certainty that she had been born and had lived only to come to this place at this time. It was an eerie feeling, but now she welcomed it.

Move, act, be brave, a voice said within her.

Holding her rusty knife at her side, hoping that the barker hadn't seen it, she moved toward Joey. "Honey, are you all right? Did he hurt you? Don't cry. Don't be afraid."

She concentrated all of her attention on Joey, so that the barker wouldn't think she was making a move against him, and when she stooped down toward Joey, she abruptly changed directions, turned, launched herself at the carny, and drove the rusty knife through his throat.

His hateful eyes popped open.

He fired the pistol reflexively.

Amy was aware of the bullet's slipstream kissing her cheek, but she wasn't afraid. She felt as if she were protected.

The barker gagged and dropped the gun and put his hands to his throat. He went down hard, and he stayed down, dead.

Liz scuttled backwards on her hands and feet, like a beautiful spider, along the earthen floor of the funhouse basement, until she backed up against the softly vibrating metal casing of a large piece of machinery. She crouched there, her heartbeat so forceful and rapid that it seemed capable of smashing her apart from within.

The freak watched her. After pulling her down through the trapdoor, he had cast her aside. He hadn't lost interest in her. He just wanted to see what she would do. He was teasing her, offering her an illusive chance of escape, playing the cat to her mouse.

Now that she had put fifteen feet between herself and the freak, Liz stood up. Her legs were weak. She had to hold on to the humming machine in order not to collapse.

The creature stood half in shadow, half in yellow light,

its green eyes glowing. It was so tall that it had to crouch a bit to keep from hitting its head on the low ceiling.

Liz looked around for a way out. There wasn't one. The lower level of the funhouse was a maze of machinery; if she tried to run, she wouldn't get far before the freak would be all over her.

The thing took a step toward her.

"No," Liz said.

It took another step.

"No. Stop."

It shuffled closer, until they were only six feet apart, and then it stopped and cocked its head and stared down at her with what appeared to be curiosity.

"Please," she said. "Please let me go. Please."

She had never expected to hear herself begging anyone for anything. She prided herself on her strength and toughness. But she was begging for her life now, and she found it easy to grovel when so much was at stake.

The freak began to sniff at her as a hound might sniff at a new bitch. His wide nostrils flared and quivered as he snorted with increasing excitement.

"Smell good," the freak said.

Liz was startled to discover that he could speak.

"Smell woman," he said.

A spark of hope flickered in Liz.

"Pretty," the freak said. "Want pretty."

My God, Liz thought, almost giddy now. Is *this* what it comes down to? Sex? Is that the way out for me? Why not? Hell, yes! That's what it's always come down to before. That's always been my way out.

The freak shuffled closer, raised one of its huge, rodent claws. It gently stroked her face.

She tried to conceal her revulsion. "You . . . you like me, don't you?" she asked.

"Pretty," he said, grinning, showing his crooked, sharp, yellow teeth.

"You want me?"

"Real bad," he said.

"Maybe I could be nice to you," she said quaveringly, trying hard to slip back into the role of the sexpot, the teaser, the fun girl, the party image she had sanded and buffed and polished until it was smooth, comfortable, and splinter-free.

The thing's wickedly taloned hand slid down from her face to her breasts.

"Just don't hurt me, and maybe we can work something out," she said shakily.

The thing licked its black lips; its tongue was pale and speckled, utterly alien. It hooked one claw in her T-shirt and shredded the thin fabric. One razorlike nail made a long, shallow cut across her right breast.

"Wait," she said, wincing. "Now wait a second." Panic rose in her again.

The freak pushed her against the purring machine.

Liz squirmed, tried to shove the creature away. It seemed to be made of iron. She was powerless against it.

The thing appeared to be far more excited by the thread of blood that decorated her bare breast than it was by her nakedness. It tore off her shorts.

Liz screamed.

The freak slapped her, almost rendering her unconscious with that single blow, and then bore her down onto the floor.

A minute later, as Liz felt the creature spreading her legs and entering her, she also felt its claws piercing her sides. As a cold, maroon darkness swept over her, she knew that sex was indeed the answer, as always; but this time it was the *final* answer.

Amy thought she heard Liz scream. It was a distant sound, a short, sharp cry of terror and pain. Then nothing but the usual funhouse noises.

For a moment Amy continued to listen, but when she couldn't hear anything except the eerie music and the laughing clown, she turned to Joey again. He was standing to the left of the barker's corpse, trying not to look at it. Amy had untied the boy. Although tears were streaming down his face, and although his lower lip was quivering, he was trying to be brave for her. She knew that her opinion mattered more to him than did that of anyone else; and she saw that even now, even under these circumstances, he was concerned that she think well of him. He wasn't sobbing. He wasn't panicked. He wasn't going to break down entirely. He even made an effort to be nonchalant; he spat on his rope-burned wrists and gently smeared the saliva over the angry red marks, soothing the chafed skin.

"Joey?"

He looked up at her.

"Come on, honey. We're going to get out of here."

"Okay," he said, his voice cracking between the syllables. "How? Where's the door?"

"I don't know," Amy said. "But we'll find it."

The feeling of being watched over and protected was still with Amy, and it buoyed her.

Joey took hold of her left hand.

Holding the barker's pistol in her right hand, Amy led the boy through the shadowy funhouse, past mechanical monsters from Mars and wax zombies and wooden lions and rubber sea beasts. Eventually she saw a shaft of light coming up from the floor, back in the darkness to the left of the track, where the glow from the work lights didn't reach. Hoping the light represented a way out, she led Joey behind a pile of papier-mâché boulders, where she found a trapdoor in the floor.

"Is this the way out?" Joey asked.

"Maybe," Amy said.

She got down on her knees, leaned forward, and looked into the dimly lighted basement of the funhouse. The place was filled with humming motors, with rumbling machines, with giant pulley wheels and gears, with banks of levers, with enormous drive belts and drive chains—and with shadows. She hesitated. But then that reassuring, inner voice urged her not to retreat, and she knew she was meant to descend into the lower chamber; there was nowhere else for her to go.

She sent Joey down the ladder ahead of her, covering him with the gun. When he was at the bottom, she followed quickly. *Very* quickly—because suddenly she wasn't sure Joey was protected by the unseen power, as she felt herself to be. Perhaps Joey was vulnerable.

"This is the cellar," Joey said.

"Yes," Amy said. "But we're not underground. The

cellar is really the first floor, so there's almost sure to be a door to the outside."

She held his hand again, and they eased down the aisle between two rows of machinery, turned a corner into another aisle—and saw Liz. The girl was on the floor, on her back, head twisted and bent unnaturally to one side, eyes wide and sightless, stomach torn open, dressed only in blood.

"Don't look," Amy said to Joey, trying to shield him from the awful sight, even as her own stomach flip-flopped.

"I saw," he said miserably. "I saw."

Amy heard a deep-throated growl. She looked up from Joey's tear-stained face.

The hideous freak had entered the aisle behind them. It was crouched to avoid hitting its enormous, gnarled head on the low ceiling. Green fire flickered in its eyes. Drool coated its lips and matted the wiry fur around its mouth.

Amy wasn't surprised to see the thing. In her heart she had known this confrontation was unavoidable. She was walking through these events as if she had rehearsed them a thousand times.

The creature said, "Bitch. Pretty bitch." His voice was thick. It came out of cracked, black lips.

As if drifting through a slow-motion dream, Amy pushed Joey behind her.

The freak sniffed. "Woman heat. Smell nice."

Amy didn't back away from it. Holding the pistol at her side and slightly behind her, hoping the freak would not see it, she took a step toward the thing.

"Want," it said. "Want pretty."

She took another step, then a third.

The freak seemed surprised by her boldness. He cocked his head, stared at her intensely.

She took a fourth step.

The creature raised one hand threateningly. The claws gleamed.

Amy took two more steps, until she was only an arm's length from the freak. In one smooth, swift movement she raised the gun and extended it and fired into the thing's chest—once, twice, three times.

The freak staggered backwards, driven by the fusillade. He crashed into a machine, throwing several levers with his outcast arms. The wheels and gears began to turn all over the basement; the belts started moving, and the drive chains clattered from one steel drum to the next.

But the freak didn't fall down. He was bleeding from three chest wounds, but he was still on his feet. He pushed away from the machine and moved toward Amy.

Joey screamed.

Her heart pounding, Amy raised the gun, but waited. The freak was almost on top of her, swaying, eyes unfocused now, drooling blood. She could even smell its fetid breath. The thing swung one massive hand at her, trying to rip open her face, but it missed by inches. Finally, when she was absolutely sure that the bullet would not be wasted, Amy fired another round into the creature's face.

Again, the freak was flung backwards. This time he fell hard against the heavy, main drive chain that operated the gondolas overhead. The sharp-toothed chain caught in his clothes, jerked him off his feet, and dragged him violently down the aisle, away from Amy and Joey. The creature kicked and screamed but couldn't free himself. The legs of his trousers tore as he skimmed across the floor, and then his skin was scoured off with equal efficiency. His left hand snagged for a moment where the chain passed under and then over a steel drum; for a second or two the mechanism jammed, but then the powerful motors pulled the chain into motion again; the freak's hand came through the huge gear with a couple of fingers missing. Then the beast was being dragged back toward Amy and Joey. It was no longer struggling with the chain; it hadn't the strength left to resist; it was howling in agony now, spasming, dying. Nevertheless, as it passed them, it reached for Amy's ankle. Failing that, it managed to hook its claws through one leg of Joey's jeans. The boy yelped and fell and started sliding after the freak, but Amy moved quickly; she grabbed the boy and held on tight. For a moment the chain froze again, and the freak stopped moving, and they strained in a macabre tug-of-war, but then one of the thing's claws snapped, and Joey's pants tore, and the chain began to clatter again, and the freak was carried away. It was tossed and battered like a rag doll until it finally became pinned in the huge, main cogwheel, where the thumb-sized teeth of the gears ground most of the way through its neck before freezing up.

The freak was motionless, limp.

Amy threw down the pistol she had taken from the barker.

Joey was staring at her, wide-eyed, shocked.

"Don't be afraid," she said.

He ran into her arms and hugged her.

Suffused with joy in spite of the blood and horror all around her, overflowing with the exhilarating joy of life,

Amy realized that the barker had been wrong when he'd said that God could not help her. God *had* helped her—God or some universal force that sometimes went by the name of God. He was with her now. She felt Him at her side. But He wasn't at all like poor Mama said He was. He wasn't a vengeful God with a million rules and harsh punishments. He was simply . . . kindness and gentleness and love. He was caring.

And then that special moment passed, the aura of His presence faded, and Amy sighed. She picked up Joey and carried him out of the funhouse.

Before we get started, remember this: The best thing about good fiction is characters and the best thing about life is people.

So . . .

This is the second afterword I've written for *The Funhouse* at the request of Berkley Books. The previous afterword was added to the novel when it was first published under my name, after having originally been issued under the pen name Owen West. I suppose that if I ever succumb to multiple-personality disorder and all of my early pen names struggle with one another for control of my mind and body, and if Owen West should ascend to the top of that motley heap, I will be called upon to write a third afterword from his perspective. No doubt it will be a bitter and spiteful piece in which he takes revenge for my having appropriated his novels and put them under my real name, which is (as far as I'm aware) Dean Koontz.

Dean Koontz is not an ideal name for a writer. The Dean part is all right, but Koontz doesn't fall musically upon the ear. In fact, I've said elsewhere that it sounds like (1) a warthog gagging on a mouthful of dead-snake dinner, (2) a warthog sneezing, (3) a warthog "sneezing" from the end opposite its nose, and (4) an Albanian word for decomposing fish.

Before anyone accuses me of being an anti-warthog bigot, let me hasten to assure you that I greatly admire warthogs, that I do not intend to mock them, and that if I could be any creature on earth other than a human being, I would delight in being a warthog. Their noses are cute. I referenced warthogs in three of those four examples only because it seems to me that my surname—Koontz, if you've forgotten—and the word *warthog* are equally funny. If any warthog—or an attorney disposed to representing warthogs—happens to be reading this, I must hasten to observe that the Supreme Court of the United States long ago ruled that when applied to the word *warthog*, the word *funny* is not pejorative, merely descriptive, and thus cannot serve as the basis for a ten-million-dollar defamation-of-character suit. Had I used the word *funny* to describe not the word *warthog* but instead the physical appearance or characteristic behavior of a particular warthog, I would be toast. But I did not. I will never do so. That's not the kind of guy I am. So stuff it.

The Funhouse began as a motion-picture screenplay by Larry Block. Larry—aka Lawrence—Block is such a much better writer's name than Koontz that there are at least two writers by that name.

I've met Lawrence Block, the superb suspense and mystery writer, a couple of times, including one evening in the early 1970s, for a poker game with some other publishing types. The editor who took me to the game, which Larry hosted in his Manhattan apartment, warned me that everyone at the table that night was a tournament-quality player and that as soon as I'd lost fifty dollars, which would probably be in six minutes, I should drop out and just observe from there on, or otherwise wind up destitute. Having never played poker before, I had to learn the basic rules from the editor during the taxi ride to Larry's place. Larry was a great guy and a fine host, and at the end of the evening, my $50 had become $120. It is a good thing that he chose to make a living as a writer instead of at the poker tables in Vegas; the world is much richer for his novels, and so is he.

That Larry Block is not the one who wrote *The Funhouse* as a screenplay. The Larry Block who did that specialized in movie work, and he had the good fortune to see his screenplay made into a film by then-hot director Tobe Hooper, who had made *The Texas Chainsaw Massacre* and would later make *Poltergeist*. Those of you who have had the great luck never to involve yourself in film writing will probably be surprised to learn that for every screenplay actually produced, there are 9,234 that never made it to the screen. So when it happens, the lucky writer has been singled out by Fate and is well advised to proceed with caution, as Fate might also intend to skewer him with a lightning bolt or introduce him to that deadly flesh-eating bacteria we hear about in the news from time to time, when reporters are not too busy writing stories about the latest member of the British royal family to be caught naked by paparazzi.

In 1980, Berkley Books proposed to me that I write a novel based on Larry Block's screenplay, a type of book that is for some inexplicable reason called a "novelization." I had been writing full-time for eleven years and had not yet seen a book of mine on the bestseller list. The money was good, and I had this plebeian notion that, while art for art's sake is what *should* be, starving to death for art's sake is for idiots. I took the job, even though I was expected to write a horror novel.

Let me clarify my feeling about horror novels: As a reader, I enjoy them; but I have never thought that I write them. And I certainly do not write them to the exclusion of other genres of fiction. That was one reason a pen name was essential. At the same time that I refused the horror label, I couldn't be blatantly publishing horror novels under my name. Besides, since my own fiction hadn't sold a gazillion copies, Berkley Books wanted a fresh new name that might be built into a—*ta-da!*—major brand with the help of the upcoming movie.

I was sent Larry Block's fine screenplay, and I discovered that the story therein would give me about 20 percent of a novel. This is because movies have far, far, far less story and incident than do novels. If you took the screenplay for some epic film like *Avatar*, which on the screen is a huge and rich story, you would find that translated into narrative prose, it would make, like *The Funhouse*, 20 percent of a book. The screenplay for a movie like *Transformers* would give you about 7 percent of a novel, and by chapter three you would be in serious trouble because you would already have grossly overused all the words that describe really loud noises and really catastrophic destruction. The screenplay for a movie like *Saw* will provide you with material for a short story, but don't expect to sell it to the *New Yorker*.

Suffice it to say that I wrote the novel, creating all kinds of additional characters, backstory, and plotlines. It was supposed to hit stores the same week as the movie appeared in theaters. But the film was delayed for three months for additional editing, and *The Funhouse* landed in bookstores without that much-desired support. Happily, it went through eight printings and a million copies, and appeared on the paperback bestseller list. When the film was released, we expected even bigger sales—but that was not to be. Let's just say that the film did not turn out like anyone who worked on it had hoped that it might, and if you saw it in a theater, you were not inclined to sprint directly to the nearest bookstore to relive the experience at the even greater length of a novel.

My alter ego, Owen West, subsequently published *The Mask* and wrote a third novel, *Darkfall*, that was never issued under his name. By then, novels under my name were on the bestseller list, and it seemed counterproductive to be publishing also under a less successful pseudonym. I ended Owen's career as a writer and, in fact, his very existence, which wasn't as sad as you might think because he was something of a snot.

Several years later, when *The Funhouse* was first released under my name, I finally got to know Larry Block #2, who wrote the screenplay. We've become friends. He's never had me to his house for a poker game, though I suppose that's because he heard from Larry Block #1 what a cardsharp I am. Larry #2 and I have a lot more in common than just *The Funhouse*. We both love dogs and animals in general. When you get us talking movies and books and philosophy, you can't shut us up. Well, you can, but it requires chloroform. We've both been told by powerful movie folk that we'll never work in this town again, and, in fact, I think we were both told that by the same famous producer. Larry is an observant Jew, and I am a Catholic, and I like to think that those are two sides of the same coin, regardless of what Larry might think. We both find life to be beautiful and terrifying, people to be inspiring and terrifying, and the world to be mysterious, which gives us more reasons than you might think to laugh.

If I were to write the novelization of *The Funhouse* today, I'd leave out most or all of the explicit language, since I've learned it's always a crutch and that it diminishes rather than enlivens virtually any story. And although this book is not as ambitious a work as *From the Corner of His Eye* or *Odd Thomas*, or the other novels that I have written since, I still have a fondness for it. This was honest work that sustained my wife and me when we needed sustaining, and it helped keep my career viable before I found my voice with my own work. But best of all, north of here, in the suburbs of L.A., I now have what I like to think of as a Jewish half brother—that would be Larry #2—whose enthusiasm for life has inspired me on bad days and who, I hope, might have been from time to time inspired by my jabbering.

The best thing about fiction and life is the people in each.

Afterword to the 1994 Edition

In 1980, when my novels had not yet begun to appear on bestseller lists, Jove Books asked me to write the novelization of a screenplay by Larry Block (not the Lawrence Block who writes the marvelous Matthew Scudder detective novels and other fine suspense fiction; another Larry Block specializing in film writing), which was being shot by Tobe Hooper, the young director who had made a name for himself with a low-budget horror film, *The Texas Chainsaw Massacre*. I had always thought that transforming a screenplay into a *real* novel would be interesting and demanding, so I was motivated by the challenge. To be truthful, I was also motivated by the financial terms, which were more generous than what I was receiving for my own novels. When I signed on to write *The Funhouse*, the inflation rate was 18 percent and interest rates were well above 20 percent, and it seemed as if total economic collapse was imminent. I was not receiving peanuts for my own novels, as I had for many years, but had worked my way up to compensation in cashews; nevertheless, given the economic climate, the offer for *The Funhouse* was enough of an improvement to be irresistible.

Yes, sometimes writers *do* have to take money—as well as art—into consideration. That is, if they like shoes, having something to eat now and then, and having more than a supermarket shopping cart in which to store their worldly possessions. Oh, I know some writers who are above such grubby motivations. Of course, every one of them has a trust fund, wealthy parents, wealthier grandparents, or a well-paid working spouse to fall back on. Nothing allows an artist to ignore the importance of money more than having enough of it to begin with. I've always thought that *having* to be desperately concerned about finances for at least the first decade or two of his professional life actually improves a writer's work; it puts him in closer touch with his fellow citizens and their concerns, ensuring more relevance in his fiction.

Anyway, I accepted the offer to write *The Funhouse*. The script was good *as a screenplay* but offered enough material for no more than 10 percent or 20 percent of a novel. This is not unusual. Movies are shallow compared to novels, shadows of stories when compared to *real* stories. I had to build up the characters, create backstories for all of them, and develop a plot that built toward the events on the carnival midway in the latter chapters, which were the scenes with which the movie was almost solely concerned. I didn't start to use the screenplay until I had written four-fifths of the book.

The project was fun, however, because I'd long had a serious interest in carnivals and had collected a lot of material about them. As an unhappy child in a severely dysfunctional family, living across the street from the fairgrounds where the county fair pitched its tents every August, I had often dreamed about running away with the carnival to escape the poverty, fear, and violence of my daily life. Years after writing *The Funhouse*, I made far more extensive use of my carnival knowledge in *Twilight Eyes*. But writing *The Funhouse* was satisfying in part because I knew that the carnival lore I was putting into it was not only accurate but fresh to readers, for this was an American subculture about which few novelists had ever written with any real knowledge or accuracy.

When *The Funhouse* was first published by Jove—a paperback imprint owned by the Berkley Publishing Group, which was a division of G. P. Putnam's Sons, which was owned by MCA, the media giant that also owned Universal Studios (life is more complex out here in the late twentieth century than in the carnival)—it was supposed to hit stores simultaneously with the film's appearance in theaters. However, late in the game the film was held back for additional editing, and the book was dropped into the marketplace three months ahead of the movie. Surprisingly, *The Funhouse* quickly went through eight printings and a million copies, and appeared on the *New York Times* paperback bestseller list. It was a satisfying success for a paperback original (that is, a book that had no hardcover history to build upon), and it sold steadily—until the film opened.

Now, you must understand that ordinarily a film sells

books. If a book does well *before* a movie is made, it will often do *exceptionally* well when it has the flick to support it. This was not the case with *The Funhouse*. Upon release of the film, the sales of the book plummeted.

A mystery?

Not really.

Let's just say that Mr. Hooper had not realized the potential of the material to the extent that the studio, probably Mr. Block, or Hooper himself would have hoped. Instead of serving as an advertisement for the book, the film acted as a curse upon it. Months later, *The Funhouse* had vanished from bookstore shelves, never to be seen again.

Well, almost never.

The book had been written under the name Owen West because Jove hoped to create a brand-new name (or new brand name) in horror-suspense and use the extra punch of a film to really send off the author's "first" book in a big way. The second West book was *The Mask*, and although sales were good, the success of the first book redounded to Mr. West's benefit less than the failure of the movie detracted from his reputation. By the time I delivered the third of the West books, *The Pit*, novels under my own name had become more successful than those written as West, and it seemed wise to fold his identity into mine. *The Pit* was retitled *Darkfall*—a great relief to me, as I could easily imagine the intense pleasure nasty-minded critics would get from merely adding an *s* to the second word of the original title—and was published under my real name.

I now tell people that West died tragically, trampled by

musk oxen in Burma while researching a novel about a giant prehistoric duck, which he'd tentatively titled *Quackzilla*.

Eventually *The Mask* was republished under my name and sold far better than it had for poor, luckless, ox-flattened West.

And now here is *The Funhouse* under my name at last, thanks to the efforts of people at MCA Publishing, Berkley Books, and the kind cooperation of Larry Block. It doesn't rank with *Watchers* or *Hideaway* or a number of my best novels, but it's as good as some and maybe better than others. I like it. I have books I'll *never* let see print again. Readers shouldn't have to pay for stories that a novelist wrote while he was still learning, just to be able to see how badly he was able to screw up before he found his way. *The Funhouse*, I think, is better than that. It's fun. It has something to say. The background is authentic. And not least of all, it's pretty damn scary, even if I say so myself. I hope you enjoyed it.

And a moment of silence, please, for the late Mr. West, whose remains continue to disintegrate in that field in Burma, where the herd of oxen—and the movie version of *The Funhouse*—drove his too-mortal flesh deep into the oily, black mud.